Critical Acclaim for Lorna Schultz Nicholson's

See Fox Run

"Lorna Nicholson has tremendous characters in *See Fox Run*. They really come alive. She really made me feel their pain and sadness, especially, something that is sorely lacking in a lot of what I'm reading these days. And having such real characters that I care so much about makes the suspense all the more palpable." —Steve Hamilton, Shamus and Edgar Winner for *A Cold Day in Paradise.*

"With well-drawn characters and a tight engaging plot, Lorna Nicholson's new book, *See Fox Run*, is like a brisk wind blowing in from her minister/detective's northern homeland - bracing, energizing and impossible to ignore." —Andrea Marantz, CBC Broadcaster in Arts and Entertainment

"A little known but significant part of Canada's history is the stories of Aboriginal individuals in transition and transformation in today's society. *See Fox Run* is a must-read for all Canadians." —Angus Kaanerk Cockney, Aboriginal Healing Foundation, Inuit artist and Survivor of the residential school.

"Race memories from the Arctic North seep into the badlands of Vancouver in this bold fusion of old ways and new. Lorna Nicholson's debut thriller, *See Fox Run*, offers a shaming indictment of a society that has lost its spiritual heart. On the margins of contemporary Canada, even salvation is a cover for yet another scam. But Inuit minister, Intuko, is determined to confront the ever-swelling tide of greed, violence, and hypocrisy. In every human being, as in every piece of soapstone, there lies the possibility of re-connection." —Graham Hurley, author of *The Take*, (featuring D/I Joe Faraday), One of the Independent on Sunday's five best crime novels of 2001, *Turnstone, Angels Passing* and *Deadlight.*

Lorna Schultz Nicholson

See Fox Run

Echelon Press
712 Briarwood Lane
Hurst, TX 76053

First Echelon Press paperback printing: September 2004
Cover Art © Nathalie Moore
Printed in Lavergne, TN, USA

Dedication

To the missing girls.

Acknowledgements

I always find it unbelievable when art imitates life. I started See Fox Run many years ago, before anyone discovered the real reason why girls were missing from the streets of Vancouver. As my work is fiction, and meant to entertain, I truly hope I have not upset any friends or family members of the missing girls. My heart goes out to all of you.

I have many people to thank for their help in writing this novel. First goes to Echelon Press–Karen Syed and Susan Sipal–women who believed in my story. Without them this story would still be manuscript pages. Angus Kaanerk Cockney, my wonderful Inuit friend, who introduced me to the North and Inuit art. If my story inspires you to purchase some Inuit art, Angus is the person to contact. And to his family, Rex and Alvira Cockney, Cathy Cockney, and Auntie Winnie, who graciously invited me into their homes. I also thank John and Kathy Miya for their hospitality in Yellowknife. And to Patty Schlafen, my long time friend and prison officer who answered my continuous questions at all hours of the day or night. Lisa Queen, my agent, was the first one to believe in a way-too-long manuscript and the character of Intuko–this manuscript would not be what it is today without her sound advice. Thanks to all who read and critiqued, especially my writing group pals. You know who are you are. Last, but certainly not least, my husband, Bob. He's lived through the birth of this book, and the pregnancy was a heck of a lot longer than nine months. That takes strength. But, hey now it's time for you, the wonderful reader, to sit back, relax and enjoy. I wrote it for you.

PROLOGUE

She looks around her small room, her last home on earth. Silently, slowly, her dark stony eyes stare at every corner, every crevice, every rough bump on the painted blocks of concrete. Drums beat, reminding her of pleasant childhood memories. She smiles. Soon she will be home; it's been too long.

The drums, made of caribou hide and birch, grow louder, beckoning her, drawing her into their soul. She turns her head, almost to the rhythm of their beat, to stare at the sink, the toilet bowl, the walls, the shelves. There are no photographs anywhere; no crayon scribbles, no past lovers, no smiling children who once nestled quietly in the comfort of her womb. The vision of her oldest boy, now a teenager, his eyes searching, longing, skips through her mind. As quickly as he appears, he disappears, like a sputtering, fading flashbulb.

Her room is empty, she is empty.

She looks down at her hand. It holds a whalebone carving of a mother carrying a smiling baby in a papoose on her back. She squeezes her fist until the veins running haphazardly across her wrist look like turquoise ribbons. In her other hand, she holds the sharp end of the razor she has kept hidden until today. Pressing it to her veins, she draws blood. Just a drop. A trickle. She stares at the blood, licks it, then licks the tip of the carving to spread her blood to the baby's face. The carving used to hang from her neck by a moose leather strap but that strap was not allowed once these walls became her home.

Strap or no strap, today she feels lucky. She is going to

her real home.

Repeatedly, she touches her wrist with the razor, digging the sharpness into her skin, brazing the surface for it must go deeper–into the depth of the blue. The blood spurts and she continues to slice. She wants to go where the land in winter is an enormous eternity of whiteness and the sky in summer shines a forever light. Either season, there is whiteness. And belonging. It also means drumming, dancing in parkas, sharing fish and caribou with people her soul can touch. Long gone, she sees beloved faces, her *amaamak* and *aapak*.

In her mind, she searches for the whiteness, stretches her arms to reach it, touch it, embrace it. But all she sees is the red blood dripping from her wrists. She probes the razor deeper.

Yarayuami; I am tired, she cries.

Qiqirurnigaa; it has become cold, she moans.

The drumbeat fades.

ONE

Why couldn't he think of a title for his sermon Sunday–again? Intuko rubbed his temples, reclined in his brown leather chair that was cracking from wear, and planted his feet on the floor. He tapped his pen on the chair arm, then leaned forward and jotted down a few words. As he stared at the words, he shook his head. No good. He scratched them out. Frustrated, he closed his eyes.

Every Thursday he encountered the same dilemma, thinking of the appropriate heading for Sunday's sermon to put in the bulletins. Most members in his struggling downtown Vancouver church seemed to accept the fact that there was often an empty space beside the word sermon in Sunday's bulletin. He had joked about it, asking everyone to bear with him; the title always came to him on Friday–a day too late. One Sunday he even preached about *Fumbling Towards Ecstasy*, and used this as an example. Of course, the idea also came from the fact that *Fumbling Towards Ecstasy* was the title of Sarah McLachlan's CD, which he listened to a great deal.

A knock shook his office door, and when he opened his eyes he saw Hazel peeking around the corner.

"Intuko?

"Hazel, come on in."

"It's Thursday. The bulletin needs–"

"I know."

She chuckled and stepped into his office. "Don't forget," she said jokingly, wagging her finger at him, "we should look

4

at our failures as gifts. That sermon of yours has stuck with me and helps me through some of *those* days. Don't be so hard on yourself."

He smiled at the little woman, with the short curly red hair and bright green eyes, standing by his office door. Hazel cheerfully fulfilled her job as secretary for Princess Street United Church, always staying on top of what needed to be done. With the church's financial woes, the job was only part-time but she had already raised her daughter single-handedly and was now a doting grandmother.

Hazel walked proudly and officiously, in her soft-soled Wallabies, toward Intuko's desk.

"I have some messages for you. I didn't want to disturb you earlier." She clutched a handful of pink message slips in her hand. "Let's see, Joe at Street People Ministry rang."

"Did he say what he wanted?" Intuko stuck his pen behind his ear.

"I think he wants you to help out with the teens on Wednesday night. I guess they've got so many homeless kids coming to the street bus that they're overwhelmed."

"I'll call him back. He's doing a great job with S.P.M."

"Do you miss being at the helm?" Hazel slid the message slip toward him.

"That's a tough question. It's such an emotional job. So many of our kids come for help but in the end they don't have the strength to follow through with the changes. You always hope for that one. Like Chris. What are my other messages?"

"Well, this was a strange one–talking about hoping for that one–but Lola called."

"Lola!" Intuko immediately leaned forward and held out his hand for the message. "I haven't seen her in a few years." He glanced at the pink slip. "You're right, I always wanted her to straighten out and I thought she had it in her." Concerned, he looked up. "How did she sound?"

Hazel pursed her lips. "Not good." She paused for a split second before she said, "Intuko, I saw her the other day. Wearing next to nothing, and wiggling toward a car that had stopped. I'm sure it was her. She was around the corner from here, on Hastings and Main." She sadly shrugged her shoulders. "Such a shame. I liked that girl too."

Once again, he glanced down at the pink paper. He turned it over to study the back. "She didn't leave a number? I'd like to call her."

"Sorry. I asked, but she said she wouldn't have a phone for a few more days. *Jimmy* was getting her hooked up."

Intuko slumped in his chair and blew out a rush of air. "Her pimp, I take it?"

"That's my guess. It makes me sick that these guys prey on these young vulnerable women. Okay, the last message here is from a..." Hazel stopped to read her own handwriting, "a Susan Peterson, at the Women's Correctional Institute. I'm not sure what she wanted, she just said for you to ring her back."

Puzzled, he reached for this last message slip. "This woman was at church last Sunday. When she introduced herself on the way out, she asked if I still taught Inuit art. I haven't taught in years so I have no idea how she tracked down my name. She wants me to teach a carving class at the prison where she works as an officer." He pulled his pen out from behind his ear and tapped it on his desk. "One day a week shouldn't take too much of my time."

"I still have the seal you carved for me out of that beautiful green stone." Hazel almost sang her words. "It sits on my mantel and I get more compliments on that than anything else in my house. This class would be good for you."

"You're right. It might be fun to get back to my art."

"And give you something to do besides work."

He laughed. "Are you worrying about me again?"

"No," she said adamantly. "But you're a good artist and you shouldn't let all that talent be wasted. I always say art shows what's inside the true person. And your art is charming. Intuko, stop furrowing, your eyebrows are near touching one another. Now, could I get you a coffee?"

He waved his arms to shoosh her away. "You're not here to fetch me coffee."

"I don't mind, really. Lordy-be, my old husband used to sit on his duff and wait. Sometimes, he'd wait a long time." She paused. "If there's nothing else, I do have to get back to my desk. We want to have something to hand out Sunday morning."

"You know the title will come to me tomorrow and..." His old friend stood with her hands clasped together and her head tilted to the side; a body position that indicated she had something else to say. "Hazel, what is it?"

"I don't mean to pry but this Susan woman, she wouldn't work at...that wouldn't be the same prison your mum ended up in?" Her eyes widened.

"I'm afraid so."

"Since I've known you–you've avoided that place!"

"I know. But...sometimes things happen for a reason." Intuko leaned back, thinking. "You know, ironically enough, in my daily devotion today I read the passage from 2 Kings 5:1-15. It was about Naaman and Elisha. Naaman had his own ideas about how God could use him and heal him of his leprosy but God showed him that he really wanted him to work in other ways. Naaman had to accept and trust that bathing in the Jordan River would cure him even if it wasn't the way he thought it was to be."

Hazel slipped into the chair facing him and straightened the bottom of her pale pink blouse until it covered her round belly. She locked her fingers together and placed her hands on his desk. "I couldn't do what you're thinking of doing." She cringed, shaking as if she had the shivers. Unclasping her hands, she leaned forward and whispered. "Did you ever see exactly where she died?"

"We...were in the visitors lounge." He rolled the message slip between his fingers. "She wasn't how I wanted her to be. I never saw her again after that." He sat up, flattened the message slip on his desk, and forced a smile. "It all happened twenty years ago. I was just fifteen."

"But, she was your mum." Hazel stood and patted his hand. "Just remember, you can always drink tea with me and talk."

After Hazel left, Intuko picked up the message slips. . Why hadn't he been here to answer her call? Then he ran the crumpled pink paper with Susan's number through his fingers. This little note conjured up a lot of memories. He closed his eyes, hoping to block out his childhood.

But he could hear the drone of the plane's engine. Every year, in September, the planes would land in his small Arctic hamlet of Tuktoyaktuk to pick up the school aged children. Intuko, along with his cousins, siblings, and friends all boarded the plane, knowing they wouldn't return home until June. Saying good-bye had been horrible. The women would cry in wails as their children were ripped from their arms and forced to leave. As the plane lifted, Intuko would press his nose to the small glass window and wave to his grandmother...but never his mother.

She couldn't be bothered to see him off. Once at school, Intuko would live like an orphan in a residence, not even being allowed to go home for winter solstice celebrations or Christmas. All because of government rules.

One summer when he arrived home from residential school, he had to live with his grandmother and grandfather, *Anaanak* and *Adaadak* because his mother had run away with a white man.

"Your mama, she no good," Grandmother had said. "*Tan'ngit* evil spirits have entered her. Oh, those *tan'ngit*, their white skin bad for our people."

Sitting at his desk, Intuko lifted his head and gave a silent prayer of thanks, for he would never forget his *anaanak*. He smiled wistfully, thinking of her. She had been a shaman in their hamlet. And a good one at that.

Even after his Christian studies, Intuko still didn't understand why so many religious men thought shamans were evil. His *anaanak* was the most spiritual and kind person he'd ever met. Why would God think of her as evil? Shamans had been a way for his people to commune with the spiritual world, a way for them to find the *tuktut* herds so they could eat and survive. And a way for them to visit the moon or go to the bottom of the ocean. Sometimes he couldn't understand why the church made such strident rules when God didn't.

Shaking his head, he looked down at the phone message from Susan Peterson. He never dreamed he would be offered a job teaching Inuit art at the prison which incarcerated his mother. Had his grandmother set this up from the spirit world? He wouldn't put it past her.

Intuko stroked the *nunuq* carving that was sitting on his desk, his first as a-five-year-old, and rubbed his fingers along the smoothness of the whalebone. It had been a long time since he had practised his art.

Then he picked up his fox. *His white fox.* He had carved the fox out of soapstone with his *anaanak* the summer his mother had left. The two of them had sat on the ground amidst the tufted pearlwort, the Arctic lupines, and the cotton grass and carved with the twenty-four hour sun beating down on their backs. His *anaanak* spoke to Intuko in the Inuvialuit language–which he could barely understood after being at English school–and told him to pay heed to his white fox. Always.

9

He rubbed his thumb on his fox's pointed ears and long nose, noticing that his carving was covered in dust. He sighed. His fox hadn't come to him in years. Or maybe, he just hadn't been around for its visit. Was he that far removed from his culture?

He placed his fox back down on his desk, picked up the phone, and listened to the dial tone. So many years had passed—surely he could handle an art class once a week. He punched the numbers on the telephone. Susan Peterson wasn't there so he left a message that he was available to teach but would need supplies. He put down the phone just to hear it ring again.

"Intuko speaking."

"It's me, Lola." Her voice sounded soft, feeble.

"Lola! I'm so glad you called back. It's been years. We've missed your pretty smile at youth group."

"Really, my pretty smile."

"Coffee's always on. Come for a visit."

"Could I come now? I'm right around the corner."

"Sure. Cream and sugar?"

"Just black."

Intuko sucked in a sharp breath when Lola walked through his office door, trying not to let her see his shock at her haggard appearance. The girl looked as if she'd aged twenty years. A few years back, she'd vanished from the Vancouver area and Intuko had prayed for her safety. Now here she was, standing in front of him. He hugged her hard, her body a rack of bones under his arms.

"It's great to see you." He held her at arms length, by the shoulders.

She averted her eyes and instead stared at the floor. He let go of her, got a mug, and poured her a cup of coffee.

Her hands shook when she took the cup, spilling coffee on

the carpet. "I'm sorry," she said.

Intuko motioned for her to sit on the old brown corduroy sofa that rose and fell in all the wrong places. "Don't worry about the carpet. How are you?"

"I'm...okay. I'm still alive." She lowered her head to sip her coffee, her long stringy blond hair falling in front of her face, hiding her features.

Intuko felt sick in the pit of his stomach, knowing street girls like Lola disappeared on a regular basis. Some moved and others vanished. "Have you been in Vancouver all along?" he asked, trying to be casual.

She shook her head. "I was in Toronto for awhile. Thought it might be safer there. But Jimmy, he brought me back a few months ago." She stared into her coffee cup, turning the mug around, sloshing coffee along the sides. "It's awful here," she said.

"What do you mean?" he asked gently.

"I dunno. Jimmy's got these rich friends." Lola bit at her nail and slouched in her seat, pulling her bomber jacket, which looked as if it came from a bargain basement, tightly around her. Intuko saw the fear in talk, understood the safety Lola felt in silence. With the crowd Lola ran with, extra words could cause death.

"I walked in on them once," she whispered, head still down. "They, they scare me."

"Have you been with Jimmy long?"

"You're from up North, aren't ya?" Lola asked quickly, pointing at the carvings on his desk.

"I am." Intuko went to his desk and picked up his white fox, wondering where that question had come from. She obviously didn't want to talk about Jimmy.

"My Sarah," said Lola, "she's part North-like. She kinda looks like you. Dark hair, high cheek-bones, crinkly-like eyes."

He smiled at Lola, trying to ease her tension, make her feel comfortable and not interrogated. If he asked too many questions, she'd clam up, or say too much, which either way would make her leave and not come back for a long time. And he wanted her to come back for coffee again or maybe even go out with him for lunch. The girl needed a friend.

"I didn't know Sarah had Inuit blood," he said lightly. "How is she anyway?"

Lola lifted her chin, breaking a small smile while playing with her long hoop earring, twisting it around and around. "She's five and she goes to school now. Kindergarten."

"School! Last time I saw her I think she was still in diapers."

With shoulders hunched together, elbows tight at her side, Lola stuck her hair behind her ears, scratched her chin, the back of her neck, fidgeting constantly but smiling dreamily. Her teeth were black, a mess of cavities. "She can almost read now. She's smart. Real smart. Nothing like me."

"I remember a young girl who wrote some pretty incredible poetry." Intuko reached his hand out to pat her arm, feeling the scaled flesh, the clamminess, the sickness of her skin. "I think Sarah must take after her mother."

Lola accepted the compliment with a bashful smile. She toyed with her mug for a few seconds before looking up and for the first time since she entered his office she made eye-to-eye contact. "Sarah's dad, his name was Kevin Kudlak. He...he wasn't a trick, you know. He really wasn't. He came from this place, he told me, called...Inuvik. Yeah, that's it. Inuvik. Funny name."

"What a small world. I come from a hamlet not too far from there. I actually went to school in Inuvik."

She pressed her fingers to her brow and closed her eyes. Even with them closed, he could sense the tears, the pain, the deep-seated grief that was going on inside this woman.

"Lola, if there's anything I can–"

"If something happens to me," her voice trembled.

"Lola, please, let me help you. I could–"

"No, no, don't get involved. It'll make it worse." She stood. "If something happens to me, take Sarah. Please. Don't let her go to a foster home. Please. Help her. You're the…the only one I know who's the same as her."

TWO

Angie Melville's watch beeped, reminding her it was three minutes to midnight. From her inky black sports car, complete with camel interior, she glanced in her rear view mirror. Only a few lone vehicles travelled up and down the street. Gingerly opening her car door, she stepped into Vancouver's damp, fall air and buttoned up the top snap of her black-leather bomber jacket. She scanned the street once more, jerking her head side-to-side for the sight of anyone she knew. Everything clear.

She slid her plastic card in the slot and heard the familiar drone of the after-hours bank door unlocking. When she stepped into the small area, the door latched behind her. No longer were her movements slow, as they were when she was outside on the streets, pretending to be calm and cool. Quickly, she moved to the wall machine, pushed the card in, and completed the instructions.

She punched in the withdrawal numbers and waited for the slot to open.

From her computer at home she had tapped into the bank's system, scammed a few bankcard numbers, redirected a few accounts and now she could hit two days of the maximum allotment of cash.

Then she waited, her gaze glued to the rotation of the minute hand on her watch until the time read two minutes past midnight. She punched the numbers again.

More cash!

She shoved the wad of bills into a black purse that was

casually slung over her shoulder and glided toward the door. Outside, she sucked in a breath of fresh air to temper the adrenalin racing through every one of her veins.

Jumping in her car, she started the engine and cranked LeAnn Rimes to full volume. Her quick departure from the curb left black rubber marks on the pavement, causing her miniature dream catcher with the pale blue feathers, hanging from her rear view mirror, to swing wildly.

"Hey baby, you're wild." Angie grabbed the dream catcher, fingered the feathers, and shoved it in her pocket.

She didn't want to go home, not when she was soaring like a white hooded eagle. She could try Hank's Place to see who was there. First, though, she should take her car home and park it in the underground parking to hide it from the crime that was as much a part of her neighbourhood as booze was to a liquor store.

She drove east down W. Hastings, away from the high-brow shops with mannequins dressed to perfection and glass-fronted restaurants with pink linen tablecloths. Within the span of a few short blocks, she was at E. Hastings, the *other* side of the street, where all the shops had black bars covering their small windows and the mannequins were real people dressed in torn and dirty clothing.

Angie parked her car in her designated spot, took the elevator to her apartment, and quickly stashed her cash in her lingerie drawer. Then she headed back outside to walk to Hank's. She sauntered up Main Street, quickening her steps past the Vancouver Police Department.

Passing Hastings and Main, she looked across the street at the steps and surrounding area of the Carnegie Library to see who had managed to stake a spot for the night. Elizabeth was sprawled across the top step, ranting and raving she was a queen, her long beige coat wrapped around her knees, and her tinfoil crown perched lopsidedly on her head.

So, the old loon had managed to get her favourite spot tonight, at least for a while anyway. A stubborn crazy woman, she could end up black and blue by morning, her thin orange hair matted with blood. But she came out of her hidey-hole each night regardless, telling her story of royalty.

Angie manoeuvred around the usual gang of young girls and guys, tattooed, bodies pierced, stoned, looking for more. Angie had been there. Some of them were new and not aware if they fell asleep their "friends" would roll them for shoes, money, or whatever else they could find. She remembered her first night on the streets–staying awake had meant survival.

Tonight only a handful of First Nations lounged on the steps, handing around a bottle in a paper bag, their black hair shining through the darkness. Some of that gang must have found a different spot for the night. Angie squinted to put names to shadows. One thing she'd learned–life on the streets had its own definite community.

She walked down the street, past the Bargain Centre on W. Hastings and Carroll Street, a building with painted murals, one of Bart Simpson with a light blue face. Another hangout for many. Years ago, Angie had gone there for clothes.

"Hey, Angie, you got a cig?" Straggly-haired Luc appeared in front of her like an escaping vapour of gas.

"Sure." She opened her purse.

"Heard there's some fuckin' good crack coming in soon." Luc lit his cigarette, the orange hue piercing the dark, a fluorescent period on the landscape.

"So's the word," said Angie.

"Got anything else for me?"

"Nope."

"Sure you don't, bitch."

She ignored him and continued. Another block and she passed the hookers, many of them from overseas–China, Malaysia, Korea–only the odd white girl.

Angie spotted Lola; her best friend during her first days on the streets. At least it looked like Lola, even though her blond hair was dyed black. Lola hooked to make money to care for her daughter Sarah. Angie had been around Lola during her pregnancy, and after for the first few years of Sarah's life. When Lola suddenly left Vancouver, Angie had been pissed and...she had missed the kid like crazy. Since Lola had returned from Toronto she seemed to be wasted most of the time. For Sarah's sake, Angie often offered to take her.

"Nice hair, Lola."

"It's a rinse. Something different." Lola ran her hand through her hair.

"How's biz?"

"Lots of creeps, man." Five-foot-nothing, lily-skinned Lola threw her cigarette to the ground, squashed it with the pointed toe of her stiletto, and waved at a passing Mercedes.

"How's Sarah tonight?"

Lola opened her coat, her breasts spilling out of the red tube top she had on. "It's her birthday today–we had a party together, before I had to leave."

"A party eh? Why didn't you invite me? Cake and all?"

Lola turned to Angie, tilted her head, and gave a crooked smile. "I picked up one of those iced ones with pink flowers on the sides at the grocery store. The kid thought she'd died and gone to heaven. You should'a seen her eat it, Ang."

"I bet. She likes that gooey stuff."

"I wrapped her present too, and put it in one of those fancy bags."

"Hey, maybe I'll pop by to see her? Who's with her?"

Lola quickly turned away from Angie and fluttered her eyes at a black car driving slowly by.

"Geez, Lola. You shouldn't leave her alone. She's only five."

"I had to tonight, Ang. I didn't have no choice. Look it's

not like I like doing it, but I gotta. I gotta to keep us alive."
Lola kept staring at the black car.

"You want me to check on her for you?" Angie asked.

Lola glanced quickly at Angie. "Would ya?" she asked
quietly before returning her gaze to the car, now doubling back,
anxious nervousness reflected in the shifting of her gaze.

Must not be an ordinary trick.

"Sure." Angie started to walk away.

"Ang."

Angie turned.

"I've moved. Lower rent you know. Get a key from
Candice." She paused for a moment, looking nervously at the
black Mercedes before turning back. "Take good care of Sarah
for me," she said in a low voice, "she deserves better."

The black car had slowed, inched ahead, then pulled over
and stopped on the side of the road. Lola surveyed the streets,
shifty-eyed like a cat hunting mice. She turned to Angie and
said, "Gotta go, girl."

Located on the edge of Gas Town, Hank's attracted a wide
assortment of people: druggies, hookers, strippers, and the
inner-city rich. Two extremely drunk slobbering men fought
near the front entrance where they had probably been bounced
out. Blood leaked from one guy's nose.

Angie's heels clicked on the red brick sidewalk as she
inched by the fight, taking a closer look to see who was getting
pulverized. She didn't know either guy. Pushing open the
wooden entrance door, she gazed through the dense, smoky
haze, trying to see a familiar face. Candice gyrated on a pole,
clad only in a black lace thong, her perfectly formed silicone
breasts swaying side-to-side in tandem.

"Hey, Angie."

"Hi ya, Charlie. How are ya?"

"Up, down. You want," he whispered in her ear.

"Nah." Up was crack, down was heroin. Angie didn't want either.

"Always so cool aren't you?" Charlie stuck his hand between her legs.

"Get your filthy hands off me." She slapped his hands.

"Tonight, my sweetie, there's more good stuff coming in."

"Don't call me sweetie and I've already heard."

"Okay, baby, but don't forget who thinks you're special."

Angie wove her way through the crowd and the heavy smoke, heading to the back room to talk to Candice after she finished her shift. Maybe tomorrow she'd splurge and get herself some coke for the weekend.

Angie couldn't help but think of Lola, how she was always strung out, and how nervous she'd seemed by that black car. Years ago, at the age of sixteen, after running away from boarding school, Angie had hooked up with Lola. They'd been two runaways, hanging out on Hastings and Main. Kindred spirits. They'd panhandled, combed garbage cans and grocery store dumpsters, sleeping where they could find a bed. Lola hung with pimps and prostitutes but Angie opted to make her living in the steamy, lucrative world of stripping. There was no touching when you stripped and your pimp didn't take all your money. Of course, her jazz-dance background provided by her well-to-do parents helped her bump and grind her way through her initial audition. Lola never had dance lessons, or lessons of any sort and didn't like the crowd thing. Hooking was her only option.

But Angie now wanted out of stripping and had found a way to make some money on the side. She wasn't getting any younger; all the new strippers were kids. At the age of twenty-five, she wanted to move to a nice side of town, get an apartment, a real job, settle down, live a normal life, maybe even have a baby, her own child, one she could feed breakfast, send to school, kiss good night. Or she'd like to go back to school, take some computer courses–maybe even get a diploma.

Life in this end of town only spiralled downhill and she didn't want any part of it any more. Angie smiled thinking of how much money she had made tonight. Added to her stripping money, it certainly would help.

Angie and Lola were now in two different worlds with the only connection being Sarah. So today was Sarah's birthday. How could Angie have forgotten? When Angie was little, she'd hated birthdays. Sure, she'd had store-wrapped presents that were always covered in bright paper and grotesque bows, but there had been no parties or doting parents to help blow out the candles. Her mother would get drunk and her father would hide. But then Lola had spent her own eighth birthday tying tourniquets around any limb with an open vein for her mother and her friends. She had told Angie, years ago, as they sat cross-legged in a back alley, slugging back a bottle of cheap wine, that she had made a game of it by pretending she was playing connect the dots with the needle marks on the arms of all the guests invited to her party.

Life could always be worse.

Angie pushed open the door and entered the small room where all the strippers hung out. Candice had just finished.

"Hi, there, doll. What you doing here on your night off?" Candice, clad in a red thong and an over-sized white T-shirt polished her toes with one foot on the bench.

"I need to get a key for Lola's place from you. I'm gonna check on Sarah."

"Good for you. I hate that she leaves that kid alone." Candice put her foot down and swivelled on the bench to do her other foot the same bright red. "If that loser up front doesn't stop trying to grab my crotch, I'm gonna kick him in the chops."

Angie smiled. Candice acted tough but underneath she

was a big, fluffy marshmallow. The only reason she stripped was to make money to raise her little boy, her one and only reason for living.

Candice slipped into her black, leopard-skin body suit, zipped it up, and juggled her boobs around. Then she went to her purse and pulled out a little white packet. "You want a snort?" She handed the stuff to Angie. "You do the honours while I finish getting ready."

Angie took a tiny spoon and put a little of the white powder on the end before passing it to Candice. "How's work tonight?"

"Shitty." Candice lowered her nose to the spoon, pinched one nostril shut with her pointer finger, and inhaled a big snort with the other nostril to clear the spoon. She leaned her head back for a few seconds then, gave her head a shake. "But hell, what else is a girl like me gonna do. I got me an office job once, dressed in hose every day, and the money sucked. I had hardly enough to feed us and what a bloody bore sitting on your butt all day, watching it spread. And, I tell you, there are as many grabbers out there as in here. I didn't get these boobs redone for nothing."

"I'm going to quit soon," said Angie firmly.

Candice smiled crookedly at Angie. "I hope you do, for your sake. You're smart Ang. You don't belong here."

"You're on in three minutes," Hank shouted from the door.

Candice waved. Then she turned back to Angie. "And Hank, he's not such a bad guy. He looks out for me."

Reapplying her bright red lipstick, Candice said, "How come you're not with that good-looking, dark-haired guy I seen you with a month or so ago?"

"He's got a wife. You know the type. Only wanted me for some weirded-out fantasy of his."

"Oh, girl, do I know the type. I finally got one without a wife but then I find out he's got a strange mama. Don't know what's worse. Hey, you didn't fall for this guy, did ya?"

"Nah. I know better." Angie avoided Candice's gaze.

"Ya sure?"

"I'll never let a man get the better of me. Anyway, we're kinda like scum to those big shot guys."

Candice stopped puffing up her hair and sharply turned to face Angie, her hands on her hips. "Did that jerk call you scum? Those kinds of men don't know the first thing about us. They've got no right to say anything when they're the ones ogling our bodies behind their wives backs. They sure don't go home a-showing and a-telling. If you ask me, he's the scum. I hate that kind of guy worse than anybody."

"You're right," said Angie attempting a smile. "Listen, you want him, you can have him. Maybe you can tame him."

"Yeah, right. Like I said, I got me a mama's boy and that's more than I can handle. Oh, there's my music." Candice rummaged through her purse. "Here's the key. Give that kid a kiss for me too."

Candice wrote Lola's address on a scrap piece of paper. "Now, it's show time. Catch you later." Candice blew her a kiss, picked up her red whip, and then sauntered seductively in her bad-girl gold boots onto the stage.

Just three blocks away, three men in Armani suits sat at a table in the back of Bailey's, a crowded high-class lounge. Cigar smoke swirled like zebra stripes above the lawyer, the accountant and the politician, and olives bobbed like plastic eyeballs in their martini glasses. A lounge singer, dressed in a slinky, silky, shiny dress, sang a breathy, seductive love song.

The men bowed their heads together to finish business, ignoring the woman on stage, her words on love, and her breasts spilling out of her sexy dress. They smoked, drank, and talked in low voices, manly whispers. Business was the name of the game, business that would bring in loads of cash.

Women would come later, when the deal was cooked, when they were high on risk, high on adrenalin. Then they would be pumped enough to hump their hookers and make love to their wives all in the same night.

"That hooker knows too much and she'll talk if pressed."

"Which one?"

"Jimmy's girl. The one with the kid."

"Maybe we should take the kid, lock her up until everything's distributed and we're in the clear again. She won't be tempted to talk if her kid's in danger.

"Why don't we just kill them?"

"Can't risk it."

"She's a hooker for shit's sakes. They disappear off the streets faster than toilet paper in a can."

"Yeah, but she's a seasoned hooker. We can't have the cops anywhere near us. Let's just get the kid to keep the hooker quiet. But don't kill the kid. If she knows the kid's alive, she'll keep her mouth shut."

As they looked up, they saw their main mule approaching the table.

"About time you got here."

"Hallelujah. It's going out, men." Always pretending to be the big shot, he slapped hands with everyone. He puffed out his chest and grinned. "I'd say it's time to have a few drinks and a few women."

"What you do in your time is your business. Just keep your *actions* away from the cops. We can't afford screw-ups."

Once business was taken care of they all got up to leave. Walking out the door they ran into Charlie, slithering toward them.

"What the fuck you doing here?"

"When's it in? People are asking."

"Get back to your end of the street and wait for your distributor. You come to us again–we blow your fucking head off."

THREE

Intuko glanced at his watch. No wonder he was starving; it was already nine p.m. Where had the time gone? Hazel had left hours ago and he'd spent the time since trying to fix a leaky faucet in the men's bathroom. Had to save money wherever possible. The church had no money in the budget to call a plumber. He'd managed to stop the constant dripping but didn't realize he'd been at the task for well over two hours.

His stomach grumbled, reminding him he only had one wrinkly apple, a loaf of stale bread and a bit of peanut butter left in the bottom of a plastic container at home. His one bedroom apartment wasn't really much of a home. In fact, it was just a place for him to sleep. He ate all of his meals at restaurants.

He pushed back from his desk and stretched. Which one of his favourite restaurants should he head to tonight? He glanced out the window to check out the weather. November was the rainy month in Vancouver. When he didn't see any drops on the glass, he grabbed his denim jacket from the hook, and left his umbrella.

Outside, he buttoned his jacket and strolled toward Main Street, trying to figure out what he felt like for dinner. He'd had pizza last night and Chinese food the night before. Deep in thought, he walked a few blocks, nodding at all the familiar faces as many pan-handled in the same spots night after night. He said hello, and asked how they were, throwing down his loose change.

When he arrived at the restaurant called The Café–which

was located just up from Hastings and Main on Columbia Street–he paused outside the lighted windows of a run-down coffee shop that boasted a decent egg salad sandwich. Lots of the street girls hung out here. He hated that he hadn't gotten Lola's phone number or address when she'd come into his office earlier. If she were here, maybe he could buy her dinner or at least a coffee. After asking him to take care of Sarah– should something happen to her–Lola had bolted out of his office. And when he'd tried to catch her and ask where he could get reach her, she'd waved him off. He let her go, knowing by her shaking, she desperately needed a fix.

With a determined step, he pushed open the heavy, warped door and entered.

Most of the seats were vinyl booths with the exception of a few rickety tables scattered in the middle of the room. The room was drab, and faded dusty landscape prints hung crookedly on the walls. All the street girls wore heavy make-up and next to nothing on their bodies. High shoes, black boots, short skirts, tube tops; Intuko knew their gaudy clothes were from the Salvation Army. He glanced around the room but couldn't see Lola.

He approached one of the booths. "Hi, ladies."

"Hey, it's mister preacher man," one of the hookers said. Her eyes were glassy and she looked totally wasted. "You wanna have a good time?"

"Not tonight, thanks. Any of you seen Lola?"

"Oh, you want Lola instead." The hooker fluttered her false eyelashes and wagged a finger–which had an incredibly long red nail–in Intuko's direction. "She's expensive. I'm cheap, just for you."

Intuko held up a hand. "I want to buy her a coffee."

The hooker snarled at Intuko and slumped in her seat. "I ain't seen her. She's already working. If she don't turn 'em, Jimmy he gets fuckin' pissed."

"Do any of you have her phone number?"

A hooker wearing black spandex pants snorted in laughter. "No, Mister preacher man, we don't got no number. *Jimmy* keeps her and that kid locked up. Lola's his prize. She sucks dick faster than any ho I know." The hooker stood up, rubbed her breasts against Intuko, and threw her arms around his neck.

"You know I can't." He pried her arms loose and backed away.

"Don't I look fine?" She thrust her hip out.

"Yeah, you do. But I've got to order some dinner. How about I buy you all coffee refills?"

After wolfing down an egg salad sandwich and greasy fries, Intuko stepped outside. Most of the hookers, after the coffee Intuko bought for them, had taken to the streets. He had thought Lola might show up for a break but no such luck.

The night was pleasant enough and Intuko contemplated hailing a cab but then he decided to save his money and walk home. He didn't have anything else to do but go home and watch television, and since the Vancouver Canucks weren't playing tonight, he wasn't in a rush.

Angie didn't feel like walking so she called a cab, which dropped her off at Lola's apartment building. If only she had a birthday gift to give Sarah. In her pocket, she felt the soft feathers of the dream catcher she'd snatched from her mirror. It wasn't much, but it was better than nothing.

Angie entered the front hallway and gagged. Urine and puke. Someone had punched the walls, leaving holes the size of basketballs.

Why was Lola living here?

Angie unlocked the front door to the apartment and had to push it with her shoulders to get the door to move. Dirty underwear, garter belts, stiletto heels, clothing, and garbage had been strewn in front of the door and everywhere in the room as well. Of course, not much of the stuff, with the exception of a beat-up backpack, belonged to Sarah.

Walking down the hall, she kicked clothes and dodged needles, until she got to the bedroom at the end of the hall. She slowly opened the door to find Sarah curled up in a tight ball. In her tiny hands she clutched a bottle of pearly pink nail polish.

Angie tiptoed to the makeshift bed and squatted down to stroke the child's thick, straight, dark-brown hair. The mattress was bare and a soiled blanket covered her. What a beauty! She brought one of Sarah's soft, warm hands to her cheek, her skin feeling like silk. She didn't deserve this. No baby did.

Gently, Angie put the little hand down on a dirty pillow and when she did, she saw the polish on Sarah's nails. It was bumpy, excess smearing the skin surrounding the nails. She closed her eyes. The child had sat by herself when the apartment was empty and it was dark outside, trying her best to put on her nail polish.

She rubbed Sarah's pink-painted thumbnail, feeling every rough spot. In all likelihood, the whole time she'd been alone in this filthy apartment, putting on her nail polish, she hadn't shed one tear. The kid never cried. Even when strange noises might have frightened her into hiding in a closet. Angie had found her there a few times, in the old apartment, shivering and coiled up like an old fashioned ringlet, with just a face of stone.

Angie's face burned. Her skin prickled. She had to get Sarah out of here.

"Who's there?" Sarah sat up in the bed and pushed herself against the wall in fear.

"It's just me, Angie. I wanted to check on you."

"Angie." Sarah pushed a tangled strand of hair from her face. "Did you see my birthday present? My mom gave me some nail polish."

In her pocket, Angie felt the dream catcher and the

downiness of the feathers that were attached to it. "I did see it. I love the colour. Happy birthday, Sarah. I brought you a little present too."

"You did? Really. Two presents. I'm sure lucky."

Angie gulped back any crass words, not wanting to spoil Sarah's moment, hardly able to believe this child, so ratty and dirty, thought she was lucky. She pulled out the dream catcher, letting it dangle in front of Sarah's awed eyes.

"Here you go. A wise old street friend of mine told me it's supposed to ward off the evil spirits that try to come into your dreams. So, no more nightmares, kiddo."

"Is it really for me?"

"Yup."

"Thanks. You're my best friend you know."

Sarah flung her arms around Angie's neck. Angie hugged her, patting her on the back, resting her cheek against the child's matted hair.

"You want to come home with me tonight?"

Sarah shook her head. "I have to go to school in the morning."

"I could drop you off."

Sarah twisted a lock of hair around her finger. "My mom said she'd walk me 'cause it's my birthday." She stopped uncoiling her hair and looked up at Angie, her eyes wide, innocent. "She only ever walked me the first day so tomorrow's special. Can I come another day?"

"Yeah, of course. We'll make a plan and have a sleep-over party." Angie pulled Sarah onto her lap. "How about I sing you back to sleep?"

Lola slouched in the back seat of a black Mercedes. Another hooker sat beside her and a blond woman who wore a big floppy hat that hid her face sat up front. Lola could care less who she was with; she just wanted the high. They passed around a coke-filled cigarette. The conservative-looking trick driving the car had parked near GM Place, and gone into Bailey's.

As Lola inhaled a deep drag, the car door swung open and Mr. Puffed-up-chest slid into the front seat. "Fini fuckin' complete," he said to the blond woman. Then he turned to Lola. "Give me some of that, bitch."

Lola sucked on the cigarette one more time before passing it on. Grinning, the guy slipped the cigarette onto a roach clip and took a long hard drag. Then he pounded his fist on the steering wheel. "Tonight we're going to have some fun."

The smoke eddied through the small space. Lola watched it shift and shape. When she was a kid she used to lie on her back and watch the clouds do the same thing. So long ago. Now she lay on her back for money.

The hooker sitting beside Lola in the car started talking about something. Lola turned to look at the white teeth talking in the dark. Perfect white teeth. Her tongue, dry, parched, skimmed over her own two crooked front teeth, how they overlapped like the letter X in the alphabet. She always wanted nice teeth, like Ashley Hendry and Britney Parady, two girls at her school. She remembered in Junior High when they got their braces, the silver glint of the metal, dazzling, the coloured elastics for every occasion–red and green at Christmas, orange and black for Halloween. Then when they got them off in high school, they showed off their perfect smiles to the popular crowd hanging by their lockers. Lola's tongue hit a hole, where a tooth had been punched out.

Tonight she could forget about teeth, about everything. This trick had offered great money for a full night orgy and...she could go up-down, up-down all night. What luck! Plus, she could get off the streets for a while and get away from Jimmy. He'd been a mean bastard lately. She shivered thinking of walking in on him and his rich "friend." They were in some sort of a meeting. Jimmy, he beat her bad for that. Punched that tooth out. Then made her hit the streets.

She ground her teeth and jiggled her leg. She liked the up. Her throat dry, she slugged back some rum. Everything in her life, with the exception of Sarah, was so fucked up that getting off the streets for an entire night seemed too good to be true. The cigarette passed her way again. She inhaled. Deeply. The effect amazing, making her body vibrate.

She looked at the other girl holding her head back in ecstasy, a smile curling her lips. The chick had to be new to the Vancouver streets; she'd tried to walk Lola's turf. At first Lola had been pissed but just after she told her to beat it, find her own street, the car had pulled up. Fortunate for Lola, the girl was young, fresh–fourteen, fifteen perhaps–and probably some new little runaway. With those nice teeth, she looked as if she came from money. Like Angie. The trick had wanted "fun sex." Lola remembered being twelve and on the streets. Boy, had she been sought after then even though she'd not been a virgin since she was maybe four.

She thought she recognized the short-haired, clean-cut guy who'd picked them up; he wasn't a regular trick but he might be someone she'd had once. He looked like he had loads of money too. He drove a nice car. They'd cruised by her, picked up the young one, then come back to get Lola just when she saw Angie. Perfect timing. Angie would take care of Sarah, and Lola could get away from Jimmy and all the other pervs.

Lola stared out the window. Sarah would be okay with Angie. God, how Lola loved that kid, ever since she saw her baby dressed in a pink blanket in the hospital. Kevin had visited her then and Lola thought they'd be a family. But when she arrived home from the hospital, he got tanked all the time and Lola had to take to the streets again to make money. Kevin left her when Sarah was only two months old.

Then she met Jimmy.

Jimmy. At first Jimmy acted nice to her. He bought her fancy clothes, took her to real restaurants. Lola had eaten steak, shrimp, and lobster. She'd never had such good food. He bought Sarah candy, toys, pretty pink clothes, and bows for her hair. And he gave Lola crack and heroin, as much as she wanted–sometimes they had up to twenty fixes a day. Then it had all turned bad and he shoved Lola back on the streets to turn trick after trick, only now all her money went to him. Lola knew if she tried to leave, he'd find her and kill Sarah. Worse– he'd cut her off. He had told her as much.

But tonight, Jimmy, he might not care if she disappeared all night, not if she brought in the cash they'd offered. He just wanted the money she could make. She hoped.

Lola watched the other girl tie her arm. She shivered thinking of how good it would feel when it was her turn.

Sarah couldn't get back to sleep. Her mom should be home soon. She wondered what she'd be like tonight. Nice or mean. Maybe she'd comb Sarah's hair, put it in braids, or play Go Fish with her. Sarah hoped she'd come home without Jimmy. Her mom hadn't combed her hair in weeks 'cause she was always with Jimmy and he was always mean. Sometimes he hurt her mom so bad she had bruises all over her face. And he hurt Sarah too although her mom always tried to protect her.

Sarah heard the door open. She got up and inched to the door. Sticking her head around the corner, she saw a strange woman.

"Kid, get out here," the woman yelled.

Sarah slowly walked down the hall, clutching her nail polish and dream catcher–her birthday presents. The woman grabbed her by the arm, pinching her skin. "They didn't tell me you'd be such a dirty little thing."

She dug her long red nails in Sarah's skin piercing the flesh. "You're coming with me you little brat."

31

* * *

Angie opened her apartment door, kicked off her heels, and hung up her jacket in the front closet. A tan-tiled entrance led to a carpeted living room in her basic one-bedroom apartment. A crushed-velvet, black sofa and love seat sat kitty-corner to each other in the living area across from her black wall unit that held a stereo, stacks of CD's and a small television.

Angie immediately put on Sarah McLachlan's CD *Surfacing* then went to her lingerie drawer for the cash. She dropped the money on the coffee table and headed to the fridge located in the kitchenette that was openly joined to the living room. After she'd grabbed a beer, she sank into the sofa.

She thumbed through the money she'd made tonight. Three thousand dollars. She counted every last bill. All of this cash for diddling around with computer passwords. As a kid, Angie's parents had invested in technology to keep her occupied. Hours upon hours she'd spent, alone in her perfectly decorated room with the canopy bed, in the company of the computer.

The thrill of victory for Angie, of the hope of one day soon getting out of this end of town, was clouded by the memory of Sarah lying on that mattress, nails dirty and hair tangled as if it hadn't been properly combed in weeks. Tomorrow, Angie would pick her up and take her shopping again. Sarah loved the clothes Angie bought her–last time it had been denim overalls and a plaid tam hat–and she had looked so darn cute in them. Angie stashed her money in her purse.

For two hours after she had gone to bed, Angie tossed and turned, thinking of Sarah alone in that filthy apartment. Finally, at three in the morning, she kicked back her covers and left the bed. She had to go back and check on the kid. Leaving had been the wrong thing to do. Even if she just checked on her, made sure Lola was with her.

Thirty minutes later, Angie entered Lola's and immediately saw that the garbage on the table had been cleared and replaced with a drug scale, vials, and plastic pouches. No one seemed home though. She quickly scanned the room, also noticing that Sarah's backpack was gone. Angie ran down the hall toward the bedroom and flung open the door. Sarah's dream catcher, nail polish and Peter Rabbit book were gone too.

Angie heard the front door open and she stepped into the hallway, hoping to see Sarah and Lola, sucking on ice drinks, possibly just coming in from a trip to the all night grocery.

"What are you doing here?"

Angie recognized Jimmy, Lola's pimp. "Checking on Sarah," she said.

"She ain't here, so get the fuck out of here."

"Where is she?"

"Didn't you hear what I said?"

"Is she with Lola?"

Jimmy pulled out a knife from his socks. "I could cut that pretty face of yours for asking so many questions."

"Okay, I'm going." Angie, shaking to the core of her bones, held her shoulders back and quickly walked by Jimmy and toward the door.

But he got there first, blocking her from leaving. He pressed the knife against her throat. "You say one word and I'll cut you good."

"I won't say anything."

"You didn't see a thing."

"I know."

He flung her around and she fell to the floor. "Keep your fucking mouth shut girl." He loomed over her. "Stop asking for the kid too. They find out you're asking, you're dead meat."

FOUR

Intuko awoke the next morning still thinking about Lola. He hoped she would come back to see him at the church. Maybe he could talk her into bringing her daughter, Sarah, to Sunday school. He doubted it–but the suggestion was worth a try. If he could find out where Lola lived, he could arrange for someone to pick Sarah up. Intuko hadn't seen the child in years. He thought back to his conversation with Lola. Was Sarah's father really from Inuvik?

As Intuko searched through his sock drawer, trying to find a pair without holes, he spotted the carving his mother had given him ages ago. He stopped and stared but didn't touch. The carving depicted a mother with a happy baby in a papoose on her back. Since her death, Intuko had kept it hidden in a drawer.

He snatched a pair of grey socks and quickly shut the drawer. Then he sighed and sat on the end of his bed. What was he thinking?

He couldn't go to that prison and teach a carving class. He put on his socks, ignoring the holes in the heels, and finished getting dressed for work.

Maybe that Susan woman from the prison wouldn't call back.

Susan Peterson pulled a marine blue, collared shirt from her closet. There were four other shirts exactly the same lined up in a row, taking up a good portion of the space in her small clothes closet. Did she have the right bra on though?

Yesterday, she had worn one of those flimsy bras and had ended up sprinting after an inmate trying to escape.

Scheduled to work in living unit "A" today, also called Alpha, she had to work with some of the institution's most aggressive criminals. She hated working "A" because the mix of people didn't work. They lumped the aggressors with the mental disorders, creating a brutal combination. Susan knew the mix wasn't right and lobbied all the time for changes.

Taking the shirt off the hanger, she buttoned it up, tucked it into her navy pants, and did up her black belt. Next, she stuck her feet in a pair of black, sturdy, rubber soled shoes, sitting on the edge of the bed to tie the laces. Finally, she was ready for her twelve-hour shift that ran from seven a.m. to seven p.m. No breaks, a hard shift, the inmates were awake the entire time.

Despite all of this, she got a satisfaction from her job. No one in her family could understand why she wanted to spend her days at a prison when she had a degree in marketing.

She walked quietly from the bedroom to the kitchen where she pulled a traveling mug from the shelf and filled it to the brim with black coffee. Snapping on the plastic lid, she heard a quiet rap on the door.

"Mary, hi," she said opening the door. "Eh-gads, it's chilly out there, come on in."

"Cold is not the word." Mary stepped in the house rubbing her hands. "Is Hilary still sleeping?"

"Yeah, she needs a few extra minutes."

"Was she up later than usual?"

Susan rolled her eyes. "When I work these shifts and I get home at seven-thirty, I don't have the heart to put her to bed an hour later."

Mary walked over to the coffeepot and helped herself to a cup of coffee. "Don't beat yourself up, hon, you're doing this alone. Has that ex of yours been around lately?"

"The support payment comes regularly but Eric sure doesn't. The only person he hurts is–"

Mary stopped Susan by pointing toward the hallway.

Susan turned. "Morning, sleepy-head."

Hilary pushed a lock of red hair from her face and rubbed the corner of her eyes. "Do you have to leave soon?"

"I do, sweetie. But not before I give you a great big hug."

"Are you going to be here after school?" Her daughter's whine sounded like a noisy kitten meowing for more milk.

Susan shot a look at Mary who mouthed the word "guilt," then sipped her coffee.

"No baby," Susan squatted down to be eye-level with Hilary. "I have to work. But after today, I have four days off…which means I'll be off for the weekend and we can do something really special. Why don't you think of what you'd like to do and tell me when I get home tonight?"

"Well, okay."

"Your Mom's got to go so let me get you some breakfast." Mary winked at Hilary. "What would you like?"

"Cereal. Mommy, don't forget to sign my field trip form. My teacher said it was supposed to be in *yesterday.*"

"Oh, right. Where is it?" Susan took a heavy, quilt-lined, navy jacket, that was also a part of her uniform, from the closet and put it on as she walked to the kitchen counter.

"I don't know, but it *has* to be in today," moaned Hilary. "It just has to be today or I can't go. I'll have to sit in the office while all the other kids get to ride on the bus and–"

"Okay, Hilary. I get the picture," said Susan.

"Can you volunteer for the trip?"

Mary placed a bowl of Cheerios and a glass of apple juice in front of Hilary. "There you go mighty mite. Eat your breakfast so you can be the smartest kid at school."

Hilary took a sip of juice. "Can you volunteer, Mom?"

"I'll have to look at my schedule."

"Can you look now?"

"I'll look later."

"All the other moms go on *every* trip *all* the time. It's no fair."

"I'll write a note to the teacher. How's that? I have to get going Hil or else I'll be late for work." Susan scrunched her nose to Hilary's nose then kissed her on the forehead.

Hilary heaved a dramatic sigh but then perked up and asked, "Have I said I love you yet today, Mommy?"

"Have I said I love *you* yet today?" Susan winked.

Hilary shook her head so hard her red curls flapped back and forth like a dog wagging its tail. Her smile showed her two front adult teeth. "No you haven't." She crossed her arms, keeping her smile plastered on her face.

Bending over, Susan brushed Hilary's hair away from her ear and, using the same voice she used every morning when they played this game, loudly whispered into Hilary's ear, "I love you."

"Me too," said Hilary. "Bye, Mommy."

The damp morning air nipped Susan's skin right through her heavy coat. She hopped into her blue Honda Prelude. The car rumbled and coughed smoke out its back end before deciding to fire completely, obviously needing a good expensive tune-up before winter set in. And with the weather today, that didn't seem too far off. The extras always ate away at Susan's bi-weekly pay check: house repairs, car repairs, groceries, and Hilary's gymnastics.

She took a sip of her coffee then put it back in a sticky plastic holder. Just yesterday Hilary had spilled her orange soda all over the place. If Eric saw this car, he'd have a fit. At least since the split, Susan didn't have to be reminded about her undesirable housekeeping skills.

For years she had struggled, fussing and cleaning to please Eric. When she stopped trying to be someone she wasn't and tried to be herself, her marriage fell apart. Susan had spent many nights awake crying, wondering if she had done the right thing by leaving.

At first Hilary had commented on being happy that she didn't have to listen to any more fighting. And Susan was sure her daughter felt relieved that her father wasn't around to scold her for every misplaced toy. But after a couple of months, Hilary, out-of-the-blue one day said, "I wish you and daddy would get back together." Susan saw the sadness in Hilary's eyes and felt it in her own heart.

She backed out of the driveway sloshing coffee everywhere. And Eric wasn't making things any easier. Why did he feel being a father was only important when the marriage was together? He claimed *she* had broken the family, *she* had no family values, and his not seeing Hilary was all *her* fault.

Enough of Eric; she needed to think of work and how she could help the inmates with *their* many problems. Her minuscule challenges paled in comparison to their lives.

A long, windy gravel road led to the prison gates. The large frost fences, with the barbed wire meshed at the top like a crown of thorns, surrounded the prison. A roaming light with the power of at least a thousand light bulbs scrutinized the grounds, remaining on day and night, searching for those potential escapees. Some inmates dug holes and crawled under the fence while others risked ripping their bodies to bloody shreds by climbing over the barbed wire. Once a prisoner had stolen cutting shears from the prison hair salon and tried to cut through the fence. The prisoner would have become an escaped convict, running from city to city, dodging police cars if she had been forty pounds lighter. As it was, she got caught in a fence hole that was too small for her body and consequently was charged and given a heftier sentence.

Susan opened the heavy side door, hearing it slam behind

her. Shut in. At least she could leave at night.

"Morning, Susan."

"Hi, Joelle."

"You on Alpha again?"

"Looks that way. How about you?"

"I'm in Golf. I don't know how you do it. I have refused to work the units you always get stuck on. I'd rather quit first."

Susan picked up her shift summary to read what had been going on in the hours previous to her arrival. Once finished, she glanced at the clock. She'd better get a move on–breakfast for the inmates appeared on the trolley cart at seven-thirty. Grabbing her radio and Personal Alarm Transmitter, and snapping her keys onto the key clip attached to her pants, she started through the first of eight doors to get to her assigned unit. At each door, she flashed her sign-in card against the black terminal to gain access. When she entered the man-trap hallway, she listened for the heavy metal door to click behind her. Once it shut, she was safe to walk the hall. She hurried as the trapped-in feeling gave her the shivers.

Speeding down the hallway, she glanced through the small window into the front entrance of the prison and the lobby for visitors. Some of the women never had visitors and others had friends who tried to sneak in drugs through their vaginas. Hooping, they called it. Good friends they were.

Finally, after more corridors and stairs, she reached her unit. Immediately, she looked through the small window of each cell to take a count and make sure every body in every cell was breathing.

All accounted for, she went to the small office and phoned in her head count. Then she checked her Personal Alarm Transmitter, better known as a P.A.T., just in case trouble brewed and she needed back up. Tired today, she hoped there would be no need to press the alert button. Once she knew her alarm would respond with just a touch, she ran her hand through her hair. Time to unlock their doors for breakfast.

A fighting troublemaker barrelled out and headed to the coffee machine, almost knocking over a mental disorder inmate who was meekly coming out of her cell.

"Hey, watch where you're going," Susan snapped.

"She's always in the way, stupid bitch."

"Slow it down and she won't be in your way."

"She should move," the inmate snapped, then under her breath she whispered, "Asshole."

"Watch your mouth. You talk to me like that again and I'll have you charged and your sorry butt thrown in seg. I tell you, you've got to learn how to live with other people or you'll spend your whole time locked away by yourself." Susan shook her head. It could be a long day.

But the morning sped by; there was much to do and much attention to dole out. And Susan thought Hilary, a soon-to-be-nine-year-old, demanded a lot of attention; she was an angel compared to these incarcerated women. Considered too violent or disturbed, the women in Alpha were not allowed to leave their unit. They either performed job tasks on the unit or took part in therapy programs like colouring, crafts, or music therapy.

Lunch arrived for the inmates at noon, then they were locked up between twelve-thirty and one to give the staff time to eat. By the time Susan ploughed her way through door after door, signing in every time, she had to rush to microwave her leftovers and gobble them down. She got up from the staff table to wash her hands when the front desk receptionist, Miriam, walked in the staff room.

"Hey, Susan. You got a message. I left it on the bulletin board. Boy, is there a buzz around here."

"You talking about Lola?" Susan walked to the board and took the pink sheet of paper.

"Yeah," said Miriam.

Joelle zipped up her purple lunch kit. "Baby-faced Lola. The one in a hundred who might go straight."

"They say she's missing," said Miriam. "Got in a car and never came back."

"How do they know she's not gone back to T.O. or high-tailed it down to Seattle?" Joelle scrunched up her face in doubt.

"I heard two girls who were brought in last night talking," said Miriam. "They sounded scared."

"Lots of hookers get in cars and don't come back. Until morning," said Joelle sarcastically as she stuffed her lunch kit in the fridge.

"If she is missing," said Susan, "I hope the cops do something about it this time. Too many girls have gone missing."

Susan looked down at her message from yesterday. The minister of the Princess Street United Church returning her call, telling her he was interested in teaching art. Good. She'd start spreading the word, get some signs up. No time to call him back now though, she had to get back to work.

Lola woke up on a hard floor, her eyes heavy slits, her throat dry, her body sticky, sore, bruised, nude. Shivering, she tried to wrap her arms around her breasts but she couldn't. Her hands…her feet, were tied together with coarse rope that dug into her skin. And her mouth was…taped. Her clothes. Where were her clothes?

She tried to stand but toppled over, back onto the dusty wooden floor. Dried blood cracked near her ankles, her wrists. Her body shook. She needed a fix.

Footsteps. She opened her eyes to see boots. Then she felt the kick to her sides, her head, her mouth.

More footsteps, a different voice. "I think this is Jimmy's main girl."

"She's not Jimmy's girl. Jimmy's girl is blond."

Lola heard the voices but they seemed to fade in and out. She thought of Sarah, walking to school. By herself. Lola felt tears on her own face, knowing how disappointed Sarah would be. Someone grabbed her by the hair.

"Look closer at her. She's got dye in her hair."

They pushed her head back on the floor.

"What about the other one?"

They walked away from Lola; she tried to open her eyes and scream but nothing came out. She tried to scream again. Nothing. They dragged the nude body of the girl she had partied with last night by the hair, across the rough floor.

"Set up a video," said the man. "I can't believe how these videos are selling. Did I tell you I'm cooking a deal in Germany?" The man laughed. "We're making good cash with this."

Lola faded in and out. *Dreaming*–about Sarah–the two of them sitting on a log at Kits Beach, the sun high in Vancouver's amazingly blue summer sky. *Dying*–Lola opened her eyes–no sun, she needed a fix–so bad–Jimmy got her hooked–nauseous, dizzy, her head pounded, her body shook. *Dreaming*–she watched Sarah run into the water, squealing when the cold water lapped her little toes, rising to her ankles before she had time to run back to mommy. *Dying*–Lola threw up.

"What should we do with Jimmy's girl?" They stood above Lola.

"She's still alive. She's seen our faces. Jimmy will go berserk." The woman was the one talking. "And you know they said stay low with the cops."

He pulled out a gun. "I'll…I'll shoot her. Then I'll…bag her head and… oh, fucking eh, this will be great. You can shoot the movie with her dead and bagged. I'll give it to her good." He laughed. "It'll be a great show. Then…I'll dump her. Yeah, that will work. The other one I can bury in the back, but if this one's dumped it will look like a regular john. The police will run in circles, they'll never link us."

Lola opened her eyes to see a gun pointed at her head.

FIVE

Angie stood behind a plant, peering at her mother as she hovered at the top of the stairs. She always looked as if she belonged on the cover of a fashion magazine. Tall and slim, she flowed instead of walked, her body swaying almost as if she could hear music amidst the silence of the air. Thick wheat coloured hair hung to her shoulders with a perfect little flip fringing the ends. Her lush red lips and sapphire blue eyes were more like doll's features, the china dolls that stood behind glass in expensive toy stores. Then there was her milky skin. She had creamy, opaque skin that to Angie looked like pearls.

But not the soft ones that were completely round, the other ones that were bumpy and odd-shaped. Especially when she started screaming Angie's name. Then her skin changed from pearly-pale to bumpy-blotches. Her lips filled with blood as she drew them in a straight line to mash her teeth together, and her sapphire eyes took on that cut-glass look, jagged edges ready to slice.

By her wobbly steps, Angie knew her mother had been drinking so she quickly darted into the dining room to hide under the table.

Shaking, she curled into the smallest ball. Why didn't her daddy come? She hated her mother. Even when she was dressed in silks and furs, smiling happily, linked to Daddy's arm. Angie hated them both, her mother for hitting her, her father for never telling her to stop.

Jolting up from her dead sleep, and horrid dream, Angie felt nauseous. Every time she dreamt of her mother, she vowed she would never treat her own flesh and blood the way her mother had treated her.

Angie got out of bed and made herself some breakfast, hoping that the food would make her feel better. But she could barely get a piece of toast down. Her nerves were frayed. Probably more from Jimmy's threats then her dumb dream. Nothing Jimmy said, however, mattered. She had to get out and see if she could find Lola and Sarah.

Taking the only snapshot she had of Lola and Sarah, a grainy picture that had been taken with one of those instant cameras two years back, Angie took to the streets. The morning light made the corner of Hastings and Main an ugly sight. At night people jived, moved, ghetto blasters played rap music, sirens screamed and bodies narrowed the streets. In the morning, the streets suddenly widened, empty, silent. Bodies could be seen sleeping off the binge from the night before, some revelling in puke and urine, others covered in blood probably unaware they had even been in a fight. There were the odd few who stumbled with bloodshot eyes, already looking for their next fix. Angie's forceful steps seemed to scream as she walked the cracked concrete that desperately needed repair.

The first place Angie went was Lola's. With every nerve in her body quivering, she approached the apartment building. If Jimmy had stayed up all night, he was probably in a deep sleep right about now. She tiptoed to the door, carefully sticking the key in the lock, her hands shaking with every click of the metal hitting metal. When it was secure, she let out a breath. Then she slowly turned the key, the familiar catch of the door unlocking sounded like a loud beat of a drum. She gently pushed the door open enough to peer inside. The scale that sat on the table last night was gone.

She stepped in.

No Jimmy sleeping on the ratty sofa.

She tiptoed down the hall, her heart pounding like a junkie's vein. She passed the bathroom. Light off and empty. Creaking open the bedroom door, she found it empty as well. No one was in the apartment. Angie ran her hands through her hair and closed her eyes. They were gone. Sarah too. Where to next?

Candice's.

"Did Lola show up at Hank's last night?" she asked Candice, in her pink satin pyjamas. A kid's movie blared in the background.

"Geez, Ang, you're here early. I didn't see Lola."

"She's missing. So is Sarah."

"She's probably sleeping off a hangover somewhere. Look, let it go. I'll see you at work tonight. I wanna finish watching Peter Pan with my kid."

"I think something's wrong, Candice."

Candice turned to stare at her little guy, sitting cross-legged in front of the television, an empty cereal bowl by his knees. She crossed her arms over her chest and turned back to Angie. "Ang," she whispered, shaking her head, "don't involve me in nothing. He means the world to me."

Angie walked away from Candice's clutching the photo of Lola and Sarah in her hands. Back to Hastings and Main.

She found Elizabeth on the front steps of the Carnegie Library.

"Hi, Elizabeth."

"Did you know I'm a queen?"

"Yeah, and I'm a princess." Angie sat beside Elizabeth and fixed her crown. "And I have a friend who's a princess, her name's Lola. Have you seen her?"

"Does she twirl and spin in her long velvet gown?" Elizabeth stood up and started to spin in circles, her long beige coat flapping by her knees, her tin foil crown once again sitting lopsided on her head.

Sometimes Elizabeth talked semi-sane but Angie knew that time was not right now. Angie patted Elizabeth on the back. "See you later, Queenie."

"I'm a queen you know. I can spin and twirl…"

Angie headed towards the Bargain Centre–which was located next to a small city park–to check out who was there. Luc lay huddled in an old torn sleeping bag under a relic oak. His makeshift bedroom was close to the dilapidated play structure, displaying a red tunnel slide defaced with graffiti.

"Luc, wake up." Angie shook his shoulders.

"What the fuck you want?" He pulled the sleeping bag over his head.

"You seen Lola?"

"Fuck you."

Two hours later, Angie was no closer to finding Lola than when she started. Frustrated, as everyone she knew didn't really care that they hadn't seen her, Angie decided to stop to get a coffee at the Starbuck's around the corner on West Cordova.

Cardboard cup in hand, she walked away, deep in thought. Maybe Lola was just out partying. But what about Sarah? Angie wondered if Paul, the lawyer she'd been seeing, could help.

She used her cell phone to call his cell phone.

"What are you calling me for? I'm busy," he snapped.

"I think a friend of mine is missing. I just wanted to see if…if you could help."

"Who are you talking about?" He sounded exasperated.

"Lola."

"For shit sake's, Angie. Isn't she a hooker? You working tonight? Maybe we could get together after. I've got candy for us."

And I'm a stripper she thought.

"I'm not on tonight," she answered.

Rounding the corner to head back onto Hastings, she ran into Charlie. He whispered in her ear. "I got coke. It just arrived in town."

Angie thought of the scale she had seen at Jimmy's last night. "You seen Lola?"

Charlie tucked his shoulders to his ears and glanced up and down the street, like he was an animal being stalked. When he looked back at her, he whispered, "Don't mess around, Ang."

"Sarah's missing too."

"You're asking for trouble."

"Why? Why do you say that? What do you know?"

"I don't know nothing. But Ang, Jimmy's a mean bastard. You know that. And Lola, she's Jimmy's girl."

"Did Jimmy do something to her?"

"No. No."

"You know something, I can tell."

"Jimmy's looking for her. Big time. Asking everyone."

Angie tilted her head in disbelief. "You're telling me Jimmy doesn't know where she is?" She paused. "Where could Sarah be?"

"Don't ask any more questions Ang. The big boys, they don't care who they knock off."

Angie raised a questioning eyebrow. "Big boys? Who you talking about?"

Charlie shoved his hands in his pockets. "The top guys, ya know. Your guy. Those pricks got cash, loads of it. And they got nuts bigger than…bigger than fuckin' boulders."

"Nice description, Charlie."

"They can do away with us, just like that." He snapped his fingers. Then he scanned the streets again, his grey, saggy skin swinging with the rotation of his neck.

"I seen 'em all at Bailey's," he said, finally looking at

Angie. "Your guy–"

"Stop with the 'my guy crap.' He's not my guy, okay. He's got himself a wife."

"Come on, Ang. Listen to me. He was with that big city guy. I saw 'em together. Those guys, they look all snazzy in their suits but they don't give a fuck about us."

"Us? Don't lump yourself with me." She watched him, angry with him; angry with everyone she had run into today. Lola could end up in a zippered bag and everyone would zipper their own lips, pretend nothing had happened just to save their own hides. They'd rather have a friend dead then deal with idiots who thought they were God because they were rich. Man, oh man, she didn't want to deal with them or the cops either.

"Hey, listen, you need a hit? I'll give you a deal." He winked. Then he jerked his head toward the alley. "Wait here, I'll give you a little extra."

Charlie was trying to make himself feel good. Angie shouldn't get so pissed at him; so many people treated him like scum. Maybe a hit would help her frustration. She had promised herself a little on the weekend. A treat. She nodded. "Okay, Charlie. Why not?"

He slipped in the alley and within seconds returned to slip a plastic bag of white powder from his hand to hers in a handshake. She slipped the coke in her purse, pulling out money at the same time.

He smiled at her. "You're always good for the dough. Go in the alley. I'll stand watch for you."

The day, so far, had been a total disaster. Angie knew she had to work later and maybe a hit would help her get there, get dressed and on the stage, just to take it all off again for leering men. In her mind, she saw Paul with a rum and Coke in his hand, gawking at her, hoping for something afterwards.

Paul had only ever wanted her for sex.

Nothing more.

An ache swelled in her chest.

She slipped into the back alley, scanning its length to see if anyone was curled in a ball, sleeping under a cardboard box. No one had claimed this alley for their home. Yet. Or maybe they'd just moved on. She crunched cans and kicked garbage and dirt as she moved to get out of sight. She'd rather be here than in her empty apartment, wondering if Paul was going to drop by and make love to her. No, not make love. Have sex. Her throat constricted.

Litter lay everywhere: beer cans, empty liquor bottles, foil from cigarette packages, candy bar wrappers, condoms, and needles. Angie tramped over it all.

Finally, when she figured she was safe from onlookers, she hid behind a blue garbage dumpster and reached in her purse, pulled out her cigarettes and stuck one between her lips. She leaned against the wall, her shoulders slumping, and stared at the black graffiti spray-painted on the red brick. "Go to hell" and "Fuck You" seemed to dominate. Paul could do both as far as she was concerned. What an idiot she'd been.

She cupped her hands to shelter the match from the cold wind and bent her head forward, moving her hands closer to her face. Although Vancouver's winters were mild compared to the rest of Canada, there still was a winter. Rain, more rain and the odd sprinkling of snow often caused a dampness that penetrated the bones.

Angie's cigarette sparked. Her long and hard first puff sank deep into her lungs. She closed her eyes and tilted her head, willing herself to stop thinking about Paul.

Instead she thought of Sarah. The first time she and Sarah had gone shopping, they'd walked the red cobblestone road in Gastown just as if they were mother and daughter. At the end of the day, little Sarah had looked like a doll all dressed up in her new jeans, red T-shirt, jean jacket, and high-top sneakers.

Sitting on the bench eating ice cream, Sarah had slipped her hand into Angie's. Warm shivers had run up and down her spine and when she'd looked down, little Sarah stared up at her with all the trust in the world. "Thank you, Angie," she'd said. "You're the nicest person I know."

Now Sarah always said, "You're my best friend."

Her cigarette down to a stub, Angie inhaled one last drag then threw the butt against the graffiti on the wall. She watched the sparks fly. Her parents had shipped her off to boarding school as soon as they could. It had been her dad's idea. Get her away from Toronto and the bad seeds. Ha. The only bad seed had been right smack at home.

Her father phoned her once in awhile and her mother–only when she was pissed. Angie hated the school. Finally, when she couldn't stand being there any more and it was either beat the crap out of a teacher or run away, she'd opted to run away. No Juvey for her. Carrying a stolen credit card and identification in her wallet, she'd been able to hop a bus, head to a brand new city. And a life on the streets.

Now she wanted something different, a normal life, a job she liked, friends who went to the movies. She reached into her purse for the coke she'd just bought off Charlie. To straighten out her life out, she would have to stop snorting. This would be it, the last forever. The coke seemed a bit course but that was good, maybe it wasn't mixed with talc.

After filling each nostril, she held her head back, letting her hair fall down her back. Then she sniffed, long and hard, sending the drug even further into her blood stream. This really would be her last high.

Her blood rushed through her veins. And her chest pounded. Suddenly, she felt her body temperature rise. Sweat beaded on her face. The pounding in her chest made her slump forward. The effect of the stuff was too much...too much. Everything inside her exploded.

* * *

Intuko pulled the collar of his leather jacket up to ward off the biting wind. Being November, winter was just around the corner, which meant his Sunday morning parish could be full of an odd assortment of people, all looking for a warm place to rest for a few hours. Most of his regular parishioners accepted the harmless grubby faces, expecting them in a downtown church. He looked up, face exposed to the wind. Not much further to the church.

Then something flashed in front of him. Intuko squinted into the wind to see a white fox. It darted across his path and disappeared down an alley. Breaking into a run, he felt compelled to follow his fox.

At full sprint, Intuko ran towards the back downtown alley full of garbage and graffiti, bumping into a man just as he hit the entrance to the alley.

The guy, nervous, agitated, eyed his collar then said, "There's a woman down there. Help her." Then he took off in a run.

About thirty feet down the lane, Intuko saw a heap, crumpled on the ground. He squashed tin cans, kicked liquor bottles, and trampled over empty cigarette packages as he ran toward the body. Moving closer, he realized the heap was a woman, flopped over sideways, motionless among the litter. When he squatted down to check for a pulse he noticed her black purse was open. Had that guy robbed her? Beside her purse a plastic bag of white powder shone in the dirt. Cocaine.

And he saw the photograph beside it.

Intuko picked it up. It was a grainy, off-centered picture of...*Lola and Sarah.* This woman knew Lola.

He shoved the photo in his pants pocket then leaned over the woman and felt for a pulse. It was faint. He gently shook her shoulders. No response.

Intuko raced down the alley to the street. Just off to the

right he spotted the green awning of the Castle Restaurant. He sped inside and made his way to the bar, ignoring the stares at his frantic behaviour.

"Someone in the alley needs an ambulance!"

"You sure it's not just someone sleeping?" The bartender wiped a dishcloth along the bar.

"Call an ambulance!"

"Whatever you say, Father."

Intuko waited while the bartender dialled 911 then took the receiver to answer all the dispatcher's questions. Confident the ambulance was on its way, he ran back outside and toward the alley. Standing on the street, he looked up and down, again and again, listening for a wailing sound. Finally, he heard the siren, saw the blinking red lights. The ambulance screeched to a stop and two paramedics jumped out.

"Down this alley!" Intuko pointed.

Quickly and efficiently, the paramedics moved down the alley with their stretcher. One medic lifted the woman's eyelids then checked her carotid artery for a pulse while the other strapped a blood pressure cuff on her arm.

"Rapid pulse."

"BP's critical. Let's move."

Within a few seconds, the woman was on the stretcher and the paramedics were hustling down the alley towards the ambulance. Intuko followed behind, staring at the woman in a comatose. Such flawless skin and silky hair that shone like a yellow Arctic poppy even in the greyness of the alley.

They had her in the ambulance and applied an oxygen mask to her face. Intuko stared into the back of the ambulance. "Can I come with you?" he blurted out.

The paramedic looked up and eyed his clerical collar. "You make the call?"

"Yeah."

"Hop in."

Intuko jumped in and knelt beside the woman as the paramedic sat in front of the shiny metal equipment that occupied a large portion of the ambulance. The vehicle lurched forward and Intuko almost toppled forward. The body of the woman, secure on the stretcher, didn't move an inch. He was sure if he had looked out the back window he would have seen smoke and black skid marks. With the siren blaring, he bowed his head and prayed.

"Oh, my good Creator, if ever someone needed you it's now. Be with this woman and let the power of your healing surge her lifeblood. Thank you for all that you are and all that you have the strength to do."

He gently touched her face and for some reason pushed a few stray locks of hair from her face. It felt as soft as the caribou fur he wore around the hood of his parka when he was a boy growing up in the Arctic. So much time had passed since he'd felt anything as soft as fur, for life in the city overflowed with harshness.

He shivered and strangely enough, thought he heard drumming. It got louder and louder and he…closed his eyes. He saw his fox. And his mother's desperate face flashed through his mind. She had died too young. His body went slack. His shaman grandmother's voice called to him. He traveled downward, hoping to find her. What was she trying to tell him? Where was she taking him?

He was alone with his *anaanak*, inside her small house. And he was a boy again. "Your mama got bad spirit," she said.

She closed all the curtains and set her caribou drum in the middle of the floor. He'd watched his grandmother out in the ice hut go on her shaman drum journeys, but he'd never been on one before. This time she said she wanted *him* to travel down the road through the earth to enter the Lowerworld.

But just as she began to beat her drum, a knock pounded on the door. He had never seen the little woman with the curved shoulders and wrinkled face move so quickly. She hid her drum under the worn-out sofa then scuffled across the bare floor to answer the door.

He heard her voice. "Don't be afraid of our people. They say we're evil but we're not," whispered his *anaanak*.

"I know," he whispered back.

The driver cranked the steering wheel, skilfully manoeuvring the ambulance around a corner. Intuko opened his eyes to see the paramedic, who sat in the back with him and had been continually working on the woman, staring at him.

"Are you okay?"

"I'm fine...I just...uh, needed to pray." Had he talked out loud?

"It's a shame, isn't it? Young, beautiful. My daughter looks like her. But she's finished her Masters degree, got a good job and engaged to be married." The man returned his gaze to the machine the woman was hooked up to.

Intuko reached for the woman's hand.

The ambulance braked to a halt. Intuko grabbed onto the side of the wall to brace himself. Looking out the front window he realized they were at the Emergency Entrance to the hospital.

The ambulance driver opened his door and jumped outside.

Suddenly, there were people everywhere, each with a specific job. Intuko was barely out of the vehicle and the woman was being wheeled through the automatic doors, nurses working on her from either side of the gurney. He followed the action of the professionals, running to keep up until the gurney moved through a set of doors and out of his sight. He felt a hand on his shoulder and jumped.

"There's a coffee machine down the hall." The paramedic who had been in the back of the ambulance pointed to the metal vending machines.

"Thanks and thanks for helping her."

"I'm just doing my job."

Intuko turned in the direction of the coffee machines. He stuck his hand in his pockets, hoping he had enough money. Being a minister in a struggling downtown church didn't exactly pay much. Arriving at the vending machines, he dropped a loonie in the slot, and watched something that didn't resemble coffee spurt into a cardboard cup.

He walked back to the waiting area with his coffee, collapsing into a brown and green tweed sofa. Across from him sat a coffee table piled high with newspapers and glossy magazines with dog-eared corners. Absentmindedly, he picked up a newspaper only to put it on his lap and stare into space. He so wanted to see someone, anyone, come running through the doors obviously concerned for that woman's welfare. But no one did. Had anyone visited his mother when she had ended up in hospital, time after time?

Intuko glanced over to the nurses' station and saw two police officers and a nurse holding a black bag. He remembered the black purse lying beside the woman in the alley. Tossing the magazine on the table, he headed toward the counter. As he got closer he overheard the officer talking to the nurse with the nametag, Vicki, on her white uniform.

"It was on the stretcher and the paramedics confirmed it was with her when they found her."

A siren rang in the distance.

"Keep the purse in a safe place. We'll have to obtain a search warrant from the justice of the peace before we check the numbers on the cash."

Nurse Vicki nodded. "I was shocked when I found there was so much in there. I was just looking for any information about this overdose."

"We appreciate your immediate attention. Here's my card. We'll want to talk with Miss Angela Melville when she awakens."

Vicki stared at the police officer and softly said, "If she awakens."

SIX

His feet rooted to the floor, Intuko shivered at what he had overheard.

Old words, old visions sliced through his mind.

He was on the playground of the residential school. A boy approached him by the swings with taunts, "I heard your mama got high on gas and took off south with a white man and your daddy's a big old fat drunk."

Intuko had looked at the boy and shrugged. It didn't much matter; his family seemed so far away anyway. He had stared at the stupid boy then up to the bright sky. How was he to react when it was March already and the sun shone again? He had lived through the darkness of winter without his family.

Years later, that same boy had come to the dorm room late at night and said, "Hey, I heard your mama's goin' to jail for putting the knife to a white man." Intuko didn't answer back but lay still on his back, on his small cot, in the dark, listening to the other boys snicker and laugh. Maybe his mother's white knight in shining armour had hit her one too many times and she didn't want to do the hospital thing anymore. So she killed him.

Intuko rubbed the back of his neck and slowly edged toward the nurse. She now stood alone at her station. "Excuse me," he said.

"How can I help you?" Nurse Vicki looked up.

"There was a blond woman, Angela Melville, brought in a few minutes ago," said Intuko. "Could you tell me how she is?"

A siren shrieked in the distance, obliterating Intuko's question. Nurse Vicki stepped into action mode, leaving Intuko standing alone, watching and waiting, as death knocked in a fit of haste.

He waited for another hour, until he finished the last sip of his second coffee. He should go. He had a ton of work to do at the church and tonight the youth group met. Crumpling his cup, he stood to find a garbage can, eyeing Vicki again for some hint of information.

Once again, he approached the desk.

Frazzled, Vicki looked up. "I'm sorry, I have nothing to tell you except we're terribly short-staffed. Phone later. I'm on seven to seven today and tomorrow. Just ask for me, Vicki." She smiled. "What church are you a minister at?"

"Princess Street United."

"I go to an Anglican church myself although I often only get there on Easter or Christmas."

Intuko smiled at her. Why did people always feel the need to validate their religion? "Thanks for your help." He turned and walked away.

The air outside was gelid, dank, and the sky appeared as one shade of grey like a big slab of concrete. Intuko stuck his hands in his pockets and looked to the ground. He hated to leave, hated what he had witnessed. With every step on his walk home he thought about what to do.

He knew his white fox had appeared to tell him something important. He hadn't seen it for five years, since the time it guided him to the Princess Street United Church. He thought since he was involved with the church, he wouldn't ever see it again. But…it had come to him. Had his grandmother sent it?

And who was this Angela Melville? Intuko had never seen her before; she'd never been involved in Street Ministry. But she obviously knew Lola. If his Grandmother were alive, she'd tell him to get busy, stop stalling–the spirits had told him something important. But what?

By the time he arrived at the church, Hazel had finished her half day but had left him a stack of work and a note. Susan Peterson had called. She'd had a great response from the women about his class and more than twenty had signed up.

Intuko sighed. He had to teach the class now.

Susan wanted to know what kind of supplies she should order. Could he call at his earliest convenience? He wrote her name in his agenda. He would definitely need soapstone and a few tools. But he would call tomorrow. Right now, he had to work on a talk for the youth group meeting.

Intuko scanned the rest of Hazel's note. The feeling of love he felt from her note sparked some thoughts for tonight's talk. Love really was the answer; the allusive love, slippery in its existence, hard for many to grasp and keep. He didn't want to talk about romantic love but nurturing love. Even love for a pet. So many troubled youngsters, like Lola, had never experienced basic love.

He jotted some notes but kept getting distracted, thinking about Lola and the woman in the alley. He tapped his pencil. How could he help? What could *he* do? Lola was addicted. Rehab maybe? He shook his head. Rehab only worked when the individual made the decision, not when someone else forced them. Lola, right now, was too scared of her pimp and too much of a junkie to accept any help. Intuko should have set an actual lunch date with her or even a coffee date. Or at least found out where she lived so he could visit Sarah.

He glanced at his notes. He had only written a few sentences when his phone rang. Still absorbed, he picked up the phone, and tucked it under his chin.

"Intuko, Joe here from Street Ministry."

"Hi, Joe."

"I've got some bad news."

Intuko put down his pen and leaned back in his chair. Joe

sounded serious. "What's up?"

"Remember Lola?" Joe asked quietly. "You've worked with her before."

"Sure, I know Lola." Intuko straightened his back. "She came to see me yesterday. What's wrong?"

"I don't know how to tell you, but...oh shoot, this is so–"

"What is it?"

"She's been...murdered. Beaten bad in a back alley and...shot."

Intuko closed his eyes, put his hand to his brow, and leaned forward in his chair, elbow resting on his desk. Dead?

"Intuko, are you still there?"

"Yeah, I'm here."

"I just thought...you'd want to know."

"I appreciate the call."

"No problem."

"Joe."

"What?"

"Where was she found?"

"Behind a dumpster on West Cordova."

Intuko hung up the phone, sitting for a minute with his eyes closed. He thought of Lola in his office, shaking uncontrollably, begging him to help her daughter, refusing his offer of help.

Now she was dead.

SEVEN

Intuko grabbed his coat off the hook and once outside broke into a sprint to West Cordova. As soon as he rounded the corner, he saw the yellow sticker tape and the people crawling around the crime scene.

Breathless, he pushed through, asking questions, finding out the investigating officer was Detective Anderson. Intuko knew him from the work he'd done with Street Ministry.

"What happened to her?" he asked, panting.

"Beaten. Shot. Possible sexual assault," Detective Anderson said in his usual official police voice.

"Who would do something like this?"

Anderson shrugged and looked at him. "She's a hooker."

"Do you think it might be related to some of the other missing girls?"

"Doubt it. We've never found the bodies of the others. Lola was shot. This is probably the work of a john."

"She's got a daughter."

"You know that for a fact?"

"I've known Lola for years–from my work with Street Ministry."

"Yeah, I guess you would. Better than I ever did. A lot of the girls like to bug us, but Lola, she hid from us." Anderson paused. Then he looked at Intuko. "I'll pass the information on to child services."

Intuko ran his hand through his hair, thinking of the last time he'd seen Lola, what she'd said, what she'd asked of him. If Sarah went through child services, she'd become a ward of the court and a foster child. "This kind of thing has got to stop," said Intuko. "You have to find out who killed her."

"I'm sorry, but I'd better get back to Crime Scene," said Detective Anderson.

Brushed aside by Anderson, and not allowed to go under the ticker tape, Intuko figured he could do nothing else at the crime scene. Shoulders slumped, hands shoved in his pockets, he retraced his trek back to his office.

As he approached Hastings and Main, he noticed Elizabeth sitting on the steps of the Carnegie Library. Could she have possibly seen Lola last night? Intuko went over to her and sat beside her. "Hi, Elizabeth."

"I'm a Queen, you know, I used to twirl and spin in my long velvet ball gowns."

Intuko smiled at Elizabeth. "Did you see Lola last night?"

Elizabeth pirouetted in her shabby shoes, holding her tin foil crown, swirling her long dirty coat. "She's a princess, you know."

"A princess. Was she walking her beat last night?"

"She danced with me. She wore a velvet gown."

"Did you see her with anyone?"

"Another princess. But she went away in a carriage. A dark carriage." Elizabeth waltzed with an invisible partner. "I think she's gone to the ball."

"Thanks Elizabeth."

"I'm a Queen, you know. I can twirl and spin in my long velvet gown." Elizabeth stuck her nose in the air and waved to Intuko as if she really was royalty. "Ta-ta. Ta-ta."

Since Intuko had a few hours before youth group started, he decided to walk the streets, talking to anyone who would talk. Hastings, Main, Columbia, Powell, West Cordova. Maybe if he searched for info on Angela Melville, she could help. She had Lola's picture.

He found out Angela was a stripper not a hooker and she

had been looking for Lola that morning. But that was it. No one wanted to talk.

Only one girl told him she'd seen Lola on a different street last night. Apparently, she had staked a new beat, had even put a black rinse in her hair. They were supposed to meet up at the coffee shop, just after midnight, but she hadn't shown up. Jimmy, her pimp, had shown up mad as hell, not knowing where she was. When Intuko asked the girl for Lola's address, the girl said she didn't know where she lived–they only ever met for coffee.

Even the guy who told Intuko about Angela Melville being in the alley wasn't cruising the streets. Such a difficult process to get any answers as most people by late afternoon were already wasted.

Intuko found Luc under a tree.

"So Lola's fuckin' dead." Luc dragged on his cigarette. "Maybe she squealed to the pigs. That pimp of hers would knock her dead for that or those rich fucker-friends of his might have pow-powed her." He held up his hand, making gun motions.

"What rich guys?" asked Intuko.

"Life is better if you just go up, down. Hey, you got something for me mister preacher boy? You can buy off Charlie. Up, down, he's the guy. Anything will do. He's the guy who'll tell you shit. Give him some money and he'll like a pig. ." Luc threw his head back to make the sound effects.

"Who's Charlie?"

"I bet he saw Lola last night. How about some hair spray? You got a can?" Luc got up, his clothes hanging like rags from his body, his eyelids half shut, and threw his cigarette butt on the ground. "You're no fuckin' good. You got nothin'."

Obviously, Luc was a dead end. Glancing at his watch, Intuko realized he had to get back to the church.

But when he walked by the Vancouver Police Department

building, he quickened his step and headed into the building. This would only take a few minutes. Maybe they had discovered something new, or located Sarah.

The lobby buzzed: druggies yelled, hookers swore, drunks snored.

"Is Detective Anderson around?"

The receptionist looked frazzled. "Uh, yeah, he...just got back. I think he's at his desk. Let me check for you."

Intuko waited patiently.

"Intuko, what brings you by?" Anderson approached Intuko in a hurry, his words a rush of syllables, his face drawn, and his eyes bloodshot.

After moving back a step to be out of anyone's earshot, Intuko asked quietly, "Anything on Lola's daughter?"

"I passed the info to child services. But, Intuko, if they don't have a file on her, it's going to be hard for them to track her." Anderson blew out air. "I'm sure someone has the child. Maybe one of Lola's friends."

"But who?"

"Look, we're working round the clock, trying to find out who murdered her. This case is piled on top with the rest of them."

"Yeah, right, with the rest of them."

"We do our best. We're swamped. Narcotics is working on something big and homicides in this end of the city come in left, right and centre. We deal with dead bodies just about every week."

"But the child is—"

"They all have kids. And I feel sorry for them but we can only do what we can do."

"Where did they live?"

"We've already been there."

Intuko remained silent.

"Intuko, I'm warning you, don't take this on. Make it your

mission. You may have worked with Street People Ministry but you have no idea the rest of it. So butt out. This is ours to handle."

Intuko nodded, knowing full well he couldn't butt out and wouldn't until he knew Sarah was okay. He'd promised Lola he would help Sarah and he wouldn't go back on his promise. Angela Melville had a picture of Lola and Sarah; he needed to talk to her.

Intuko worked well into the evening with his youth group. The church had just received four old computers from a local business and the teenagers plugged in lines and fiddled around with the programs to get them up and running.

"I'm off, Intuko." Chris Temple, the youth group helper, shut off the last computer and picked up his black leather Vancouver Canucks jacket. Putting it on, he said, "We worked out a few bugs."

"I still don't understand technology," said Intuko. "But one day I will. The kids are jittery."

Chris snapped up his jacket and bent over to tie the laces on his beat-up high-top runners. "Lola's murder isn't sitting well. And there's new crack on the streets and I've heard there's more coming. I'm glad I'm out of that crap." Chris tied the last knot on his shoe and stood. "A lot of these kids will end up dead or doing time."

Intuko had to look up to make eye contact, as Chris was well over six feet. "You ever heard of a guy named Charlie?"

"I think he's a street seller. Low guy on the rung. Why? What's going on old man?"

"Who you calling old?" Intuko gave Chris a quick jab on the arm.

"No way. I'm not getting sidetracked here. Why do you want to know about Charlie?"

Intuko looked Chris square in the eye. "I heard his name

today. He may know something about Lola's murder."

"Let the cops handle this, Intuko."

"Do you know Angela Melville?"

"She's a stripper. Look, I've been hearing things about Lola's pimp. You ask questions, you're gonna look trouble in the eyes. Big time."

"Where can I find Charlie?"

"Oh, man, I can tell you're not gonna let up. He frequents Hank's."

"Hank's? That place is close to Gastown, right?"

"Yeah, you know–the strip joint. Naked women. Not a good place for a man of your position." Chris paused. "Speaking of women, Intuko…have you ever thought about getting a little…"

Blush red crept from Chris's neck into his cheeks as he shoved his hands in his pockets. "You know, having a woman in your life. Like, I guess what I'm trying to say is, maybe having a wife, kids, you know–the family thing."

Intuko smiled.

"I'm sure," continued Chris, spewing his words like a water fountain, "a guy like you would probably want to get married first instead of just shacking up. Heck, say something would you, instead of just looking at me like that. You're not getting any younger and you'd be a great old man." Chris ran a hand through his hair and blew out some air. His face was the colour of a ripened tomato.

"I think, Chris," said Intuko, folding his arms across his chest, "this is what I'm meant to do."

"I know *that*. But can't you do both? I mean, that doesn't mean you should hole up without getting it your whole life."

"But I *get it* here at the church."

"No, you don't *get it* here at the church. At least not since I've been here." Chris shook his head. "Anyway, what about kids? Don't you think of stuff like that?"

"Every once in awhile when I'm at home in my little apartment, I do think of the family life, but–"

Chris poked Intuko on the upper arm. "Don't bail on me. You think of a woman, right?"

"But then, I always come around to thinking that I have a family. The church and people like you are my family. I've made a choice. Believe it or not, I knew lots of women when I was your age, before seminary school. And, sure, I'm human, I do think now and again of having someone to share my life with."

"I knew it! You can't be as perfect as you come across."

"I'm far from perfect, Chris."

"Yeah, well, perfect or not, if it wasn't for you making me your family, I'd still be boozing, snorting, fighting in bars and waking up hung every morning. Now I got a construction job making some honest money and I get to help with these kids.

Chris let the conversation lapse and a thoughtful silence like a swirl of cool fog encased the small room.

"Don't do anything stupid, okay," Chris said softly. "And call me if you need help."

Suddenly, Intuko's day caught up with him and his revolving mind slowed, like a toy car running out of batteries. Exhaustion seeped into his muscles and bones, draining the life force from his body.

Chris broke the silent spell both men seemed to be under and said, "I should get going. I have to work in the morning. The big bosses just started a new project down at False Creek. It's great. Good dough and steady work for a while. And tomorrow night I got a date. A real date."

"Good for you." Intuko yawned. "Have a good time, okay. Thanks for your help tonight."

After Intuko heard the heavy wooden front door close, he flipped off the lamp sitting on the table and all the light switches before going into the sanctuary. One small light

above the organ–that was used for reading sheet music–
remained lit. Chris had been playing earlier in the evening and
must have left it on. The teens loved to jam with Chris–he
once played keyboard in a rock group–and he actually,
although self-taught, was quite talented.

Intuko slipped out of his shoes and walked toward the
pulpit where he spoke from every Sunday. The hardwood floor
needed sanding and varnishing. Stu, the church custodian, a
retired old gentleman, worked for next to nothing because he
wanted something to do with his time. But he only did the
basics. Maybe next spring Intuko would sand the floor
himself. The thought made him weary. He ran his hands along
the oak pews with the ornate ends that were chipped and
cracking with wear. The hymn books were frayed and tattered
too–some day soon they would have to purchase new ones.

At the front, two steps led to a platform and the pulpit, and
a few choir pews sat to the side. In the five years he had been
with the church they had tried numerous times to form a choir
but it had always failed. He knelt on the step to pray.

He closed his eyes. His words were full of heart-felt
messages for the sick woman he had stumbled upon. No.
There had been no stumbling. His white fox had guided him.
Suddenly, he remembered the short trance he'd had in the
ambulance. What was that all about? Had he gone on a short
shaman journey? He'd never really gone on a drum journey.
He remembered as a child, out in the ice hut, his grandmother
would throat sing while someone else drummed. And she
would go into a trance. When she finally opened her eyes, she
said she had glided down a long tunnel, as if falling through a
tube, and had gone into the ocean, her Lowerworld. There she
had met with her spirits who had guided her to the fish. She
said her power animal was a whale and he traveled with her.
That is why she told Intuko to always take heed of his fox.

He continued praying to give thanks to his grandmother

for her shaman teachings. Then he prayed for Lola. And Sarah. He vowed he would fulfill his promise to Lola and he would take care of Sarah if he could. He prayed Sarah was okay. And he asked his grandmother to embrace Lola, love her in the spirit world.

Then he prayed for his own family. The family he hardly knew, hardly seen in the past twenty years. His sister, Ruby, her drinking. People lost, unable to see the beauty of life. She had been born when Intuko had been away at school. Intuko remembered coming home, seeing his baby sister, touching her, thinking of her as a stranger. And she had been only four when their mother had run away. Then, at school, her body had been a pawn for the priests.

When he lifted his head, the silver effulgence of the moon cast light prisms through the stained glass of the nativity scene. It was a small, old and rundown church built with many turn-of-the-century features: vaulted ceilings, wooden beams, stained glass, large frosted windows and ornate designs etched into every newel post. Intuko inhaled. Other than the Arctic, this church was his home.

He slowly arose from his kneeling position, turned off the light above the organ, and walked back down the aisle. Tomorrow he'd try to see Angela Melville. Then he'd hunt for a man named Charlie.

Lola's murderer had to be found.

And Sarah was now his responsibility.

EIGHT

Angie awoke and pried her eyes open. She felt as if loose pieces of gravel were stuck under her lids. When she moved her arm, she encountered tubes and a needle sticking in her vein. Slowly, she turned her head to see the IV hook up. Dripping liquid moved through the tube and down into her arm.

She stared at the white walls, white sheets, and green hospital gown. She rolled her head back and forth trying to calm her stomach.

"You're awake?" A cop loomed over Angie.

Angie's mouth felt as if it had broken pieces of chalk dissolving into the cracks and holes in her teeth. "Where am I?" she whispered.

"St. Mary's Hospital." The cop flashed her badge. "You're under arrest for fraud. You have the right to obtain an attorney."

Angie's head throbbed and she was momentarily blinded by the one little fraction of light trying to enter the room through the drawn beige curtains. She closed her eyes, laid her head flat on the starched pillow, trying to reduce the cop's stream of words to a murmur. She remembered looking for Lola and Sarah. After a couple of smokes, she'd had a hit of coke and that was the last thing she could remember.

Hearing the clanging sound of metal, Angie opened her eyes to see the cop shackling her to the bed. Even though she felt sick, she sat up. Her stomach rolled as if she might spew her guts all over the drab bed sheets. *"Where's my purse?"*

"It's been confiscated for evidence."

Angie's face reddened and sweat beaded across her forehead. Dizzy, she groped for the side of the bed and tried to stand up but she couldn't...she was chained like a wild animal. She had to get out of here if she wanted to find Lola and Sarah. "Get these things off me!" She kicked her arms and legs, ripping the intravenous out of her arm, shooting bright red blood onto the white sheets.

"The more you fight, the harder it will be."

Angie plopped her head on the pillow and stared at the ceiling. A wave of nausea rumbled in like a tidal wave and she clutched her stomach and vomited all over the floor. Wiping her mouth, she moaned.

The shackles attaching her to the bedposts felt icy cold and she started to shake as if rain pelted her skin. Waves of nausea kept rolling in.

"You have the right to make a call to arrange for a lawyer."

She gulped. Who should she call?

She thought of Paul but remembered their last conversation. He wouldn't help Lola; she was a hooker. Why would he help Angie? She was a stripper. Maybe Candice could help her find a lawyer, and possibly help Lola, or even just find Sarah.

"Where were you last night?" Candice asked on the phone. "Hank's pissed at you."

"I'm in the hospital. I need your help."

"Hospital? What's wrong?"

"Have you seen Lola?"

Silence.

"What is it Candice?"

"Ang, I don't know how to tell you this...but...Lola's dead."

"Dead? How? What about Sarah?"

"They found Lola in an alley. She was beaten pretty bad

and...shot."

"Shot! Oh, shit. What about Sarah?"

"I don't know. I don't know who's got her."

"You have to find her for me!"

"I can't. Lola was stupid. In way too deep. I'll pop by and see you though, okay."

The hospital room door opened as Angie, shaking, passed the phone to the cop. A nurse, dressed in her whites and looking all too perky, strode toward the bed. Without even a sniff or a curled lip, she cleaned up the vomit and reached in the side table to pull out a pan, placing it beside her. Then she took Angie's arm to fix her IV hook-up.

The nurse fidgeted with Angie, swabbing her arm, changing tape, and pricking her skin.

"What...happened?" Angie asked quietly.

"You overdosed."

"I didn't take that much though."

The nurse picked up a blood pressure cuff from the table beside the bed, strapped it around Angie's arm, and pumped the little black bulb. When all the air was out, she ripped the Velcro on the cuff. "The cocaine you had was somehow mixed with some MDMA." The nurse put the cuff down and reached around her neck for her stethoscope. "Take a deep breath." She plugged it onto Angie's back.

The nurse manoeuvred her shoulder and put the round, cold, heavy button of the stethoscope in between her breasts. Angie breathed in and out. Ecstasy mixed with her cocaine? How could that have happened? What was wrong with Charlie? Did he crush it and put it in himself or was it already in the coke and maybe he didn't know?

"Everything sounds good," she said. "The pregnancy could be causing some of the nausea. I would suspect, however, most is from the drugs in your blood stream."

"*Pregnancy?*"

"They ran blood work."

"Pregnant? I didn't...I didn't know I was...*Oh shit*." Angie slumped back onto the starched pillow.

"Ring me if you need anything," said the nurse softly.

"Wait," Angie said, sitting up. The nurse who was now a few steps away from her bed turned and looked back at her.

"Is...the baby okay?" Angie asked quietly.

"There was a heartbeat." The nurse nodded. "The doctor will be in to see you later."

Angie fell back against the pillow and closed her eyes. Emptiness invaded her, the power of the feeling shocking her. She tentatively touched her flat stomach, the word sorry sticking in her throat like a piece of stale bread.

She remembered when Lola was pregnant. Angie had to find Sarah.

The shackles on her legs weighed her down.

By the time Intuko finished with his regular Friday morning Men's Breakfast Fellowship meeting–complete with eggs-over-easy, bacon and toast–and had looked into the leaky roof, written up his sermon, answered three phone calls from board members and cleared his paper work, time had slipped away. Two o'clock, already. All morning, he'd used every spare minute trying to find out if he could get to visit Angela Melville. He'd called the police station four times, leaving messages for Detective Anderson each time but there had been no return phone call. Maybe he should just go to the hospital.

He had his coat on when Hazel squeaked the door open and poked her head around the corner.

"I hate to bother you but I have a feeling he's in the rest room again."

Intuko sighed and nodded. "Okay, I'll go check."

Hazel followed Intuko down the hall, her short legs taking two steps to his one. "I could smell him."

Intuko opened the door of the men's rest room and walked in. Sure enough, there was Harry, slumped in the corner by the urinal, passed out with his pants wet in the front. At the start of every winter they found him hiding in the rest room trying to escape the cold. Right from the first day he discovered him, asleep in a corner, he hadn't kicked him out, put him back on the streets. Harry had fallen asleep in the shelter of God's house. But he couldn't let him just wear off his binge in the men's rest room. Little children often ran in and out here.

In the beginning, Intuko tried to help Harry by sending him to the detox centre, but it never worked, he always showed up again, reeking of alcohol. Intuko needed to call the police. At least in a city cell, Harry could sleep in a bed, eat a proper meal, and warm his body for a short time.

"Harry?" He gently shook his shoulders.

"*Umph.* Top of the morning to you, Father." Harry smacked his lips to generate some saliva in his dehydrated state.

"Top of the morning to you too, Harry. I hope you had a good sleep." Intuko arose, knowing Hazel was waiting.

"Was he in there?" Hazel asked when Intuko came out of the rest room.

He nodded and they started down the hall. "It's that time of year."

"Would you like to call the police or should I?"

"I will."

When Constable Carter arrived, Intuko met him at the front door and they warmly shook hands. "Is he in his usual place?"

Intuko swung the door to the rest room open and watched as Constable Carter roused Harry who had fallen back to sleep. "Hey, guy," he said, "you're coming with me. Take my hand and I'll help you to your feet."

Harry swayed but stood on his feet and Constable Carter

gently pulled his arms behind his back and cuffed him. "Come on. We've got a bed waiting for you."

Intuko walked outside and stood beside the police cruiser. "Would you know anything about Lola's case?" he asked as nonchalantly as possible.

Constable Carter put Harry in the back seat and shut the door. "Routine investigation. I know they're working round the clock."

"Any family been located?"

"Don't think so. Her mother was a junkie who died a few years back."

"Does any family ever come in for these girls?"

"Sometimes, but not often enough. Sad, eh?"

"What do you know about Angela Melville?"

Constable Carter smiled and patted Intuko on the back. "I thought you handed the reins of the Street People Ministry over to Joe. As a matter of fact, Miss Melville's been picked up for fraud. She's at St. Mary's until tomorrow I think. We needed to close that case." He nodded his head as he spoke. "Free some men. You should see the case files in homicide."

"Do you think I could get in to see Angela?"

"Corrections has a chaplain. She won't be allowed to see anyone in the hospital but I'm sure you could see her when she gets to Corrections. She has to agree though."

Friday night. Nine-thirty p.m. Intuko took off his collar and put on a navy golf shirt, jeans, and a baseball hat. Then he pulled on his fleece-lined jean jacket and left his apartment building. The crisp, night air penetrated his lungs, making him shiver. He quickened his pace. Maybe he should have taken Chris up on his offer of help.

Chris was having his doubts. He didn't want to hit a smoky bar and drink when he could sit outside and stare at the constellations glimmering against an ebony backdrop. He took his date's hand and said, "I could give you my coat."

"I'm not cold. I'm bored."

Chris had thought this girl to be different. But he'd gone and done it again; assumed her packaged good looks–nice face and body–were enough. He glanced at her pretty silhouette in the silvery moonlight: perfect little nose, straight teeth, and long thick red hair. What a knockout, and he was the one who asked her out. Chris looked at her, bouncing up and down like a basketball.

"Okay, let's go for one."

"Murphy's will be happening tonight." She jumped up and grabbed his hand. "Come on."

Murphy's was jammed with bodies of all shapes and sizes. Women in provocative clothing hung over the bars and guys strutted, beer glasses in hand. A meat market for sure.

Chris's date spotted some girlfriends. He strolled to the bar, ordered two beers and by the time he returned, she had boogied onto the dance floor.

Her friend, dressed in skin-tight black jeans and a red T-shirt, yelled in his ear, "She wants you to leave her beer here. She said she'd be right back. I'll dance with you if you'd like."

The dance floor was as hot as a sauna with all the fleshy bodies gyrating to the forceful downbeat pounding from the speakers. Lights flashed for visual effects. Arms and legs flailed every which way and although Chris liked to dance, all he wanted to do tonight was get outside in the fresh air. After the song ended, he wandered back to his beer, anxious to leave but not wanting to ditch a date. Or appear jilted.

When she returned to her drink, however, with her arms looped around her dance partner, she looked at Chris and said, "I had a good time tonight, but you don't have to drive me home."

He wanted to sock the guy standing beside her but instead

he leaned across, put his hand on her forearm, and said, "I'm outta here."

The black night and fresh air felt like the sun shining after a long day of rain. Chris breathed deeply to rid his lungs of the smoke and his lousy feelings. He shoved his hands in his pockets, and after kicking a garbage can, walked to his car. His first date with her, the other night in a coffee bar, had been okay, but tonight was a big joke. This dating thing sucked.

Through his teens he'd never committed to a steady. When he played Junior hockey, puck-bunnies hung around the dressing room doors, waiting, willing, and he'd often ended up in the back of a car with a stranger. Then in his early twenties he drank and played the pick-up game. Just as his date did this evening. She'd probably go home with that guy. Well, it was her loss.

When he got in his car, he looked at the clock on his dashboard. Eleven p.m. on a Friday night. Still early. He'd better check to see if that crazy Intuko was at Hank's.

Intuko ordered a beer. The woman on the stage–her body wrapped in silver chains and plastic wrap–doused herself with water. It streamed down, running the length of her body, bubbling in the creases created by the wrap. Intuko averted his gaze and instead looked around the bar. Charlie or Jimmy could be any one of the men watching the stripper.

"That's five bucks." The waitress plunked a beer in front of Intuko.

Intuko pulled out his wallet, taking out a five-dollar bill and a loonie. "Keep the change." The waitress stuck the bill in her cleavage and the dollar in her apron.

Intuko took a sip. Then another. Not knowing what else to do, not wanting to look out of place. How could he to find a name in this crowd? The place overflowed with prostitutes, pimps, dealers, and…men still dressed in suits from the workday. They were the ones with their eyes stuck like Crazy Glue to the woman on the stage. Charlie was probably a jeans-guy. Intuko finished his beer and ordered another.

"Hey, man."

Intuko jumped.

"Whoa. I didn't mean to scare you." Chris smiled and took a swig of his beer straight from the bottle.

"Chris, glad you're here."

"How long you been here?"

"An hour or so. I've no idea where to start, how to approach people. Do I ask questions or will that get my face punched in?"

"No one likes questions."

"Do you recognize Charlie?"

Chris scanned the bar, eyes lingering longer on the girl on the stage who, still at the beginning of her set, wore a fragment of clothes.

"I've always liked Candice, she's got a heart of gold," said Chris. He turned to Intuko. "I don't see him, man. But that doesn't mean he won't be here later. Let's get another beer."

Two hours and three beers later, Intuko and Chris were still sitting on their stools scouring the bar.

"Hiya, Chris." Candice, makeup off, clothes on, smiled sweetly at Chris. "I haven't seen you here in a long time. It's good to see ya."

"Candice, good to see you too. This is my friend Intuko."

Intuko smiled and nodded. "Nice to meet you."

"Wow, a polite one. Never seen you before."

"How you keeping?" asked Chris. "How's your little guy?"

"He's great. A real doll. As for me, I'm tired. Working overtime these days. Hank's got to get some new girls. Did you hear about Angie? She took a bad hit and ended up in hospital. Then, they arrested her! I tried to see her at the hospital but 'cause she was under arrest, they wouldn't let me in."

"Angie? What did they arrest her for?"

"I heard, but don't quote me, fraud. She phoned me from the hospital but didn't give me no details."

"Is this the Angela who's a friend of Lola's?" Intuko butted in the conversation.

"Lola, hell, I feel sick about her too. Look, I got to go. Relieve the sitter." Candice kissed Chris on the cheek and turned to Intuko. "Maybe, we'll see you again?"

"You wouldn't know where Lola lived?" Intuko asked quickly.

"Nah. I didn't know her that well."

Intuko watched Candice walk away until she was out of earshot. Then he turned to Chris. "She sure took off in a hurry."

"She stays tight-lipped to protect her kid."

"Do you think she knows something about Lola?"

"Possibly. Stay low with her though. Her kid's her life." Chris jerked his head. "There he is. Over there in the corner. Must have come in through the back door. I'm pretty sure that's him." Chris kept his eyes on the back corner of the bar.

Intuko pulled the brim of his cap down over his eyes and slowly turned. "That's the guy."

"What do you mean?"

"He told me Angela Melville was lying in the alley."

"Are you sure?"

"I think so."

Charlie, toothpick in his mouth and drink in hand, was talking to a greasy-looking guy wearing a silk-shirt unbuttoned to mid-chest and loads of chains and another expensive-suit, Italian-loafer, short-haired guy.

"It looks as if he's leaving." Intuko watched Charlie pick up a black leather coat and fling it over his shoulders.

"Let's follow him," said Chris. "But don't look obvious."

Intuko nodded, slipped on his jean jacket and slid off his seat. His legs were wobbly and his head fuzzy from the beer. "Wait a sec."

"You okay."

"I need to get outside."

"Come on. He's leaving from the front."

The cold air jolted Intuko, clearing his brain a bit anyway. He tried to look around but knew he was moving in slow motion.

"There he is," said Chris. "Getting in the front of that black Mercedes. Classy car for a street seller."

Intuko stared at the black car, pulling away from the curb and tried to focus on the license plate. "I got the first three numbers." He talked as if he had marbles in his mouth.

"I got more than that," said Chris.

NINE

Saturday morning, Susan awoke early. Although she was supposed to have the day off, they'd called her in for a special assignment–to escort a new inmate who had been arrested for fraud after being admitted to St. Mary's Hospital. The pay was double time.

And it was just a pick-up. Susan had often sat in the Emergency Room with someone who was sick or injured or with someone who hated her skin so much she had sliced and slashed. Those were hard shifts.

Once at work she checked in and picked up her issued van keys. Driving out of the prison gates, she cranked up the radio and relaxed, enjoying the sun that shone like a polished lemon in a sapphire sky.

Susan had been informed this new inmate was twenty-five, which meant she'd had a few years to harden her edge, but she *was* entering the prison for the first time. Nine times out of ten, the fear new inmates felt came out through aggressive behaviour, especially in the first few days. Survival mode.

Stripper, street girl, once teen-age runaway, young, and smart. No one got away with stealing from bank machines through computer manipulation without possessing a few brains. Now she had to fit into a new system. The challenge for each woman was to find her place in the pecking order.

At the hospital, Susan took the elevator to the second floor and walked the length of the hall to Ms. Melville's room. She pushed open the door to see a woman, sitting, shackled to the wheelchair, ready to be released. Susan evaluated her presence; straight posture, rigid muscles, and solemn face–the woman was trying desperately not to look scared.

"She's all yours," said Susan's fellow blue, handing her the forms.

Susan pushed the wheelchair out the door and down the hall toward the elevator, avoiding small talk.

Outside, she wheeled Angela toward the van. Now came the tricky part. If she didn't do the transfer correctly, she could end up sprawled on the pavement and Angela could be running with the speed of a fleeing deer.

With a final snap of the leg iron, Susan said, "Time to get in the van."

Taking her by the elbow, she helped Ms. Melville into the van and when she was seated, Susan buckled her seatbelt. Then she slammed the side door of the van, locking the new inmate in until their final destination.

Sitting in the driver's seat, Susan snuck a quick glance at Angela Melville through the wire mesh fence that separated them. She wore that frightened child look, her vulnerability seeping through her tough persona.

The only thing Angie could do with her cuffed hands was place them in her lap. Every time the van went over a bump or they come to a sudden stop, her body lurched forward, and to brace against the jerk, she had to lift, not one, but both hands. She took a deep breath and closed her eyes.

She was on her way to the joint.

And Lola was dead and Sarah…where was she?

Angie's stomach, a bundle of knots, careened with every bump. She glanced at the officer driving the van. Should she say something? Ask her for help? She had to get someone to help.

Suddenly the road changed, became bumpier, gravel-like, with lots of potholes. Out the front window, she saw a large, lacklustre grey building that looked like an oversized warehouse. High metal fences surrounded the building and sharp coils of barbed wire swirled like cyclones above the fences. Her palms and face began to sweat. Drops rolled from her armpits down the side of her body. This was no joke. The fence looked hard and cold, the metal glinting in the sun like the edge of a razorblade.

Her gaze followed the fence around the four corners of the square it formed. Once inside, she would be locked behind that fenced area like a caged animal at the zoo.

She turned her attention to the trees, standing tall in the distance, to the high grass and the stretching field that spread for miles…outside the fence. The trees, grass, and field led to the paved road, the highway back to life. She wouldn't be able to touch the trees, or freely run through the field feeling the grass brush against her legs. Nor could she stand on the side of the road and thumb her way back into the city and her apartment and her car. Or drive her car at insanely high speeds, just to feel the rush of the risk.

She wouldn't be able to find Sarah.

The thought of Sarah sitting beside her in the car with the top down, her dark hair flying in the wind, her eyes glistening in joy made Angie breath in short gasps. Maybe she could escape, dig a hole or climb the fence.

Closer to the entrance now, the fence appeared higher and she stared at the glinting pointed needles of the barbed wire. Escaping over that looked impossible, unless you wanted to end up covered in gouges, looking like a bloodshot eye. Angie tried to lengthen her gulps, take them into the middle of the knot in her stomach so it would loosen.

The officer steered the van through the parking lot, then stopped, grabbed the remote from the visor and pressed a button. A large heavy looking, garage-type door opened and the van inched into a covered grey, brick garage. Grey like the clouds that stalked the sky, day in and day out, during the winter months.

Without turning her head, Angie knew the heavy door was lowering by the screeching and rumbling of it running down metal runners. The officer remained in the van until the noise stopped then she got out and walked around to the passenger side.

"I'm taking you to admitting."

"I...I need your help."

Angie felt a hand on her elbow. The woman helped her out of the van. Her throat dry, Angie tried to talk. "Did you know Lola?"

The officer walked her forward. "Sort of."

"Her daughter, Sarah, I need to find her."

"You know how many requests I get? I can't help." The officer unlocked a heavy door and gently guided Angie into a room that reminded her of the gym equipment room in her high school.

"Hi, Joelle," said the officer. Once the door shut, she dropped Angie's elbow.

"This escort must be a nice change for you, Susan, after all the time you've been putting in seg lately." Joelle sat behind a counter, folding a towel.

"Here's the paper work." The officer named Susan handed over some forms. "I'll unshackle her."

"Perfect. I've got the admitting forms ready."

The weight of the leg irons fell from Angie's ankles. The officer stood and faced Angie, looking her square in the eyes. "Be careful in there."

"Find Sarah," Angie whispered. "Please. Go to the low rentals on West Cordova, number–"

"Take care of you first," the officer interrupted. "You got a baby in *your* body that needs you to be a decent mother." Then she turned and left.

Angie endured the many questions, (no, she didn't know who the father of her baby was), the Polaroid picture taking, and it was only when she stripped down in the shower area that she started to shake. Although she stripped for a living, she felt the need to turn her back, hide her body.

She stepped into the shower and turned on the cold faucet. A silent scream simmered in her body like boiling lava and she had to continue to breathe deep to keep it from erupting from her mouth. This abrupt turn in her life had occurred in less than forty-eight hours. The icy water drenched her skin like a hose on full blast, like the one her mother would use on her in the backyard. In those days she never screamed or cried, she just ran to find shelter under the picnic table or in the shed knowing the hose couldn't reach that far. Here, she had no place to hide–her entire life was open for everyone to view.

Finally, she turned the shower on warm.

When she stepped out of the shower, the clothes she had left on the bench were gone. In a neat little pile sat grey sweat pants and a sweat top, a white T-shirt, a pair of cotton briefs that looked like they belonged to someone's Grandmother, white tube socks, a plain white sports bra and slippers.

"The nurse needs to see you in Health Care," said the woman on the desk when Angie was dressed.

"Not more questions," mumbled Angie.

"Consider yourself lucky; they pertain to your pregnancy."

The nurse asked questions but also showed Angie pictures from pregnancy books. Although only the size of a robin's egg, her fetus had the beginnings of a real heart, brains, limbs, ears, nose and eyes. The baby was due to be born, according to the calculations, on June 15th. The nurse put her on a special diet and everyday they would give her special vitamins.

Angie still couldn't believe she was pregnant. Could a life really be growing inside her body? Her throat constricted when the nurse talked about her baby. Her baby.

Back with the unfriendly woman in admitting Angie was given a paper bag filled with a second set of clothes, a stick of deodorant, a toothbrush, toothpaste, comb and a plastic cup and cutlery. She followed her through long corridors and doors and each time the door clicked behind them, she flinched. They walked deeper and deeper into the cold heart of a prison.

Intuko tossed and turned until finally he got up, downed a couple of aspirin with a huge glass of water and phoned Chris.

"What time is it?" Chris mumbled on the other end.

"I have to find Sarah. I have to find out who killed Lola."

"You're crazy."

"Phone that Candice for me, get her address. Then phone me back."

"You almost passed out on me last night. I barely got you in your door."

"And that plate. We need to track it. How do we do that?"

"Phone the cops, I guess. They can track anything. What about that cop who always comes for Harry? He likes you, he'll help."

"Good thinking. I'll call you back when I find out more."

Intuko hung up the phone and drummed his fingers against the table. He had to think of a strategy. Chris was right, if Constable Carter was in, he might help. He picked up the phone, put it back down, and decided to go to the station. He'd visit Harry and go from there.

"Harry's gone already. He was released after breakfast." Constable Carter patted Intuko on the shoulder. "Good of you to care though. I'm sure you'll see him again."

"Yeah, I'm sure I will." Intuko wondered if he sounded a little too glib. "Is Detective Anderson in today?"

"Day off."

Intuko nodded. "Say, listen." He knew he was stumbling for words. "Can you track a license plate for me? Fellow came to church last week and I never got his name. Wanted to send out a welcome card, you know, something to say, thanks for joining us."

"Sure."

Constable Carter went to the nearest available computer and punched in a few numbers. Intuko closed his eyes, giving a quick prayer to God, saying he was sorry for his little white lie. Opening his eyes, he could see the computer screen change but it was too far away to read anything. He watched as Constable Carter picked up a pen, found a scrap piece of paper, and jotted down a few words.

"You're back again, Intuko."

Intuko immediately turned to see Detective Anderson standing behind him in a ball cap, jeans, hockey jacket, and sneakers.

"Lennie, I thought you had the day off," Constable Carter said, walking to the counter.

"Got tons of paperwork to catch up on. Plus I need my hockey sticks. I've got a game later tonight."

Constable Carter handed Intuko the paper. "That black Mercedes is owned by Harrison Fleming. Isn't he that television Evangelist from BCTV?"

Sheepishly, he took the paper from Constable Carter. "Thanks." He turned to face Anderson. "I thought you were working round the clock."

"I've got men on the case. What's all this about?" Detective Anderson jerked his head at the note in Intuko's hand.

"Intuko wanted to track someone down who came to his church. He had the license number."

Anderson nodded, staring at Intuko with his lips pressed together and his eyes drawn into slits.

86

"I guess I'll be on my way." Intuko faked a smile.

Once outside, he took a deep breath, sighing in relief.

"I want to know what you're up to." Detective Anderson pronounced every letter in every word while breathing down his neck.

Intuko pivoted on his heels to face Anderson, meeting his gaze head on, waving the paper with the number. "Lola was seen with a guy named Charlie the night she was killed. I saw Charlie getting into a black Mercedes last night. I wanted to find out who that car belonged to, in case there's a connection."

"You're not a bloody detective." They stood facing each other. "Charlie got in the car, *not Lola.* You're grasping at some pretty small straws. We've got men and strategies. I'm warning you, Intuko, butt out. This is more dangerous than you think."

Intuko backed up a step.

"Let me see that paper." Anderson snatched the paper from Intuko's hand and stared at it, shaking his head. "This is not concrete evidence. Why dredge the guy through hell for no reason? Which is exactly what you'll do. Drop it."

"Okay," said Intuko. "I'll drop it."

Intuko approached the big BCTV building and stood outside for a moment, looking at the aerial standing on top of the building, pointing to the sky like an overly large needle. He licked his lips and swallowed, his throat dry. He'd never been inside a television station before, had no idea what to expect. Straightening his clerical collar, he sucked in a deep breath and walked toward the front door.

"Excuse me," he said standing at the front desk.

A woman wearing a head set glanced up. The phone rang and she held up a finger for him to wait and pressed a button.

"BCTV." She paused. "He's not in at the moment. I'll transfer you to his voice mail."

She looked at him. "How can I help you?"

"I'd like to see Harrison Fleming."

"Do you have an appointment?"

"No."

"He doesn't see anyone without an appointment."

"I really need to see him. It's important."

The receptionist shook her head. "I can't buzz you in, sorry." Then she smiled. "I know he's open to visitors at his church, Divine Intervention, later today. It's located in Kerrisdale, on the corner of 41st and Granville."

Kerrisdale boasted old Vancouver money, high real estate prices, fancy cars, and furs even though there was rarely snow. Intuko whistled as he stared up at the state-of-the-art church. Divine Intervention. Home of Harrison and Hope Fleming. One thing he knew for sure; this church had money and it wasn't struggling in the downtown area of Vancouver, like Princess Street United. On the marquis out front, along with all the information on service times, there was a picture of Hank and Hope, smiling, arms wrapped around two beautiful little children. A boy and a girl. The perfect family.

He walked up the stairs to the front door feeling as if he was on that game show, *The Price is Right*. He'd already been through door number one at BCTV and now he was entering door number two. Would he get the free trip or the dud prize?

When he approached the front office, the clock read twelve on the dot.

"Hello," he said to the girl sitting behind the desk. "I'm an architectural design student and I'm wondering if it's possible for me to take a look at the main part of the church." He paused to smile. "I watch Harrison Fleming's show every Sunday and I love the design of the church. I'm working on a research project. Could I just peek in for a moment?"

The tall, slim, young and so-unlike-Hazel front desk

receptionist tilted her head. "Why don't you just come to a service to check out the design of the church?"

"Because…because I'm from out of town. And anyway, if I was privileged enough to actually attend a service I'd be so engrossed by the truly wonderful inspiring message of Reverend Fleming I don't think I'd be able to sketch a straight line." He leaned forward and whispered, "I think it would be a bit sacrilegious, anyway. Don't you?"

The receptionist shrugged her shoulders. "Yeah, I guess you're right." She looked around. "I'm only on temp here today. It seems kind of quiet right now and seeing as Reverend Fleming won't be back until two, I guess I could help you out."

Intuko breathed a quick sigh of relief that his rehearsed spiel and his quick answer had worked. When he entered the church, he pulled out the notepad and pencil he had just purchased at the drug store and drew a few lines, carefully hiding his paper from the receptionist. A much better carver than sketcher, he turned to her and faked a smile. "If you have work to do, don't feel as if you have to stay with me. I just want to do a quick draft then I'll be on my way. I still have another church to look at."

"Oh, okay. Be quick though, I don't want to get into trouble."

"I sure will and thanks."

As soon as she left, he put his book away and started toward the front of the church, knowing, from all his experience with churches, that there had to be a door in the front leading to Harrison Fleming's office. He moved quietly down the aisle and through a door off to the right hand side that led him to a hallway. He stopped. A woman's voice. He pressed his back against the wall and edged toward the door.

"How about Bailey's at ten Monday night? I'll wear the blond."

Pause.

"I know it's dangerous but it's the only way."

Another pause.

"Mercedes. I'll drop her off first."

The woman's voice became a murmur. Intuko leaned against the door but couldn't make out any words. Footsteps walked toward the door. Jerkily, he scanned the halls. He had to get out of here before this woman caught him snooping around in the back wing of the church. At the end of the hall, a red exit sign glowed. He scooted down the hall on tiptoes, creaked open the door and stepped outside. Into sunshine.

He pressed his hand to his chest to stop his heart from beating through his skin. Detective Anderson was right, he was no detective.

All the way home, Intuko tried to think of how he could continue his search. He phoned Chris when he got back to his office.

"Did you get Lola's address?"

"Candice wasn't home."

"Someone has to know where she lived."

"I'm sure someone has Sarah, Intuko."

"Yeah, but who? And if no one does, where would she go? Maybe she's alone in her apartment.

"I thought the police went to her place."

"She may have come back. She's a kid. And more than likely very scared. Or she might be on the streets."

"She'll probably know enough to go to school on Monday."

Monday, to Intuko, seemed a long way off.

TEN

Sunday morning arrived and it was another magnificent Vancouver day–two in a row was a rarity in November. The amber hues of the sun shone in a sky the colour of a sedate mountain lake.

Sunday climaxed Intuko's week and he usually awoke feeling energetic and ready to meet the world head on. This morning, however, an undefined worry chewed away at his stomach. He didn't want to don his white robe and preach.

Yesterday had been a total disaster. Even after searching the streets, he hadn't come any closer to finding Sarah. Or who had killed Lola.

In his boxer shorts, he walked out to the living room, turned on the television, and flipped through the stations. At six-thirty in the morning most of the shows were reruns. He stopped when he hit BCTV and television evangelist, Harrison Fleming. Must be one of his earlier shows. Without taking his eyes off the screen, he sat down on the edge of the sofa and watched Vancouver try to put a Hollywood spin on a religious show. Harrison Fleming was oil slick and smooth like creamed butter, a strange combination.

Then his wife walked on the stage, her long flowing dress swirling in the breeze of her stride, her jet-black hair pulled back, accentuating flawless skin and dark, deep-set eyes. She smiled, praised God for his magnificence, picked up the microphone, and began to sing, her lush and vibrant voice making melodies to Jesus her Saviour.

Mesmerized, Intuko listened to her sing until she hit her

long, last note, finishing in a deep breath to bow her head in prayer. Hope Fleming–wife of television evangelist, mother of two. She looked a lot younger than Harrison, but then, Intuko wasn't much of a judge when it came to the age of women. He had been celibate by choice for the last six years now since he'd graduated from seminary.

Harrison Fleming seemed to have it all.

Intuko shook his head. He had been ready to pay Harrison a visit yesterday but Chris had convinced him to have a game plan in mind before barrelling in to ask questions. Now he wondered how he should approach a perfectly polished, powerful man like Harrison Fleming. He felt intimidated by this man. And saddened.

How did *he* know Charlie?

Glancing at the clock on the television, Intuko realized he had to start thinking about his own sermon. He shut off the television and entered his bedroom to see crumpled bed sheets, a frayed comforter, books heaped in piles and loosely scattered photographs. What a mess. A picture of his siblings that he had put into a cheap brassy-looking frame sat on his nightstand and a few other pictures hung crookedly on the wall.

He walked to his nightstand and picked up the one picture he had of his family. It had been snapped with a Polaroid camera by a white boyfriend of his mother's, so many years ago–her first white boyfriend of many. The four children in the photo looked young, innocent, and trusting. He sighed. Maybe later today, after church, he would call Ruby.

Intuko stared intently at the little girl with the chubby cheeks, wearing a handmade dress and moccasins. She was a baby when the picture had been snapped. If he called her later this afternoon, he'd probably wake her up from a drunken Saturday night. Six years younger than Intuko, she had few memories of a loving grandmother. Their *anaanak* and *adaadak* had died the year after their mother had left.

The three other children posing in the photo were boys: Intuko and his two brothers. They wore traditional clothes and held their harpoons proudly. Hunting and fishing had been a wonderful way of life. His brothers were both married; one lived in Yellowknife and the other in Norman Wells.

Time and money hindered Intuko's return to his homeland, or at least those were the excuses he used. He rubbed the dust off the glass with the cuff of his sleeve. He'd removed himself from all these people and they from him. None of his siblings could understand why Intuko wanted to be a minister when they had been treated so poorly by the priests.

The priests had often snuck up on them in the playground of the residential school. One man had been the worst. "I hope you're not whispering secrets in your native tongue," the man-in-black had said with contemptible coldness. "You know the consequences."

Intuko had stared at the toe of his boot. He didn't even know enough words in his native tongue to be whispering secrets on the playground, but to say so would mean he was talking back.

"No sir, I'm not sir."

"Look at me when I'm talking to you," the voice threatened.

Anaanak had always said to never look a bigger person in the eyes as it showed you had no respect. Animals too. Don't look in the eyes. Before he could lift his head, Intuko had been cuffed across the ears. And sometimes, if the priest or sister was in a bad mood, he hauled him inside to be whipped. Bloody red welts.

Intuko shook his head and quickly placed the family photo back on his nightstand. Enough. He had a sermon to preach.

Sunday morning. Susan awoke to Hilary shaking her. "Mommy, time to get up."

"What time is it, Hil?"

"Eight o'clock. Come on, get up."

Blurry-eyed, Susan walked to the window and pulled up the blinds to dazzling sunshine. "Oh, what a gorgeous day. Maybe we should go for a hike."

"Let's go to Sunday school first. They're practising for the Christmas performance and I want to be Mary."

Susan tweaked Hilary's nose. "You wouldn't settle for being an angel, now would you?"

"But Mary is so cool, Mom. She's the best part. Hey, I wonder if Mary, you know real-live Mary, wants to come with us to church. She'll keep *you* company. Do you want me to phone her?"

"Are you worried about me?"

Hilary stared up at Susan. "I think you need some friends besides me. All you do is work."

Susan tousled Hilary's hair. How perceptive.

The one social function Susan had attended, after the separation, astonished her. Every time she began a conversation with a man, the wife of that man seemed to appear from who-knows-where to cling to his arm, coo in his ear, purr like an annoying kitten. They honestly thought she was after their men because she no longer had one. These women were friends; she had been one of them. Now they treated her like a man-hungry woman, an out-cast, a divorced woman. She lost them as friends and had not yet made new ones. Except Mary. The crazy writer who lived downstairs.

"You know, Hil, I bet Mary would love to come with us to church. Why don't you wait an hour before calling her though? You know her sleep patterns on the weekend."

Susan and Hilary cuddled on the couch, watching cartoons and eating Honey-Nut Cheerios until it was time to call Mary.

"I just love Vancouver on days like today." Mary sat on

94

the top step of the veranda, looking up into the crystal-clear sky. They decided to meet at ten to get to the service by ten-thirty.

Susan stepped outside, took a deep breath, and closed her eyes. "Beautiful." Opening her eyes, she shut the front door tightly then turned the knob just to make sure it was locked. "I could do without the crime, though," she said walking toward the steps.

"I wonder how many vagabonds will be at church today." Mary shook her head in amusement. "This minister is something else. He keeps his voice so quiet and just keeps talking when people of all sorts wander up to the front, mumbling and burping and letting it out their back ends. I've never been a church goer but this place is highly entertaining." Mary stood and brushed small pieces of leaves from her black jeans.

"How about we take my car?" Susan walked down the front steps of the brown house she lived in, on West 18th–a turn-of-the-century house renovated and made into apartments. Hilary and Susan occupied the ground floor–a spacious, bright, two-bedroom apartment with high ceilings, moulded archways, big window ledges, French doors, and an alcove in the front room–and Mary lived in the basement suite. After her separation, Susan wanted out of the newer suburban house in Richmond that she had shared with Eric. Of course, Eric was appalled that she'd *rent* an older house, in a funky neighbourhood as he was into the suburbs.

"Come on, Hil, let's get in the beater." Susan took Hilary's hand and began skipping toward the car. Hilary squealed in delight and quickly joined Susan's stepping pattern.

Sitting on the hard wooden pews, Mary leaned behind Hilary who sat sandwiched between her and Susan, and whispered in Susan's ear. "You know what else I like about this church?"

"What?" Susan whispered back.

"Two things." Mary held up two fingers. "The service is one hour exactly, no rambling on and on, and the minister is gorgeous."

Susan covered her mouth to stifle her giggles.

"Mom, don't. You'll embarrass me." Hilary nudged Susan with her elbow. Then she turned to Mary. "What? Tell me? Come on, I want to know what you said."

An older woman, with a crocheted bun holder positioned at the nape of her neck, sitting in front of the trio, turned her head sharply to stare at them. This brought on more snickers from Susan and Mary and from Hilary who wanted to join in.

Only the organ music, pounding out *Great Is Thy Faithfulness*, signifying the beginning of the church service stopped their shoulders from shaking in laughter.

Susan and Mary managed to procure proper church manners until Hilary left for Sunday school. Then Mary slid over beside Susan. "Come on," she whispered, "you have to agree with me, he is cute."

Susan nodded her head. The first Sunday she'd attended Princess Street United Church with Mary, she'd been so stunned by his looks, her jaw had almost fallen into the hymn book she held in her lap. She expected some guy with a holier-than-thou, neatly-coiffed, grey-around-the-temples look, like Harrison Fleming, the evangelist on a Sunday morning television show. But this guy had been down to earth. Every week, that she did go, she was awed by the quietness of his sermon, and the amount he managed to say without any fire and brimstone pulpit-banging.

Intuko's sermons—he insisted on using his first name only, Susan didn't even know his last name—were always life messages. He took passages of Scripture from the Bible and related the verses to the everyday perils of life. No judgement involved. He didn't call people sinners and saints, distinguishing between the two. Susan remembered his sermon on failing; it was just after she moved out. That sermon had comforted her.

She wondered how he was feeling about his upcoming art class and she decided to talk with him after the service.

They stood for another hymn, this time a modern let's-clap-your-hands, wave-your-arms hymn. "Hey man, let's groove," whispered Mary.

"Would you stop it? You're going to make me laugh again."

"That's what I'm trying to do. You're always so serious."

"I am not."

"Are too."

"Would you be quiet and sing."

Mary smiled at Susan, picked up the hymn sheet inserted in the bulletin and belted out the words in a lovely soprano. When the song was over and the congregation seated, Intuko called up a guy named Chris Temple, to say a few words regarding the youth group.

"And I thought the minister was good looking!" Mary whispered.

With her finger on her mouth, as if they were small children needing a warning, the woman in front of them turned around again. "*Shh.*"

After the woman turned to once more face the front, Mary leaned over again, "I can't help it. Look at the bod on that guy."

"He's too young for you."

"I wasn't thinking of me, I'm always only thinking of you."

"I don't want a man. I'm not ready for that. But I think you do. You're obsessed."

This time when the woman turned around to glare, Susan smiled sweetly while elbowing Mary in the ribs. Then she turned her attention to hear what the youth leader had to say. He seemed to genuinely care and she wondered what his story was, why he was willing to give his time to help with the youth when most guys his age were still party animals.

Mary very quietly and seriously whispered, "How old do you think he is?"

She shrugged her shoulders. "He's the kind of guy where age wouldn't make a difference."

After the church service, Mary and Susan queued in line to shake hands with the minister who stood at the doors, greeting the congregational members.

Mary, who had jockeyed to be ahead of Susan, shook hands first. "It was a nice service."

"What was your name again?" Intuko took her hand and smiled warmly. "I'm terrible with names, but I know I've seen you here before."

"Mary. Mary Perkins."

"Glad you could make it today, Mary."

Susan was next. "Hi, I'm Susan Peterson." She stuck out her hand. "Thank you for agreeing to teach the art class."

"Susan! Nice to meet you again. Did you get my message about the soapstone?"

"It's already ordered."

"Thank you for coming this morning and I look forward to my class."

The line-up behind Susan was long and she moved ahead to let the next person have their turn with the minister.

"Susan."

Intuko spoke so low, she barely heard him. Startled by his tone change, she turned sharply and ended up staring into a pair of dark, questioning eyes. "I have something to ask you." He moved a step forward and leaned into her. "Has an Angela Melville been admitted to Corrections?"

People were randomly scattered everywhere in the small foyer and Susan, taken slightly aback by the question and his approach, stepped back.

"I'm sorry." Intuko backed up, resuming his position at head of the line to shake everyone's hand.

Something about the look in his eyes, Susan couldn't pinpoint what, it wasn't desperation, but something, told her to nod her head.

Turning, Intuko continued his duty of shaking hands and thanking everyone who took the time to wait in line after the service. He knew his actions had been inappropriate but *Angela Melville was in prison.*

"It's nice to see you again, Gladys." He smiled.

He would need to visit Angela.

"Hello, William, glad you could make it out today."

Maybe Susan could help with that.

"Mr. Stillwell, how nice…"

"What was that all about?" Mary whispered, leaning into Susan.

Susan slowly shook her head. "I'm not sure. He wanted to know about a woman who came into the prison."

"Is she a friend of his?"

"I don't know."

"What's she in for?"

Susan stared at Mary. "Fraud. She's smart. Stripper. She also asked me to help find this little girl." Susan glanced at Intuko again as he wrapped both his hands around a little oriental woman's hands. "It still puzzles–"

"Mommy!" A very excited Hilary interrupted the conversation. Jumping up and down she said, "Could I go to Jenna's? Her mom said it was all right. Come on, talk to her."

Grabbing Susan's fake fur coat, the one she'd bought at a

thrift store and that Eric absolutely hated, Hilary pulled her in the direction *Hilary* wanted to go.

"Okay, okay." Susan laughed. "I see Jenna's mom."

Once all the arrangements with Hilary and Jenna were squared away, Mary and Susan stepped into the blueness of the world outside.

"It feels weird to be without Hil," said Susan.

"Hey," Mary linked her arm in Susan's, "why don't we go for a bite to eat then a walk? It's a beautiful day."

"Yeah, I guess I could. It seems kind of decadent, I have a lot to do at home."

"Oh, for the love of Pete, woman, you can do those chores later. I'm taking you to lunch and then it's the Sea Wall. Where do you want to go?"

"I don't know."

"Let's go somewhere fun. How about Tomatoes?"

Energy seemed to ooze from the green, yellow, and tomato-red painted walls of Tomatoes, a hip restaurant located on Cambie Street. The restaurant boasted yellow booths, red and purple chairs, colourful art on the walls, and canned jars of tomatoes lined up and stacked on shelves. Susan inhaled a whiff of garlic and herbs, and scanned the seating situation.

"Two for lunch?" The waitress was dressed in jeans and a T-shirt.

"Can we have a booth?"

"If you want to wait. There's a couple leaving soon."

Susan nodded as she preferred the booths for privacy. While they waited for the waitress to return and usher them to their seats, Susan and Mary perused the posted notices on the bulletin board. Aside from the advertising of local theatre productions, art performances, art exhibits, and literary readings, there were phone numbers for homeopathic medicine, massages, chiropractors, and support groups. Susan finished reading all that interested her then looked out the window. She couldn't believe it when she saw Intuko, striding like a madman toward the restaurant. He saw her, waved, and pushed the restaurant door open.

"I'm so glad I caught you," he said breathlessly. "I just have one quick question then I'll leave you alone." Intuko glanced at Mary. "Oh, hello–"

"Mary. Like the virgin."

"Oh, yes, Mary." He turned back to Susan. "I need to see Angela Melville at the prison as soon as possible. When could I do that?"

"Uh, visiting hours. Tomorrow between six and eight in the evening. We have a chaplain, though. I can give her the message but she has to agree to the visit."

"I don't want to see her as a minister."

"Would you like to join us for lunch?" Mary butted in.

Intuko shook his head and smiled. "No, thanks, another time."

"Your table is ready, ladies," said the waitress, picking up two plastic menus.

"Go ahead Mary, I'll be there in a moment," said Susan.

Susan watched Mary walk toward the table before she turned back to Intuko. "I may be out of line, but–"

"I need to see her."

"Why?"

"I found her, in the alley. She had a picture with Lola."

Susan thought about how Angela had asked her to find Lola's daughter. "I drove Angela from the hospital. She..." Susan hesitated, not knowing how far to go with all of this.

"What?" He sounded earnest.

"Okay." She lowered her voice. "This is between us, but...she asked me to look for Lola's daughter."

"Sarah," said Intuko quickly. "What else did she say?"

Susan shrugged, thinking about how Angela had tried to

give her an address. "Not much, really."

"I have to find Sarah."

"Why don't you try her school?"

"Did she say what school she went to?"

Susan pictured the street in her mind and the schools nearby. Finally, she looked at Intuko, who waited for her to speak. "I bet she's at Roberts Elementary."

"Roberts. Okay. I'll go tomorrow. How should I approach this school thing?"

"Go to the front office." Susan, seeing Intuko's desperation said, "I'll meet you, if you'd like."

"Really?" His eyes popped open.

"Yeah, really."

"What...time?"

"School starts at 9:00 a.m. How about 8:45?"

"I know I asked this earlier, but, what was that all about?" Mary whispered to Susan as she slid in the booth.

"I just did something really stupid. I agreed to help him track down a child." Susan flopped her head in her hands.

"Whose child?" Mary leaned forward.

Susan looked up. "A hooker's. She was murdered yesterday. Can you believe it? Angela Melville, the woman just brought in for fraud, tried to tell me an address to go to find this child."

"You didn't give him the address?"

"I don't even remember it. Anyway, it could be a drug house. I told him to try the schools and...I said I would help him."

"Won't child services look for the child?"

"It all depends if the child's been with them before. They may think the girl is with a relative. You have to understand these hookers are transient. The kid could be in Toronto by now." Susan rubbed the back of her neck for a few moments.

"But if she isn't and I don't do anything, we're looking at another inmate in thirteen years. What kind of person wouldn't help a child?"

"Not someone like you, that's for sure." Mary patted her hand.

The waitress sat two glasses of water on the table. "Can I get you anything to drink ladies?"

"A glass of white wine for me," said Susan. "Chardonnay would be perfect."

"Double that," said Mary.

After the waitress left, Mary said, "Hey, I read the bulletin at church and they have some neat groups going. Want to come to one with me?"

"It's enough that I go now and again on Sunday," said Susan. "Church groups are as much my thing as they are yours."

"I think it would be fun." Mary's eyes twinkled as she peered over the top of her water glass.

"And what group are you going to join?" Susan asked sarcastically, shaking her head at her crazy friend.

"The youth group."

Susan laughed. "I think at thirty-five you're a bit old."

"If both the minister and that Chris guy show up at every meeting, who cares if I'm too old."

ELEVEN

Ten o'clock, Sunday night. Her door shut and the lock clicked. Angie was alone; locked away from the rest of the world, not allowed to leave her tiny space for nine hours. Tomorrow she was to meet with a lawyer from legal aid to discuss her hearing.

Although her night-light shone, the room seeped with darkness. She pulled the grey, scratchy wool blanket up over her body until it touched her chin. She wanted to go home to her apartment and her satin sheets; the only place in the world that had ever been home. As a child she'd had a big canopy bed and a yellow, goose-down comforter. The down comforter was supposed to be soft, but had scratched her face as much as the wool in the blanket she laid underneath did now. Different beds, different rooms, same feel.

Angie put her hands to her tummy. The flatness of her stomach made her wonder if she was pregnant. She remembered when Lola was pregnant; she'd liked putting her hands on her stomach to feel Sarah kick.

Angie shivered and rolled around on the uncomfortable, skinny mattress.

Sarah's little face still haunted her, crying out to Angie, her innocent voice strangled and muffled like someone had a hand over her mouth.

Angie sat up, her head falling in her hands. She sucked in deep breaths, trying to steady her nerves. Then she lay back down to try and sleep. Just as she was slowly drifting into an unconscious state, a little noise, almost as if someone was tapping her hair brush or her cup against the sink, startled her awake.

She opened her eyes and turned her head.

Angie gasped, unable to move or speak.

Standing still as a statue was a woman dressed in a long, white, thick cotton tunic, cinched in at the waist with a gold braid. She raised her arms to the side like a majestic bird getting ready to fly into the blue sky of the world beyond the clouds. But she didn't take flight–she remained poised on the brink, halcyon in her silence. Her hair, black and long, hung to her shoulders–thick like a horse's hair, but not course, more like silk. High cheekbones moulded into the curves of her round face and satin-textured, bronzed skin glowed like a well-oiled tanned body in the sun. Little eyes holding a sparkling glint smiled even though her mouth remained steady, one straight line. Around her neck, shining against the white tunic, hung a necklace. A carving. A woman carrying a baby on her back, papoose style.

Angie squinted; it was made of something white. Stone or bone? Angie continued to stare at the necklace, unable to take her eyes off its artistic beauty.

"Who are you?" Angie whispered, averting her eyes from the necklace to the woman's face.

"Learn to love, and you will free me."

"What do you mean?"

"I've watched you, as I've watched many in this cell, and I know you are the one who is going to free me. Go to the man in the cloth, I know him well, he will guide you."

"But..."

The woman disappeared.

The eerie quiet of the church, like whispering spirits, seemed to be floating through the walls of Intuko's office. The Sunday night church service was over, the last person finally gone, and he felt guiltily relieved.

His desk sat piled high with work and he wanted to throw everything onto the floor. How was he supposed to get it all done? He needed more volunteers, more people to help, and more money. Most churches relied heavily on the congregation, but his congregation...Old Joe used to come in every Monday to count the money but once Hazel discovered he was pocketing some for himself, he had to be told he couldn't help any more. Now, Intuko, or Hazel, counted the money, along with everything else.

Then he'd gone to that church. A church with more money than they knew what to do with. And instead of saying thanks to God for providing people with such a wonderful place to worship, he'd spent his time skulking around hallways, lying to people, eavesdropping on a woman's conversation.

And he still had no idea where Sarah was. The police had so many plausible excuses: she had gone with a relative, she was with one of Lola's friends, she was...Intuko had to find her.

His doubts nagged his soul, reminding him of doubting Thomas in the Bible. Did all spiritual men have such doubts? Did Jesus have doubts when he was nailed to the cross? What about his disciples? They were men, living in physical bodies. And what would his grandmother say after what he had done today?

After his freedom from residential school, Intuko had professed to right all the wrong that had been done. Ministering, he had felt, was a viable way to help the young from his culture today. Now he'd wondered if he'd ever make a difference. He'd never returned to his homeland, or his shaman teachings, and he spent all his time wading through piles of paper. He truly believed he could combine the Christian teachings of the Bible with his shaman upbringing but he'd never done so. He'd ignored Lola's pleas, another woman had almost died of an overdose and he was trying to lay blame on another minister.

He made a promise to a woman to help an Inuit child, and after another day he had not come close to keeping that promise. And he didn't want to do the work for the church any more, he didn't want to tackle the pile of files, the stacks of bills or return the many messages that came across his desk every day.

He must find Lola's killer.

And Sarah.

Sucking her thumb, Sarah curled into a small ball on the mattress in the apartment they had taken her to.

"Aren't you asleep yet you stupid little brat? Get that friggin' thing out of your mouth." The woman named Angel yanked Sarah's thumb out of her mouth. "I'm being nice to you, ya know. They told me they wanted to kill you but I said I'd do it. You see, I think I can get money for taking care of you. So you have me to thank for being alive. Can't you even say thanks?"

Sarah stuck her hand in her other hand, squeezing them both between her legs, hoping, she wouldn't be tempted to put her thumb back in her mouth. She'd not sucked her thumb since she started school, but she couldn't help it now. "Thanks," she said quietly.

Angel pushed Sarah with her foot. "Get to sleep! If you make one peep, I'm warning ya they'll kill you."

Sarah curled into an even tighter ball, closed her eyes, forcing them shut, and lay as still as she could.

She heard Angel leave the room, banging the bedroom door, punching the walls. Sarah knew she was acting mean 'cause she wasn't high no more. Then Sarah heard the front door open.

"Have you got a fix for me?" the woman yelled.

"Shut the fuck up. Did you get rid of the kid?"

"Gimme a fix and I'll make sure she's good and done. Please."

By the sudden quiet, Sarah knew they were probably tying their arms.

Curled up as still as Peter Rabbit in Mr. McGregor's field, she wondered if she would ever go to school again. She hadn't been out of the apartment in days. They'd brought her to this place in the middle of the night so she didn't even know where she was. She put her thumb in her mouth, knowing they wouldn't come to see her now. Not when they were busy tying their arms.

At six o'clock on Monday morning Intuko made coffee. At seven, he tried to read his Bible and pray. At seven-thirty, after drinking the entire pot of coffee, he paced. At eight he shut the door to his apartment, pulled up the collar on his all-weather coat, and braved the pelts screaming from a dark sky. He started the engine of his car, hoping the sound of a failing muffler would drown out his thumping heart. He'd hardly slept a wink last night thinking about his mission today.

The roads were slick and the windshield wipers on the car flipped back and forth. Their constant scraping was almost welcome, giving Intuko something to concentrate on other than the nerves he felt he was wearing outside his body. A trucker passed him on the other side of the street, sending a spray of water that blanketed his car. For a moment the road became invisible. He leaned forward and gripped the steering wheel.

He slowed down when he hit the front of Roberts Elementary School. Finding a parking spot curb side, he watched the children dressed in rain slickers and plastic boots, rushing from cars to the school doors where they huddled awaiting the bell. Colourful umbrellas, some with pictures of Mickey Mouse, were a stark contrast to the bleak sky.

Searching the vehicles stopped on the side of the road, he realized he didn't even know what kind of car Susan drove. He would never be able to find her until all the parents left and then it would be nine o-clock.

He let his car idle and flipped on the radio only to hear some guy taking phone calls on today's hot political topic. Uninterested, he shut it off to listen to the pounding of the rain on the roof of his car. He looked at his watch. Eight-forty. Susan might be waiting inside.

But she wasn't in the front lobby or at least not in his view. Intuko read the signs.

All volunteers or visitors report directly to the front office. Please remove your outer footwear.

Intuko looked down at his soaked sneakers. He didn't want to be here long enough to take off his shoes. He heard the door behind him open and when he turned, he saw Susan, shaking her hair.

"Have you been here long?" she asked, avoiding Intuko's gaze and looking down the long corridor.

"Two minutes maybe."

Susan moved toward him. "Should we go to the office?"

"I'm a little out of my comfort zone here. What do I need to do?"

"We need to ask if Sarah Block is at this school. From there, depending on the answer, we'll ask where she lives because, as the family's minister, you need that information."

"And the information I have in my directory is wrong," said Intuko.

"Sounds good."

They entered the office and Intuko smiled at the secretary who sat at a desk fielding calls. "Excuse me," he said.

"What can I do for you?" The woman put the phone in its receiver.

"I'm looking for Sarah Block. Is she at school today?"

The secretary looked over her reading glasses and stared directly at his collar. "Sarah Block. She's in Miss Clarke's kindergarten class. She wasn't here all last week and she's not here today either."

"For some reason, my church has lost her records and I have a basket of goods to deliver to her house. It would be a shame if she didn't receive what we had for her family. This was the only avenue I could think of to track down her address. We haven't seen her for awhile."

"It's not school policy to give out a student's information."

"I would hate for her to miss out."

The woman tapped her finger on her lip. Then she went to the filing cabinet, pulled out a file, flipped it open, and started to read it to herself as she walked back toward the desk. "Emergency contact is Angie Melville." She peered at Susan. "Are you Angie?"

Susan shook her head.

"How about I call Sarah's number for you?"

"I would like…to visit her."

"What church did you say you're from?"

"Princess Street United. I have identification if you'd like to see it." Intuko pulled out his wallet and the woman thoroughly scrutinized it.

"I just thought of something," she said. "My neighbour, Gladys, is a member of your church."

"Gladys Underhill."

"That's her."

"I have her husband Bill in my prayers. Awfully sad about his stroke."

"It happened so suddenly. Life's scary that way." The woman wrote down the address, handing the paper to Intuko. "I can rest with a clear conscience now. I hope Sarah is feeling better soon and that you can be of some help to her and her family."

Outside the door of the school, the heavy rain had ceased. The sky now looked like white gauze cloth and light, Lilliputian drops landed on Intuko's nose. Staring at the address written on the scrap piece of paper, he sighed then turned to Susan who was now peering over his shoulder.

"What are you going to do?" she asked.

Intuko put the paper in his pocket. "Go to 131 West Cordova, apartment four and see if Sarah's there."

"You're crazy. That place could be a drug house. This is a job for the police."

"You don't have to come with me."

"It's not safe for you or me."

Intuko looked Susan square in the eyes and said, "And it isn't safe for Sarah either. Children are gifts and need to be protected by adults. The police seem too busy to look for her."

Susan closed her eyes. She knew she shouldn't get involved in this dangerous situation but...she couldn't help but be moved by his concern for a child. Susan slowly nodded her head. "I'll ride as a passenger, if that's okay."

"You don't have to do this."

"I have a daughter of my own. If something happened to me, I'd want someone like you in her life."

In the car Susan said, "By the way, I phoned the prison and left a message for Angela Melville, telling her you wanted to see her tonight."

"Thanks." He glanced at her attractive profile, enjoying having a woman ride in his car with him.

Within five minutes, they were parked in front of a dilapidated brick apartment that was spray-painted with graffiti. Intuko shook his head and looked at Susan who sighed.

"In my line of work I see a lot," said Susan, "but it's generally in the confines of the centre. It's not often I see where they live. No wonder so many children grow up to be criminals."

Entering the front entrance, Intuko gagged and covered his mouth with his hand. The smell of urine oozed from every corner and crack. Crusted vomit lay in clumps on the floor and there were even feces, dog or human, Intuko wasn't sure, lumped in a corner. He turned to Susan who had also covered her mouth with her hand. Neither spoke.

Holes spotted the walls. Big and small. Intuko imagined some were from angry or destructive punches. He'd witnessed bloody fights in the North and many times he had been made to wait, shivering, hunkered in the corners of a hotel lobby for his mother to finish what she had to do. Men had staggered out of the bar to bash each other, too drunk to notice the boy hovered in the corner.

"It looks like number four is just around this corner," whispered Susan.

A plastic number hung precariously from a nail, looking as if it would soon fall to the filthy floor. Intuko knocked on the door. They waited. There was no answer.

"Try again," Susan whispered. "Harder."

Breathing deeply, knowing full well if this wasn't handled right there could be trouble and his head could possibly end up shoved through the wall, he rapped harder. This time someone scuffled on the other side of the door but it was hard to tell if it was an adult moving or a child. Trembling, he listened for voices, but heard none. His throat tightened and he squeezed his fingers into a tight fist. Susan, standing at his side, placed a shaking hand on his forearm.

The door opened and in front of them stood a short, portly older man with grey hair and black horned rimmed glasses.

"The other day the cops, today a minister. What do ya want?"

"Have you seen the little girl who lives in this apartment?"

"Nah. They skipped out. I'm cleaning up the mess. Got

to rent it out, ya know. How she let that child live in the filth is beyond me."

Intuko wanted to say something about the filth of the outside of the apartment, but decided against it. Better not to anger the man. "Do you know where Sarah went?" he asked politely.

"No idea. At least the mother wasn't murdered in my apartment. I had an overdose once that was bad enough."

Intuko took out one of his cards. "If you see Sarah please call me."

The man shrugged his shoulders. "I guess I could seeing as you're a man of the cloth."

Angie had been assigned to the kitchen. Sick to her stomach with morning sickness, she showed up to be given a little blue hair net by Iris, the woman in charge of the kitchen.

Iris stood by the stove, stirring a big pot of soup.

"You need to make fruit salad," she said without even a glance in Angie's direction. "All the cut up fruit is in the fridge."

Angie made salad without saying a word. "What's next?" she asked, bored out of her mind.

"Pudding. You'll find everything on the counter."

Angie stirred chocolate powder into a big bowl of milk, stealing glances at Iris, trying to figure the woman out. Short and stocky, she had a hard face and looked to be in her fifties.

"How long you been here?" Angie asked nonchalantly.

"Long enough to know what goes down."

"Why you here?"

Pause. Iris stopped stirring. "You're a nosy one."

Angie kept mixing the pudding.

"Fifteen years. Put the pudding in them bowls."

Angie spooned the pudding into the little plastic bowls sitting on the counter. "You gettin' out any time soon?"

"Maybe, maybe not. When you're done that you gotta make macaroni and tuna salad. I'm okay in here. I bin here long enough to think of it as home."

"Home? Wow."

"After fifteen years I ain't got no home on the outside. What you in for?"

"Fraud," said Angie.

"Oh right. You're the knocked-up one who ripped off them bank machines. I never used one of those machines. I've been inside too long."

Did everyone know everything about Angie? She had to change the subject. "You ever get day passes?"

"I got no one to visit."

"Oh."

"Yup, my old man made sure I had no friends and my family disowned me a long time ago. I was a drunk."

"I know about drunks," muttered Angie.

"My old man beat me all the time," continued Iris much to Angie's surprise. "We'd get pissed-up, he'd swing punches, knock me down and boot me. Then for a little extra, if he wasn't passed out cold, he'd throw me against the wall like a rag doll. I saw more of the back of an ambulance than I did of my own place."

"Did you do something to him? Is that why you're here?"

"One day, I said enough of this shit, and I grabbed a knife off the kitchen counter and stabbed him. Then I called the cops." She shrugged. "Back in them days, murder was murder. I got life."

Angie nodded. Iris had probably been stirring soup for fifteen years.

"And my kids," Iris continued, "they went to homes. It's where they should have been all along. I know that now."

"How many kids you got?"

"Three."

"Where are they?"

Iris tasted the soup. "Dunno. I had to give up any right to them when they was adopted. In those days there was none of this adoption stuff that goes on now-a-days. They don't got no letter of sorry from me but at least they got a home."

Angie stirred some green onion in with the macaroni and tuna, thinking about Sarah, and how with Lola dead she was about to become another foster case. Angie was to have a visit tonight from the minister who found her in the alley. He was a link to the outside, a possible link to Sarah. Should she ask him to help?

Iris threw a spoon in the sink. "Take my advice, girl. Don't make my mistakes. A woman never forgives herself for screwing up her kids. She bears 'em, she births 'em, she gives 'em a life. Mine were given a bad start. Coming to prison has saved my life and it probably saved those three kids of mine."

Silence mopped the room.

TWELVE

Back at his office, Intuko phoned Chris's cell number and tapped his fingers, looking at the mess on his desk, the files stacked unevenly.

Chris answered after the first ring. "What's up?"

"I had no luck finding Sarah at the school or at Lola's old address which I got from the school. I need her pimp's address. Can you get that for me?" Intuko played with his fox carving on his desk, a reminder of the art class he had to prepare for this week. He couldn't help but smile.

"Her pimp's bad news," said Chris. "Charlie's a saint compared to him."

"I'm going to see Angela Melville today at the prison." Intuko rubbed his carving with his thumb–smooth, so smooth. "She might be able to tell me something. She had Lola's picture with her in the alley."

"It's worth a try."

"Where's Bailey's? Is it a restaurant?"

"Not really. It's a high-class lounge on West Hastings, down by G.M. place. They serve some food but they're known for their music. I think Sarah McLachlan may have got her start there. Diana Krall played there years ago too. Why?"

"I overheard a phone conversation. I think Harrison and Hope Fleming are meeting there tonight at ten and they said something about it being dangerous."

"Intuko, you're going in circles. What do you expect to accomplish at Bailey's? And Anderson was right when he said Charlie got in the car, not Lola."

"Call it instinct. You want to meet me there?"

"Yeah, sure, but…nothing you're chasing seems to fit."

"Come on, I'll buy you a drink.

"Melville, you got a visitor."

"I'm coming." Angie jumped out of bed, stuck her feet in shoes, and pulled at her hair elastic. Once her hair fell freely around her face, she quickly ran a brush through it.

"When you're ready, I'll walk you down."

Angie, with the officer, (screw they called them here), walking right behind her, kept her head high and breasts forward when she walked past the other loitering inmates plopped in front of the unit television.

She heard the familiar click of the door, allowing entry into the next hallway. Two more doors and she would be in the visitors lounge for her first, and maybe only, visitor.

She spotted him immediately–his collar giving away his identity–way in the back of the room sitting on a sofa. They tried to make it comfortable in here, nothing luxurious, but decently civilized. At least she had been granted an open visit so she didn't have to talk to this guy behind glass like in the movies.

All the sofas faced toward a glass partitioned office manned by a woman, obviously on watch for any kind of illegal interaction.

When he saw her, he rose. Walking toward him, she couldn't help but notice his slight swagger, (no puffed up chest though), his smooth skin, his white teeth that shone like snow bergs in the sun and his small, semi-sweet chocolate eyes that seemed to be smiling even when he looked serious. He actually looked somewhat like Sarah too–same caramel colouring, dark eyes, high cheekbones and round face.

"Angela." He stuck out his hand. "My name is Intuko. I found you in the alley."

"So I heard." Angie shook his hand, liking the warmth of his skin. She sat down, trying to thwart the sensations.

"I'm glad to see you're okay," he said, sitting beside her.

"I need your help," she blurted out.

"And I need yours," Intuko said calmly but with force. "You had a picture of Lola and–"

"You know Lola?" She immediately sat up, her back straight as a steel post.

"I met her years ago, through Street People Ministry. She came to see me just a few days back. Angela, when did you see her last?"

"Call me Angie. I saw her the night she died, getting into a black Mercedes. Something wasn't right."

"What kind of car did you say?

"Mercedes, I think. Black."

Intuko whistled through his teeth. "What time was that?"

"Around eleven."

"Did you see her after that?"

Angie shook her head. "I went and looked in on Sarah." She leaned forward, placed her fingers to her forehead, and lowered her head. "I should have taken her with me. She'd be safe if I'd taken her to my place."

"What else can you tell me?"

"I looked for Lola and Sarah the next day. No one had seen them. I went back, you know, that night, later, around three o'clock to get Sarah and she was gone. Jimmy, Lola's pimp was there."

"Did he say anything?"

"He told me not to look for Sarah. This is all related to him. I know it. And someone put something..." Her words trailed off.

Intuko squeezed her shoulder. "I know what happened to you. I was there. Who sold you your score?"

"I can't say."

"This could be important. Someone might have wanted to kill you because you were asking questions. We don't know. I need all the help I can get."

"Okay, okay. But the street dealer is a nobody. Even the cops don't care about him. They want the big guys."

"Who Angie?"

"Charlie." She dropped her head. "There, I've said his name."

"Is there anything else you heard that you think would help?"

Angie bit her bottom lip, closed her eyes, and then opened them. "Charlie talked about the big boys. The guys at the top."

"The top of–"

"The ring," she whispered, looking around. The screw leaned against the door, supervising them.

Intuko nodded.

"They're the guys in the suits and ties." She pressed her fingers to her brow. "They don't get their hands wet, 'cause they make the overseas deals and the money."

"Do you know any of them?"

Angie shook her head as she picked at the threads on the sofa.

"Are you sure?"

She looked up. "Charlie sort of mentioned one guy but…" Her words trailed off as she couldn't stop thinking of Paul. Paul Redman. Father of her baby. Rich, snazzy dresser, user of women. Was he involved? All the time she'd been with him, she'd never put two and two together. But the fact was– Paul *was* friends with that big city guy, Brad Black. Angie had been to Bailey's with Paul, and Black had been there. They'd talked, leaving her sitting by herself. But…that always happened. She'd never connected them to the drug shipment until Charlie mentioned names.

"Angie."

She turned.

"Tell me," he said.

She closed her eyes for a moment, squeezing them shut to get rid of the images swirling in her mind. "He said the city guy," she whispered, "I think he might mean Black."

"Black?"

"Yeah, you know, from city council. He owns that condo development in Whistler."

"Brad Black? Are you sure?"

"No. I'm not sure. Ignore what I said, okay." She stood, ready to end this conversation. Now.

"Angie," Intuko said her name in such a low, intent voice that she made direct eye contact with him. His eyes were filled with compassion, unlike the men she knew who leered. *Unlike Paul.* "I have to find Sarah," he said. "Can you think of any place she could be?"

She tilted her head upwards to think. "I've been racking my brains, trying to figure out where she'd go. Maybe she's still with Jimmy. Or one of Lola's friends–although most of her friends, except me, wouldn't want Sarah. It doesn't make sense. Unless Sarah saw something she shouldn't and then if she did…" She held her hand to her chest, and breathed, trying to rid herself of the sharp pains that punched at her chest.

Once she'd caught her breath, she asked, "Why do you want to find her?" She paused to stare at his skin, his eyes, his small nose. "Is she yours?"

He stood in response. "Not biologically. No. But…she is culturally. Lola told me Sarah's father was Inuit, actually Inuvialuit from the Western Arctic, and…" He closed his eyes for a minute. When he opened them he stared at the landscape prints on the walls, the ones framed in cheap brass, and he let out a painful sad sigh. He turned to Angie. "Lola came to me, she asked me to take care of Sarah if something happened. I made a promise."

"Maybe… if we work together on this, we can find her. We have to believe she's okay. But you have to promise me one thing."

"What?"

"If and when you get her, keep her. She can't go to the courts. She just can't. It's the one thing Lola wouldn't want. Keep her for me. I want her."

"Melville, your time's up." The screw stood in front of them.

They waited until the screw had walked away, then shook hands, their fingers intertwined, holding firm their grip for a few beats.

"No contact, please," said the officer as if she could see through the back of her head.

They both dropped their hands.

"I'm teaching an art class here Wednesday," said Intuko. Please come."

She gazed into his eyes. "I'd like that. "Promise me, you'll be careful," she whispered.

Exactly at ten, Intuko sat in Bailey's Lounge, at a small table, off to one corner, but still in open view of the stage and other tables. He sipped his lime garnished soda water and listened to the alluring music of the woman singing. What a voice. Rich, husky…her love song plunged straight to his soul. Love knew no bounds, knew no limits. The words rang through the air, sinking into the walls.

"I told you they had great music here." Chris pulled up a chair and plopped down. "This place has a little different atmosphere than Hank's, eh."

Intuko stared around the room at the small oak tables, clean and polished, each adorned with a glazed candle. Flames flickered seductively, creating smoke that swirled upwards. People leaned into one another. Men were dressed in suits, women in jewels. Talking, whispering, kissing, touching.

Intuko turned back to Chris. "I don't see them."

"Maybe something came up." Chris shrugged, looked around the room, waved to the waitress then turned back to Intuko. "You're really bugged by all of this."

"It's so convoluted."

"You need a life, maybe a woman."

Intuko had to chuckle. "That's your answer for everything, isn't it? I saw Angie Melville today."

"Angie. She's a cutie. And she's got smarts. Too bad she used 'em the wrong way."

"She's got a big heart, she really cares for Sarah." He leaned forward. "She told me she last saw Lola getting into a black Mercedes."

"Whoa. Was she sure?"

"She seemed sure." Intuko snapped his fingers. "Elizabeth, she told me Lola went to the ball in a dark carriage. Maybe she meant black."

Chris puckered his face then doubled over in laughter. "Intuko, buddy, pal. I'll take Angie's word but Elizabeth's? Come on. You're really grasping here."

"Okay, okay. You're right." He waved his hand at Chris.

"Now, did *Angie* mention anything else?" Chris asked.

"She said Charlie mentioned a city counsellor being involved. We put a few pieces together and came up with Brad Black."

"You can't mean the Whistler mega-millionaire on city council?"

"Yeah." Intuko rubbed his forehead. "So far we've got Harrison Fleming and possibly Brad Black. Both unlikely characters." He paused. "Angie also feels Sarah might be with that Jimmy."

"I told you Jimmy's a bad one." Chris watched the lounge singer for a few seconds before pulling a paper out of his pocket. "But...I got his address for you."

"You're a good man." He took the paper, studied the number then shoved it is his pocket. Sipping his drink, he stared over the rim to the back of the room where a couple sat side by side.

"Don't go to his place by yourself," said Chris adamantly.

"That woman over there," said Intuko. "Sitting at that table pushed in the corner. I think that's Hope Fleming."

Chris slowly turned. When he looked back at Intuko his eyebrows were pushed together. "From what I've seen of her on the tube, Hope Fleming is a knock-out brunette. Like dark brunette. Not a blond. And that guy is not Reverend Fleming."

"Yeah, but it's her. I can tell by the eyes, the smile and by the way she walked when she came in." Intuko squinted. He was sure it was the woman from the television and the marquis out front of the church.

"If it is her, then who's the guy? Chris asked. "It's not her husband and they don't look like they're just friends. She's all over him like a fly after shit."

Intuko didn't want to know anything more about Hope and her man. He thought he was going to figure out something from this meeting about Sarah and Lola. He was disgusted with himself for dragging Chris out to see this when they should be finding Sarah. "Let's get out of here, Chris."

"I think we should get his name."

"Why?" Intuko put his coat on.

Chris didn't take his eyes off the back of the room. "If you visited him, and asked some questions about Fleming and the black Mercedes, he'd have to answer or else you'd tell his little secret."

"That's blackmail, Chris."

Chris leaned forward, elbows on the table, the candlelight illuminating his face. "Intuko, you're trying to find who murdered Lola. And you're trying to find a child in trouble.

You need to use every resource you have."

Intuko sighed and shook his head. "I'll go as far as little white lies but blackmail–I can't do that."

"I can. Let me handle that. Somehow tonight we'll get his name."

Angie awoke in the middle of the night screaming. Something was wrong with Sarah. She could feel it.

The officer on duty rapped on her glass. Angie wiped the sweat off her brow and sat on the edge of her bed nauseated. This morning sickness was no longer just a morning thing; it plagued her all day, all night. Leaning over the toilet, she heard her door click, unlocking. Hair totally dishevelled, eyes watering, she kept her head in the darkened toilet bowl.

"Are you all right?"

"Yeah, I'm fine."

"I'm just checking on you." The voice sounded soft, gentle. "Other women who have been in this cell have had nightmares. There's a rumour about an Inuit spirit living in this cell."

"I know, everyone's been telling me." Angie kept her head still in the toilet, not wanting to look anyone in the eye in case she revealed that she did believe the rumours. "I'm okay, really."

"This type of sickness usually only lasts the first three months. I was sick with my pregnancy and I know the feeling. It's not fun." The officer shut the door so Angie was alone again.

Shivering, she crawled under the blanket and stared at the ceiling, watching the shadows jerkily dance. They were bothering her, making her think too much, jumping in her face, so she turned on her side, facing the wall, closing her eyes, trying to eliminate the world. But it wouldn't go away.

Paul's face appeared.

"You can't keep my baby from me," he said.

"Yes, I can," whispered Angie. "She's not yours, she's mine."

Angie heard a scratching and it sounded as if someone was using her hairbrush.

She wouldn't look, couldn't open her eyes, she must be imagining things. She curled into a tiny ball and pressed her cheek against the pillow. Then she stretched her arm, feeling the coldness and course texture of the brick that formed the cell wall. The concrete blocks were thick and hard, not easy to penetrate. There was no way out.

She pulled her hand away and placed it on her tummy. A dull ache burned inside her body like the amber coals of a fire.

Sarah crouched in the closet in the dark. Angel had put her there and told her to be quiet. No one was supposed to know she was still alive. Angel had dragged her by the arm, shoved her in the closet and told her to shut-up or she was dead. In the closet, Sarah tried to imagine she was Peter Rabbit in the watering can and how quiet he had to be.

THIRTEEN

Waking up, Angie jumped out of bed and threw her head over the toilet bowl. Then she rinsed her mouth with water and put on her grey sweats. The hall was still dark. Her clock read six.

Why couldn't she sleep? Out of energy from the seemingly monumental task of getting dressed, Angie sat on the edge of her bed, running her fingers through her tangles. They were nothing in comparison to how Sarah's used to be. Sometimes after combing Sarah's hair, strand by strand, she had put it in French braids. Thoughts of the kid were driving her insane.

She picked up her brush and yanked it through her own hair, untangling the little knots that had mysteriously appeared during the night. Her mother used to comb Angie's hair until her scalp bled, then she would pull it into a ponytail that was so tight her head would ache. And if she came home from school without the ponytail in place, the belt appeared.

When Angie grabbed her brush to clean the excess hair from the bristles, she noticed the blond and dark hair woven together like marble cake. Had that woman spirit visited again?

She shook her head, tossed the hair in the garbage can, and threw the brush on her desk. Then she lay on her bed fully dressed to wait for her door to be unlocked.

Intuko arrived at church at six in the morning, knowing he had tons of work to do before he left the office to visit Jimmy.

Then he had to hook up with Chris at two at Divine Intervention Church to meet with Steven Campbell, the man from Bailey's; the accountant for Hope and Harrison Fleming's church. They'd stayed late last night and Chris had sweet-talked the hostess into giving him a name after Mr. Campbell had paid with a credit card. Back at his office after midnight, Intuko had gone on-line, looked up the Divine Intervention web site and found out that Campbell was the church accountant.

Dark and quiet, Princess Street United Church had a powerful peacefulness that seeped through the cracks of his skin. In reverence, he trod softly towards the altar. Alone in the quiet, he really became close to the spiritual world, baring his all, every stored secret, every frustrating moment.

He knelt and bowed his head. "Please, tell me what to do," he whispered. "Show me a sign, any sign that I am following this path for a reason. I feel so lost right now. A young woman has lost her life, a little girl is in need, and I'm the one who has been summoned to help. And I'm failing as a minister. I have a congregation of people I'm not attending to and I'm letting everything slide."

Intuko lifted his head to stare at the minute fraction of light struggling to squeeze through the stained glass. God worked in strange ways. So many assumed when you prayed a voice would speak in return or a big clap of thunder would rumble or an angel would fly out of nowhere. But the answers to prayer could be found in the oddest ways–a person walking by, an article in a newspaper, a road sign, a picture, a phone call. All you had to do was look.

As he prayed he felt himself floating downward, plunging through a long tunnel. He heard his grandmother telling him to relax, enjoy his journey. Suddenly, he started to sing, old Inuit words from the past. Intuko saw two rivers, flowing in opposite directions and...he saw his fox, sitting at the exact point where the rivers met. It motioned for him to come closer. Intuko shook his head. What was happening?

He quickly opened his eyes. His mouth felt dry. He bowed his head. "Thank you for listening," his entire body trembled as he spoke out loud, "and... and now I know it is up to me to listen to you."

When he arose, his knees cracked.

In his office, Intuko plugged in the kettle, sat down at his desk, and pulled out his notes and his Bible. When the kettle whistled, he quickly made himself a cup of tea and returned to business.

Within an hour he felt he had made a dent in his church work, even though he had done nothing about getting the leaky roof fixed. He had no money in the budget for repairs. Reaching for his full-to-the-brim mug, he took a sip of cold tea. He glanced at his watch. Starbucks would be open and their coffee was a whole lot better than cold tea.

He closed the door to the church and stepped outside into the cascading rain that fell like Niagara River going over the falls. The cold, damp, empty streets reeked of loneliness. He shoved his hands in his pockets and walked by bodies huddled in corners, sleeping on cardboard, the rain drenching them. November was a bleak month, a high suicide month, a month when the shelters became full, all beds taken. Had his mother ever ended up curled in a ball in an alley? The cold hit his face, reddening his cheeks.

He entered the coffee shop, shook the water from his hair, ordered a grande coffee to go, and glanced at his watch. Almost nine. He needed to get to Jimmy's, catch him first thing. With the rain, he should go back to the church and take his car but he had to hurry. Hazel always arrived at nine-thirty, and he needed to get away before she could ask a zillion questions.

Before he started his walk back he lifted his face to the

rain, to the heavens sending the rain, closed his eyes and...prayed...for his own safety.

Angel opened the car door and pushed Sarah outside into the pouring rain.

Sarah only wore a thin coat and the rain soaked her skin, causing goose bumps on her arms. She rubbed her freezing cold hands together as there were no pockets in her jacket. She knew her clothes smelled stinky, were spotted with food and that she hadn't combed her hair or brushed her teeth in weeks. The rain dripped off her nose and she stuck out her tongue, licking her chapped lips.

"Are you coming to get me when school's over?" Sarah shivered.

The woman laughed. "Fat fuckin' chance. You're lucky I *borrowed* this car to drive you. You're not worth a fuckin' penny to me, kid. So just consider yourself lucky you're alive. I couldn't kill you 'cause you made me think of my girl, the one they took from me. But so help me God, you tell anyone I let you go I'll find you and kill you myself. Remember our deal, I drive you to school, you keep your little trap shut."

"Where do I go after school?" Sarah's teeth felt as if they were rattling in her mouth.

"Ask your teacher. Or go home with a friend."

Sarah nodded, she had no friends except Angie, but she liked Miss Clark.

"Shut the damn door."

Angel drove away from the curb before the car door was even shut, splattering rain all over Sarah. The old rusty car chugged down the street and out of sight. Sarah turned and looked at the school, the kids on the pavement, most holding umbrellas, some huddled by the doors. The bell rang and she watched all the kids running. She saw her teacher, Miss Clark, open the door. Maybe she could ask Miss Clark to phone

Angie to come and get her. Angie had come to the school before, and picked Sarah up, and Sarah knew Angie's phone number off by heart.

Sarah walked to the schoolyard, wondering where her mom had gone. Jimmy had said she'd run away 'cause she hated Sarah so much, 'cause Sarah ate too much peanut butter.

Sarah's stomach growled.

Chris swung his car door open and sprinted toward the side door of Princess Street United, dodging the puddles that were spotted across the pavement like dots on a Dalmatian dog. Stomping the excess water off his high tops and swinging his head side to side, spraying water in all directions, he entered the office.

"Hi, Hazel. You're looking good so early in the morning. But then you always look like a million bucks to me."

"Oh, go on with you." She looked up from her computer screen. "You're always buttering me up when you should be saving your sweet words for the young ones. Someone just rang you here. Her name was Mary Perkins and she said it had something to do with teaching writing to the youth group this week. Now, I know I said young, and this one here, I think, may be a trifle too old for you. Here's the note with her phone number."

Chris took the pink message paper from Hazel. "Thanks. Old or not, this one's kind of cute. By the way, you don't look a day over twenty-nine."

She stood up and put her hands on her hips. "Flattery will get you nowhere."

"Not even a cup of coffee? I showed up for work this morning but got sent home because of the rain. I thought I'd drop in on Intuko. Is he in his office?

"You can have a cup of coffee but not with Intuko. I think he might have been in earlier but he's sure not here now."

"Where is he?"

"I don't know. He's been so distracted lately that I don't know what's going on with him." Hazel plopped back down in her especially-designed-chair-for-bad-backs and stared at her computer screen.

Intuko shut off his car, eliminating the noise of the windshield wipers. After ten minutes or so he opened the door, stepped into the downpour, and walked slowly toward the apartment building. He licked his lips, ran his hand through his sopping hair, and tried to breath through his constricted airways. His body almost moved as if it was out of his control, his feet stepping forward without being told.

He had to do this.

The red brick apartment building was closer to Gastown than Hastings and Main, in a nicer section of town. Intuko stepped with caution up the five steps that led to the arched front entranceway. Jimmy was making money from his girls and money from something else to be living in this apartment. Looking at the twelve names on the list, Intuko wondered how to get through the locked door. Should he buzz?

A dark-haired woman, dressed in high black boots, and extremely provocative clothing, pushed open the front door. He smiled at her, (wondering who requested escort girls at nine in the morning), and although she didn't smile back, she did let him into the apartment.

Intuko stood in the hallway, gathering courage. Then he went to Jimmy's door and knocked.

No one answered.

He knocked again, louder this time.

He heard a flushing toilet. He took a deep breath and knocked for the third time. Heavy footsteps thumped down the hall and towards the door.

"Who's there?" The voice sounded rough, gravely.

Intuko hesitated. He cleared his throat. "Is the woman of the house in?"

"The woman?" The voice snarled then laughed rudely and Intuko knew whoever was behind the door had seen his collar through the peephole.

"..." Intuko searched for words.

"There's no woman here." The door opened slowly.

Jimmy's long hair was held back in a ponytail and he wore a white sleeveless undershirt that showed the tattoos of intertwining serpents carved in his upper arms. Intuko thought he recognized him as one of the men with Charlie that night at Hank's. But he couldn't be sure. Unlike Chris, whose muscles bulged, this man was wiry, more like an untrained Doberman Pincher. His face had the same long lean pointed edge and his sinewy muscles tightened when he flexed. But it was the beady, wary eyes that caught Intuko off guard. He'd not want to meet him in a dark deserted alley.

Jimmy poked at Intuko's religious collar. "What the hell does a man like you *want the woman for*? You guys are just like the next guy, always wanting a bit of tail."

"Is Sarah here?" There was a flame raging inside Intuko. This man preyed on women and stood in front of him to laugh about it.

"Sarah?" Jimmy laughed. "What the hell does a man like you want with *Sarah?* You want to diddle her, do you father? You like the little ones?" He leaned on the doorframe and crossed his arms.

"Is she here?" Intuko, close to boiling, balled his hands into fists.

"You really want her father? How much ya willing to pay? I'll get you someone who looks just like her. I'll have to charge you for the cherry though. Big bucks."

Any fear Intuko had about approaching this situation subsided, any compassion and caring he had for the human race dissolved. He was overcome by an out-of-control raging fire, flaming. He didn't care about the consequences, his spiritual beliefs, right or wrong, or about this despicable man who felt he could treat a child like dirty rotten garbage.

Intuko barrelled into the room, pushing into Jimmy, driving him back with the full force of his weight. Jimmy stumbled, thrown off balance in surprise. Intuko wasted no time. He grabbed the other man by the throat and heaved him against the wall.

Another hole in another wall, so be it. Holes showed the callousness of life, the openings to fall into, the abyss of black nothing. Intuko knew he was falling into a hole of darkness, going to a place he'd never let himself go and he knew at this moment in time there was no ladder to reach for.

Falling.

He had witnessed enough bar room brawls to know how to fight dirty. He kneed the guy in the groin, doubling him over, making him gasp for breath.

"You dirty little bastard," the man spat through clenched teeth.

"Where's Sarah?" With all the strength he had and then some, Intuko grabbed him by the oily hair, thankful for the length, and drilled him in the face. Blood spurted.

"Fuck you." Jimmy lunged at Intuko.

Intuko darted out of the way, grabbed and punched him again. "Where is she?" Intuko pinned him against the wall.

"I ain't telling you nothin', man."

Intuko felt a crunching blow to his own nose. But nothing, not even his own blood running into his mouth could stop him. He went back with a vengeance, spitting fire lashed out from his pores. He shoved Jimmy down and kicked him.

"Did you kill Lola?" He kicked Jimmy again.

Jimmy peered through his hands with a shocked look on his face. "Lola? I didn't have nothin' to do with that. *Why would I want my best girl dead?"*

Jimmy tried to get up but Intuko pushed him down again. Intuko was about to keep kicking, while Jimmy was down, huddled on the filthy floor with his hands over his head but...something jolted him to his senses.

What did the creep say?

"If you didn't kill her, who did?" Intuko had Jimmy pinned.

"How the hell should I know?"

"Where's Sarah?" Intuko shouted.

"The stupid ho said she killed the brat but I bet she dumped her. I'll kill the bitch if she let her go. That is if they don't kill me first." Jimmy could hardly spit out his words.

"What do you mean dumped?"

"On the streets asshole."

"Where? Tell me!"

"In a back alley for all I know."

Intuko drilled Jimmy one more time then ran for the door. Near the door, he bumped into a table, sending it toppling to the floor, knocking over beer cans, ashtrays, and a soft and downy dream catcher with feathers that were blue and pink. The dream catcher shone like a piece of gold amid the dirty debris and...the gun that lay on the floor.

Intuko quickly turned, and when he saw Jimmy still moaning, his head in his hands, he picked up the dream catcher and gun. Like a wild and crazy animal that had been locked up for too long, he shoved open the door. And he didn't stop running until he was in his car. Tires squealing, he drove away from the curb, breathing in rasps, his body still shaking. Once he was a few blocks away, he pulled over.

He leaned his head forward, letting it drop into his hands as if it were a huge bag of cement. He dug his fingers into his scalp, pressing, prying, trying to get at something, trying to understand why he had acted so viciously. He grabbed his minister's collar and yanked it off, throwing it on the seat beside him.

He was no better than Harrison Fleming.

He couldn't wear his collar after what he had done. How often had he spoke about the need to control anger in this society, how violence and war were ineffective ways of solving situations? He abhorred violence, but yet he had succumbed.

He sat shaking as if he had been caught outside with no clothes on in a terrible snowstorm, white swirling around him, blinding his vision. He felt like a child again. Not understanding why he had to go to a school so far away, why he had to be taken from the only security he knew, why the men in black robes beat him so badly, why his mother left with a white man, why his people were so sad and didn't want to dance any more. Could Sarah possibly be on the streets? By herself?

The sobs started. And he cried like he'd never cried before in his life. Men didn't cry, at least, that's what he'd been told, been thrashed about at school. But nothing could stop him from releasing a dam, tearing down the wall that kept the water harboured safe on the other side. No more. No more.

Finally, he leaned his head back and wiped his face with the cuff of his sleeve. Blood mixed with tears. Where was he to go now? To the streets, with his face a bloody mess, to hunt for a child? To the church to pretend he was a good man, a man of God? He should have delved into his problems, his own anger a long time ago, then maybe he wouldn't have had to beat a man.

He glanced at his collar lying on the seat beside him. It sat amid a downy-soft, hand-made dream catcher and a hard, callous-looking, black gun.

FOURTEEN

Susan sat in her car, watching the parents park their mini-vans by the street curbs to drop off their children at school. Such a normal daily routine for many.

The women at the Centre were unable to live this kind of existence–wave good-bye to their own flesh and blood before a day of school. Some of them were unaware that this kind of life even existed. Susan watched the many parents on the playground, knowing that they, on the flip side, also had no idea of life in the prison.

With Hilary already amidst a group of girls all huddled in a circle giggling, Susan turned her gaze to watch a woman, struggling with a screaming toddler who obviously didn't want to be strapped in a car seat. There were so many similarities between that child and the women in the prison. They also struggled, had temper tantrums, hit their friends because they couldn't have what they wanted.

The school bell rang and Hilary turned and waved to her in exaggerated gestures. Susan smiled, waved back, and honked the horn.

When Susan arrived home, she ran into Mary who was carrying her garbage out.

"Hey, woman, how about a cup of tea and some girl talk?" Mary said from underneath her orange umbrella.

"Sure. I'm off today."

"Any more on that minister friend of yours?" Mary asked, sitting in Susan's kitchen with her knees pulled up to her chest, sipping tea and eating chocolate cookies.

"How can you eat chocolate so early in the morning?"

"There's only one thing better than chocolate and they're both pretty good in the morning."

Susan shook her head at Mary and her constant talk of men.

"So, answer my question. How's the minister?"

"I think I'll call him this morning, see how things went with Angela Melville last evening. She may know some of Lola's friends. One of them might have the girl."

"He's bloody determined to find this child isn't he?" Mary dipped her cookie in her tea.

"He's a good guy," she said thoughtfully. "He cares for people. Genuinely cares."

Mary squinted over the rim of her mug. "Do you...kind of...like this guy?"

"What's not to like?" Susan spun the sugar bowl around in circles.

"That's not what I meant."

"It's too quick after Eric. I got Hilary to think about."

"There's no set time frame for when you can date again, you know."

"I know," she said. "How about you? Are you going after that *youth guy?*"

Mary stood and stretched like a cat arching its back. "As a matter of fact, I'm meeting him for coffee later this afternoon to talk about me teaching writing to his group."

Susan rolled her eyes and picked up the empty mugs to put in the sink.

When Intuko entered the church, Hazel took one look at him and put her hand to her mouth. "Oh, my good Lord in heaven, what happened to you?"

Intuko shook his head. "I don't know. I really don't

know." The only reason he'd returned to the church was to clean up. If he approached a little lost girl, looking like he did, he could scare her. The fact remained; he hadn't seen Sarah for years. Would he even recognize her? *Was she even alive?*

"What do you mean, you don't know? No one gets bloody like that without knowing. Come here, sit down, and lean your head back. We need to wash you up."

"I can do it myself, Hazel."

Intuko had the gun, which he'd wrapped in a towel he'd found on the floor of his car, hidden in the inside pocket of his jacket.

"I'll get some antiseptic for you," she said, "and a clean cloth."

Intuko knew her well enough to know she'd busy herself until she had everything she needed but after that, she'd be on his heels. He pushed the door of his office opened, quickly shut it and moved to his desk. Yanking open the bottom drawer, he laid the gun under a bunch of papers and shut the drawer. Then he walked back out to the main office.

Hazel was at her desk still, standing in front of a big white metal box that held medical supplies. Her reading glasses slid to the end of her nose as she read the side of a bottle of some sort of antiseptic cleaner.

"This will do just fine," she said, handing it to him.

"I have a favour to ask you," said Intuko, staring at her, not moving forward to take the antiseptic.

"What is it?" She looked over the rim of her glasses.

"Could you call an emergency board meeting for tomorrow night?"

"Tomorrow…that's soon to call everyone."

"I know, but it has to be done. It's urgent."

"What time?"

"Seven-thirty. I teach art at the prison first."

"I'll ring everyone as soon as we get you fixed up. Is this

emergency meeting anything I can help you with?"

"Not this time, Hazel."

She bustled over to the tea kettle and plugged it in. "Use this to help your face. Oh…and I have a few messages for you. I'll give them to you after you come back from the men's room."

"If it's about the leaky roof, I already know."

"You're not calling a board meeting because of the leaky roof are you? Chris was in earlier, he knows someone who can help fix the roof for a good price. He said he'd organize it."

Hazel dumped two tea bags into a blue and white ceramic teapot. "That wasn't the message I wanted to tell you." She smiled, like a child with a secret. "Your brother from the North rang you. He said something about a big celebration happening, some sort of big Arctic dance for winter solstice that your niece is involved in. He wants you to come home. I think your sister is going to be there as well so it could be a reunion of sorts. You need to see family, Intuko. Now go to the men's room, blood is dripping everywhere. Get cleaned up. Go."

Intuko took the antiseptic and clean cloth Hazel had given to him and wandered down to the men's room. When he opened the rest room door, a waft of alcohol mixed with stale urine and sopping clothes greeted him. Harry was back for a little breather. With Hazel and Stu running around trying to fix the leaky roof, it would have been easy for Harry to enter the church and stagger his way to the shelter of the men's room. Intuko looked at the lost soul propped up against the wall like a puppet without strings.

"Was the rain just too much for you, old guy?" Intuko sat beside Harry, on the cold, hard tile of the bathroom floor. "I don't even think you're really that old."

Harry's chin dropped to his chest, oblivious to any of this idle chit-chat.

139

Intuko continued talking anyway. "Would it help if I told you I sort of understand why you drink like you do? There must be something deep you just can't face. My mother, she was the same. My people, their lives were taken from them, just like that." Intuko snapped his fingers, the sound reverberating off the walls.

"And, you know, Harry, I've been like you, hiding my pain for years. I just dealt with it a different way, by becoming a minister. But I don't want to be like you. I'm going to stop hiding, return to who I am. You can't really hide from your truth."

". Is that you, Intuko?"

"Yeah, it's me."

Harry grunted and opened his eyes, his lids lifting like they were dusty blinds being pulled on a worn out string. "Whad'ya say Intuko?"

"A whole lot if you wanted to listen."

"Be a good man. Call them guys for me." Harry stopped to hiccup. "I need me a good bed tonight, some place where there's no stinking rain."

Intuko shook his head and sighed. "I'll do it for you Harry, but this may be your last time."

Harry smiled–his teeth rotten to the roots. "You're a good man, Intuko, a good man. Don't ever forget that, you hear." He closed his eyes, slumped his head forward, and snored.

"You look a little better," said Hazel when Intuko returned from the men's room.

"Harry's here again. Call the police for me and let me know when they get here. I have some other calls I need to make."

"But Intuko you haven't–"

"I can't talk right now Hazel." Intuko went into his office and shut the door. *Where should he start looking for Sarah?*

Feeling sick, he leaned against his desk. What was he doing with his life? After one altercation, he'd suddenly decided to quit the ministry, a job he'd been at for years. He looked at the pile of work on his desk and suddenly he realized his decision to leave had been coming for a long time and that his fight with Jimmy was just the catalyst. He thought of the two rivers he'd seen last night during his prayer-time. His fox standing between them. Had he gone on a shaman journey to discover what he was to do with his life?

He picked up his fox carving, closed his eyes, shuffling it in his hands. Taking a deep breath, he exhaled, blowing the air loudly through his lips. He set the carving down. Then he opened the bottom drawer to see the towel that was hiding the gun.

The gun was unlike the hunting rifles he used up North–that was for sure. This thing looked like the handguns in the movies. Had it been used to murder Lola? *Or Sarah?* His stomach knotted. He had to get it to the police station. But not now. Not when he had to try and find Sarah. A kid like Sarah, with nowhere to turn would go–where?

Suddenly, he saw his fox run through the playground at Roberts School. It jumped and leaped and ran to Miss Clarke. She patted its head and smiled.

School! Where else! He had to try the school one more time. This time he'd go directly to her teacher. He wondered how to approach this teacher, what to say, how to make her believe he wasn't someone trying to steal Sarah. He wondered if she was in school all day or…His phone rang. He crooked it in his ear while he put his coat on.

"Hi, it's Susan. I just called to see how your visit went with Angela."

"Susan!" Intuko sighed in relief. God was still working for him, sending him signs.

* * *

141

Intuko met Susan by the metal fences surrounding the school grounds. The pouring rain of two hours ago had subsided. "Thanks again," he said, jingling the coins in his pocket.

Susan stared at his face. "No problem." She tilted her head. "What happened to you?"

"It's too long a story to tell right now. Later."

"Okay," she said, nodding her head but not taking her eyes off his swollen nose and eyes that were starting to rim with navy and crimson bruises.

"I'm not even sure she's here but...Any idea how we should do this?" Intuko turned from her to stare at the school.

"Schools have policies to protect the children. They don't let a child go home with just anybody."

Intuko tried hard to think of a way to be able to take Sarah with him today if she was indeed at school. Then he remembered something. "When we were here yesterday," Intuko said quickly. "The receptionist said the emergency contact was Angie Melville."

"So?"

"I'll say I'm a friend of Angie's and she asked me to come for Sarah. And that you're a prison officer and can verify this."

"Leave the ending out. I want to keep my job. Look it's almost time for the Kindergarten class to finish. Let's catch her teacher."

Sarah's teacher was a young woman with shoulder length, honey-blond hair. She was dressed in casual beige pants, low flat shoes, and a green turtleneck sweater. She stood outside the door of the classroom monitoring the children while they collected their coats and backpacks. Kindergarten ended at eleven-fifteen. Intuko and Susan approached her cautiously and simply asked if Sarah was at school today.

"She sure was. It was good to see her." She smiled. "Are you friends of hers?"

"She sometimes comes to my church," replied Intuko. Another white lie.

"There she is now." Miss Clark put her arm around Sarah. "Sarah and I tried to phone Angie Melville today but couldn't reach her," said Miss Clark, smiling affectionately down at Sarah.

Intuko couldn't believe how much Sarah had grown. The last time he had seen her, she had still been a toddler in diapers. He smiled at her, but she only frowned, scrutinizing his face. Intuko touched the bridge of his nose.

"Sarah, why don't you go in the classroom for a few minutes," said Miss Clark. "Finish colouring your fall picture."

Sarah nodded.

After Sarah had left, Miss Clark turned to Intuko and asked, "How did you hurt your face?"

"I fell off my bike. The rain. The roads. You know, so slippery." These lies were becoming a habit.

"That was sure some downpour. I'm glad it stopped for a bit." Miss Clark looked from Intuko to Susan then back to Intuko. "I have to tell you both, I'm worried about Sarah. She kept asking me to call this Angie Melville because she said her mother was gone and she had nowhere to go today after school. But I couldn't reach her. Sarah often walks home by herself even though it's against school policy but today she told me she couldn't go back to her place." Miss Clark sighed heavily as she sadly shook her head. "There's a few at this school with similar home life situations."

"What did Sarah say about her mother?" Susan asked in a non-threatening voice.

"I don't think she's seen her in a few days and her mother never let her know she was leaving to go somewhere," Miss Clark said disgustedly.

"Miss Clark," Intuko said softly, "Sarah's mother was murdered the other day."

Miss Clark put her hand to her mouth. "Oh, my God. I didn't know that. No one's informed the school. Are you a relative?"

Intuko shook his head. He felt for his collar around his neck, realizing it wasn't there. It still sat on the seat of his car. "I'm a minister at Princess Street United Church," he said, showing his identification. "And I'm a friend of Angela Melville's. She can't be here right now to take care of Sarah so she asked me to come and get her from school."

Miss Clark looked at Intuko's card, tucked her hair behind her ear, and said, "I'll be right back."

Miss Clarke returned in a few minutes and said, "I'll get Sarah for you."

"Where am I going?" asked Sarah quietly, once she was buckled in the back seat, her brown eyes dull like two dirty pennies.

Intuko glanced at Susan who kept the door open and squatted down. She smiled at Sarah. "How about I take you to my house for a little while. I have a little girl so we have lots of fun toys and I bet we can find some clothes that she's grown out of."

Sarah nodded. "Will I get to see Angie today?"

"We'll see."

Susan shut the back door of the car.

"You don't have to do this. She's my responsibility," said Intuko.

"She needs a bath. And she needs her hair combed. I already have everything at my place. If she goes to your place you'll have to stop and pick everything up at a store and right now she needs to settle. I have the day off. I don't mind, really. Why don't you follow me to my place and I'll make us some lunch. I have a feeling Sarah is hungry."

* * *

144

Minestrone soup, tuna sandwiches with lettuce, and caramel pudding. Angie's stomach rolled and her head pulsed at the temples. She'd been making the tuna sandwiches all morning in the kitchen; the smell of the fish was enough to make her want to run to the bathroom to heave. Yesterday, she had to work around bacon frying. She put a bowl of soup on her tray, a handful of crackers and bowl of pudding.

The tables in the cafeteria sat lengthwise and they all had attached chairs. Looking around, Angie noticed one table that was half empty.

Tray on the table, she sat down and stared down at her food. Every damn thing she did was controlled: eat, work, sleep, eat, work, sleep, every second, every minute, all day and night cooped up without contact to the outside world. She hadn't worked long enough to have enough money to buy a phone card. And she wanted to phone Intuko, find out if he had Sarah yet.

She had slurped down a few spoonfuls of soup when a woman, a hooker Angie vaguely recognized, came to her table.

"Anyone sitting here?"

"Nope."

The woman sat down. "I'm Sherry," she said.

"Angie."

"I seen you at Hank's."

Angie bit into a cracker, chewing it before saying, "Yeah. So."

"What you in for?"

"Shit."

"I heard you was into scamming from the banks. Good on ya'."

"You in for hooking?" Angie asked, stirring her soup around, trying to avoid the peas that she knew were from the can.

"The pigs did a big fuckin' sweep a few Saturdays ago.

Booked a bunch of us. Just before the crack came in. Bastards. I'll be out soon. I heard there's more gonna hit the streets. Another big shipment. I can't believe what happened to Lola." The woman bit into her tuna sandwich. "I hate fuckin' tuna."

Angie lifted her spoon full of just broth to her mouth, knowing the small world of the prison. She slurped another mouthful of soup then wiped her mouth. "Did you see her that night?"

"We work different streets. I don't think she was even on her street." Sherry threw her tuna sandwich on the plate. "I hate the crap they serve in here."

"You think that's bad, I have to make it." Angie saw the clock on the wall and knew there was only eight minutes left then it was lock-down time.

"Hey, kitchen is a good job. Try cleaning up real shit. I had to do that once for lippin' off." Sherry stood and picked up her tray. "I need a cig before lock-down."

Angie shoved her hand in her pocket, retrieving two rolled cigarettes Iris had given her. "I'll swap you minutes on a phone card for a cig."

Sherry pulled out her phone card. "I just got this card this morning. Gimme two cigs and I'll give you two minutes."

"Deal." She gave her the cigarettes and Sherry handed her a phone card.

"You know who might have killed Lola?" Angie asked casually as they walked out of the cafeteria, not wanting to arouse too much attention.

"It was probably some perv. Man, I've met a few psychos myself. Once I kicked a car door so hard I ripped the heel off my shoe. Ran away barefooted." Sherry put her tray on the pile of trays. "Lola hit up with some weirdo I bet."

Yeah, but who, wondered Angie. She crossed her fingers for Intuko's safety.

FIFTEEN

Sitting in a tub full of bubbles, Sarah looked like a different child. At first she'd been tentative when she saw the white froth bubbling under the tap and she'd clung to the wall for a few minutes before gingerly putting one foot in the water.

And to watch her now, her body so still and stiff, almost made Susan cry. Most children had the pleasure of playing in a simple bubble bath a couple of times a week.

"Would you like me to wash your hair?" Susan asked.

No answer.

"Sarah, would you like me to wash your hair?" Susan asked again.

"Mommy washed it a long time ago."

From the mess of tangles, Susan guessed that the washing had probably been weeks if not a month ago. Susan ran her fingers under the tap to feel the temperature of the water. "Has your mommy been gone a long time?"

She shrugged. Then she looked up at Susan with hollow, dull eyes. "I wonder if she misses me."

"I'm sure she does."

"Would she have left 'cause I ate too much peanut butter?"

"You don't really believe that, do you?

"I think she needed drugs."

The tone of Sarah's voice sounded so nonplussed that Susan pushed the knob on the faucet down, sending a stream of water spurting through the hand shower.

"Tilt your head back and I'll wet your hair."

Sarah closed her eyes and did what Susan asked, letting

the water stream down her back.

"Okay, how about we put some shampoo in your hair. Would you like cherry-almond or tropical-fruit shampoo?"

"Cherry-almond?"

"Yeah, here, I'll let you smell both of them then you can decide. My daughter cherry-almond."

Sarah sniffed one bottle then the next then repeated the process. "I'll have...I'll have the...cherry-almond."

Susan squirted pink shampoo into the palm of her hand and carefully rubbed it into her scalp, making sure to scrub everywhere. Before the bath, she had checked for lice and, fortunately, there were none. Massaging Sarah's scalp, she wondered what they were going to do with this child.

Although she knew there were a lot of good foster parents out there, she also knew there were a lot of bad ones too. Holding on to her today, for a few hours, maybe even for the evening was fine, but they would have to report her to child services sooner or later. There could be a relative–an aunt or a grandmother–who wanted her.

"We're just about done. Close your eyes again and I'll rinse your hair." Susan sprayed water over the top of Sarah's head, glancing at the child's tiny frame.

Bones and ribs protruded from all different angles, sticking out like sharp stones. Her once pale flesh, thin as onion paper, was now pink and translucent like a newborn baby's skin, glistening brightly from the warm bath water and showing traces of yellow bruises.

Little fingers rubbed her face, protecting it from the water that attempted to drip in her eyes. Spindly, little legs that looked like twigs stretched straight, hardly taking up half of the tub. And...immature private parts. Innocent. She had years before they would fully develop. Susan just hoped, prayed, they hadn't been tampered with already.

"There, all done." Susan grabbed a thick fluffy yellow

towel from the rack. "I bet you feel a lot better. Let's wrap this around you, like you're a queen, and this is your fine gown. Now, my lady, shall we find you some clothes?"

Sarah actually lifted the corners of her mouth, attempting a little smile, as she walked with Susan to Hilary's room. Her smile didn't last long, however, before her face turned dull and lifeless again.

Intuko stirred the tomato soup, trying to get rid of some of the lumps. He had poured the entire can of milk in at one time and great big globs of red things had immediately clumped together. He mashed the spoon against the side of the pan hoping to squash a lump. Thankfully, Susan had come with him to find Sarah–he didn't stock his shelves with soup or peanut butter or bubble bath, and he certainly didn't have clothes for a little girl in his apartment.

Intuko stopped his vigorous stirring to turn down the burner coils that were as red as the soup. He could hear the bath water emptying through the pipes and voices talking, very softly. And bathing her would have been inappropriate.

"Here she is, all clean and sparkling."

He turned to see a much different version of Sarah, her face shone like pristine purity. Squatting down in front of her, he smiled and scrunched up his nose. "You look so pretty and clean in those sweat pants."

"They're a little big but I like this kitten." She pointed to the kitten on the front of the sweatshirt. "I had a kitten once. She was black and white, too."

"A kitty! I bet that kitten sure was lucky to have you take care of it."

"It got killed." Sarah chewed at her fingernails and looked away. "One of my mommy's friends kicked it. Could I have something to eat now?"

"Of course." Intuko stood, shaking his head.

He didn't grow up with pets. In the North, dogs were kept outdoors and shot if they were found off leash, but after living in the South for so long, he understood the value of family pets. An animal may have been the only living thing that offered this child some sort of love. Her own mother didn't care enough to watch out for her.

Her own mother. The words rang in his mind like church bells gone crazy. His mother hadn't been much better.

He went to get the lumpy soup from the stove and the plate of sandwiches that he had stacked lop-sided on the plate.

"Lunch looks good," said Susan. "I'll get the bowls and spoons. It's great to see someone else cooking in this kitchen besides me. Sarah, why don't you sit here?" Susan pulled out a Disneyland place mat and set it on the table.

Sarah devoured a cheese sandwich like an animal finding food after a dry summer in the woods. Susan placed another sandwich on Sarah's plate and she immediately picked it up and took a huge bite without even a glance upwards.

Intuko turned his head, remembering his days of hunger, his first days on his own, when he was fifteen. This child was *five or six*. Despite all his mother's inadequacies, at that age he'd had extended family and his community always rallied together to feed the children. The men hunted for caribou, harpooned whale and fished for salmon and everyone ate as much as they needed.

Watching this child eat with such vigour, cheese staining her chin, as if she thought there would be no food tomorrow, made him clench his hands under the table, unable to eat in case she wanted the entire plate.

"We can make more sandwiches," said Susan, even though she had yet to take one herself. "I've got lots of bread. Eat up. Sarah would you like some crackers for your soup?"

Sarah nodded.

Susan arose and went to the cupboard to get some crackers

and Intuko finally took a sandwich, realizing when he bit into it that he was starving, and that his jaw ached from his morning with Jimmy.

When Susan returned to the table she said, "Sarah tells me Angie used to buy her clothes."

Intuko looked up at the mention of Angie's name.

Sarah stared at him. "What happened to your face?"

"I fell."

"Oh. It looks like someone punched you."

Sarah wiped her mouth with the back of her hand. Unobtrusively, Susan pushed a napkin closer.

"Angie showed me how to use one of these, one day when she took me to lunch at a real nice restaurant." Sarah used the paper napkin. "They were thicker, not made of paper and they were pink. She was my best friend. She bought me a birthday present." Sarah stopped talking, her face clouding over like a pending rainstorm. "Oh, no," she said. "I forgot to bring my dream catcher. Angie told me it would take away my nightmares, and, and it had soft feathers. I wanted to show it to my teacher."

"I have it, Sarah," said Intuko. "At my office. After lunch I'll go get it for you."

"Where'd you get it from?" she asked, puzzled.

"From Jimmy," said Intuko.

"Was my mom with him?"

"No, honey, she wasn't." Susan intervened and Intuko was extremely glad. How were they to tell this child about her mother?

"You can take it to school tomorrow," said Intuko. "How's that?"

Sarah nodded. "Am I sleeping here tonight?"

Intuko patted Sarah's hand. "Why don't you run to the bathroom to wash your face?"

She slipped off her chair, walking slowly down the hall.

As soon as he heard the bathroom door shut, Intuko turned to Susan. "I'm so sorry I got you involved in this. She doesn't have to stay here tonight."

Susan touched his arm. "I'm a mom. I've read a lot of child psychology books. Because we brought her here first, I think she *should* stay here tonight. She needs a little stability, even if it's only for twenty-four hours. She's got a tough road ahead of her."

"Should I take her to see Angie tonight?"

"I wouldn't. Not until you talk to Angie. You definitely need to talk to her today, tell her Sarah's okay, but," Susan shook her head, "she may not want Sarah to see her in prison."

"I don't know what I'd do right now without you. I'd be doing everything wrong."

"No, not everything. You care. And that means more than anything."

He stepped towards her to embrace her in a friendly hug and he ended up holding her tightly, in a hug that made him feel twice his size. She laid her head on his chest and he automatically rubbed her back, the pliability of it astonishing him, the way she so easily moulded into him, her full breasts pressing against his chest. The stimulation of her curved body made him swell. It had been so long since he'd allowed himself the pleasure of having a woman in his arms.

She tilted her head and…he kissed her. He kept his eyes open, but she… closed hers.

The flushing of the toilet broke them apart. Intuko ran his hands through his hair and Susan brushed the front of her jeans, even though she had no crumbs on them.

The awkward silence made Intuko glance at the red kitchen clock. One-thirty already. Suddenly he remembered he was supposed to meet Chris at two at Divine Intervention Church. And he had to call Angie or go visit her tonight. And sometime today, he had to visit the police station. Susan picked up the dirty dishes off the table, taking them to the sink.

"I, uh, should go to the church," he said.

Susan stood in front of the sink–her back to Intuko–opened the dishwasher and turned on the taps.

"Can I help with the dishes?"

"No," said Susan still facing the sink. "I can do these. It'll only take me a minute. Sarah should stay with me, though. I'll pull out some toys for her to play with or put on a video. Hilary will be home from school in a couple of hours, they can play together."

Sarah padded into the kitchen in her sock feet. Intuko crouched down to be eye level with her. "Sarah, I'm going out for a bit. But I'll come back later, okay."

"Are you going to get my dream catcher?"

"I sure am." He tweaked her nose. "And maybe I'll bring you back something else. Do you like chocolate chip cookies?"

She nodded.

Intuko tenderly took Sarah in his arms. Holding her, he felt her little ribs protruding through her skin and he boiled inside at the people who were responsible for this child.

"I'll call," he said to Susan who was staring at Sarah but wouldn't look at him.

"We'll be fine, just fine," said Susan. "Don't worry about us, right Sarah. We've got some books to read and some games to play."

Susan placed her hands on the counter and looked out the kitchen window, relieved to look into her back yard and not her front. She didn't want to see Intuko driving away. Rain pelted her tiny garden and ricocheted off her rickety back porch.

This man was making her crazy. She had been swept into his embrace, kissing him readily, as if she were starving for love. She hardly knew the guy. The morning had been so emotional that they'd fallen into each others arms without even thinking. The scary part though–she had liked the feel of a man again, strong arms around her.

A little hand tugged on her shirt.

"Are you watching the rain fall?"

Susan turned to see Sarah staring up at her with big brown eyes that looked like two little muddy ponds frozen in time.

"Here, let me lift you up and you can sit on the counter and watch the rain with me."

Sarah nodded. "I don't like rain; it makes me cold when I walk home from school."

"I'm like you, I like the sun." Susan pulled out the flour and a bag of chocolate chips. "Let's make some cookies."

"Angel made me stay inside when it was sunny."

"Who's Angel?"

Sarah clasped her mouth. "Nobody. She's nobody. I wish I could see Angie. She likes me."

"I like you too," said Susan.

Sarah pointed to a little sparrow flying in the rain. "Look at that bird; he's out in the rain."

Intuko wished he had a hat or umbrella or even a newspaper to stick over his head. The rain that had so pleasantly lightened a few hours ago now pelted down in full force, just like his life. Up one minute, down the next. He ran to his car

He had to phone the church soon, but he wasn't sure if Hazel would give him the silent treatment or barrage him with questions, much like a police interrogation. Then there was everything else he had to do. Meet Chris at Divine Intervention Church to find out…what? Visit Detective Anderson with the gun he'd found at Jimmy's and deal with a lecture. Prepare for his board meeting. Get Sarah's dream catcher. Call Angie, go see her again with the news and…why had he kissed Susan?

Intuko leaned his head back, closed his eyes, and listened to his car idle and the rain pound against the metal roof. Drums. Like at home. Singing, dancing. The North.

Since Lola's murder, his whole life had been turned upside down. A few days ago he had been a celibate minister, and now he couldn't stop thinking of being with a woman. Scented hair, soft curves. He had restrained himself for so many years. But he had kissed Susan when he wasn't sure if he felt anything for her. What an idiot!

Every aspect of his life swirled in his mind like one big mosaic, pieces put together randomly to create some sort of picture, only his didn't seem to fit anymore. It was as if pieces were missing or overlapping the edges, making an incomplete picture. The fight occupied his mind and seemed jumbled together with kissing Susan, his childhood in the North and Angie. His perfect mosaic had fallen, cracked, and little pieces of his life had been scattered all over the floor.

A violent fight.

Intuko gazed in the mirror and stared at an unfamiliar face with swollen eyes and a bruised nose. In one day his entire look had changed. As had his life.

Would the pieces all fit when he tried to piece them together again?

He flicked on his windshield wipers and listened to them scrape the rain away. Rain didn't fall a lot in his homeland. The Arctic had a desert climate, flat land spreading for miles. At this time of year, each day was shorter, until December came and winter solstice. Twilight took the place of day and the sun appeared as only a small arc, bending slightly just above the horizon.

His homeland was one of the fallen pieces.

Angie was going crazy working in the kitchen. She had

waited in line for the phone at lunch, but didn't get to use it before she got locked up. Now, she had to prepare for dinner and she couldn't use the phone until four when she was off work. She ripped the lettuce, leaf after leaf, unable to get her mind off Sarah, Intuko, Lola. Not knowing what was happening on the outside was enough to make her want to scream at the top of her lungs. Instead, she shredded the lettuce into little bits.

"Hey." She felt a hand on her arm. "Slow down. You got enough lettuce for three days worth of salad."

Angie, hands on the counter, leaned forward trying to catch her breath while staring at the large pile of little green pieces in front of her.

SIXTEEN

"You're crazy. You went to see Jimmy. Didn't you?" Chris shook his head at Intuko.

For the second time in days, Intuko stood on the street, his neck craned, staring at the massive, contemporary church. All glass, it was the only one of its kind in all of Canada and had been designed after a church in Southern California. Even with impressive architecture, Intuko still preferred the old and ornate features of Princess Street United.

"I hope you phoned Hazel," said Chris.

"Yeah, I talked to her."

"She's pissed."

"I know. I'll smooth it over later." Intuko brushed his hand through his hair and chewed on his lip for a minute before looking at Chris. "We found Sarah this morning."

"Holy Dinah. Where?"

"Her school. She was dumped there."

"That's sick. Child services case number two thousand and three."

"She's with Susan Peterson right now, a member of the church."

"What are you going to do with her?"

Intuko shrugged. "Any ideas? Lola didn't want her to go to child services even though I know that's what should happen."

"Find some of her relatives then. They always give kids to relatives if they're around."

"They have to want the child though."

"Yeah, and in Lola's case I'm not sure that will happen."

"The last time I saw her, she asked me to care for Sarah because I was Inuit and Sarah's father was also Inuit, Inuvialuit actually, from my area of the Arctic."

"If I were you, I'd look for her father or some of his relatives and if that doesn't pan out then–"

"Angie wants her, though. *I'd* like to keep her until she gets out–for Angie's sake."

Chris put his hand on Intuko's back. "Intuko, Angie could get a three year sentence which means she'd be locked up for over eighteen months. I know you'd do anything for anybody but…you're talking about a child here."

"Weren't you the one who told me I'd make a great old man?"

Shaking his head, Chris blew air out like a whale that had been below the surface for too long. "Come on, old man, we'd better go see Steven Campbell and find out about that black car. You found Sarah. You might as well keep going, Sherlock, to find out who killed Lola."

Fondly, Intuko patted Chris on the back. "I knew I hired you for a reason."

Inside, the church looked and smelt new like books whose spines had not been cracked. The ambiance was so different than Princess Street United: energy flowed, people bustled, phones rang, fax machines beeped.

"Hi, my name is Chris. Chris Temple." Chris smiled at a pretty young red-haired woman in a headset. "I'm here to see Steven Campbell."

"Do you have an appointment?"

He propped his elbow on the counter and leaned into the counter. "Not really."

Intuko glared at Chris and mouthed, "I thought you had an appointment."

Chris smiled, flashing his white teeth at the woman. "I've

tried a few times to reach him, but he's a busy man. I work with a youth group and I wanted to get some advice. Do you think you could call him down to the front office? I could wait here and talk to him in the hallway. Even a spare moment of his time would help our organization." Chris lowered his voice to an enticing whisper and said, "It's important for the kids."

"I can try," she said smiling, obviously captivated by a handsome man.

Within a few minutes Steven Campbell came through the side door.

"What's up, Julie?"

"Mr. Campbell." Time for Intuko to talk, work his charm. He stuck out his hand. "My name's Intuko. I'm from Princess Street United Church. This is my youth leader, Chris Temple. You run such an efficient business here and we wondered if you could spare a few seconds to talk to us."

Steven Campbell stared at Intuko's bruised face for a moment before turning to Julie. "Do these gentlemen have an appointment?"

"Well, no, not really, Mr. Campbell."

"I fell off my bike in the rain," said Intuko sheepishly.

"Julie thought you might be able to help us," said Chris. "She said you're easy going and helpful. We're from a struggling downtown church and could use some sound financial advice. We promise not to take too much of your time."

Steven Campbell hesitated, Julie looked perplexed, and Chris and Intuko smiled.

"All right. I'm sure I can spare a few minutes."

Steven's office was located at the end of a long hallway. He ushered Intuko and Chris into a spacious room where not one thing was out of order. Even his pen stood upright in a musical note holder. Intuko thought of his own desk at his office and cringed. This guy had one file sitting on his desk, with all the others resting in either the "in" or "out" basket. If Intuko had baskets the "in" would be overflowing and the "out" empty.

Perfectly framed pictures hung on the walls. Intuko was immediately drawn to them. From the family photo, which must have been taken at Queen Elizabeth Park, Intuko noticed that Steven Campbell had one child and that his wife looked an awful lot like Hope Fleming, except she was blond.

Then there was a photo of what looked to be a ground digging ceremony where Steven Campbell posed, holding a shovel, and Harrison held a mound of dirt in his palm. Both smiled like kids in a candy factory.

"When was this taken?" Intuko asked.

"It will be ten years in the spring."

"Such an endeavour to build a new church. What's the history behind Divine Intervention?"

Steven pointed to another photo, further down the wall. The photo showed a young Harrison Fleming and a young Steven Campbell in front of an old community hall building holding a sign that said *Seed of Life*. On the porch sat a young red-haired woman and a young boy, who looked to be around four. The boy had his arms around a golden retriever puppy.

"Harrison owned Seed of Life church years ago," said Campbell, staring at the photo as well. "I was there with him, just as a member. The church had a split. Harrison and his partner in the church who was also a board member didn't agree on a few things and the congregation divided. They had thirty acres of land which they divided equally between them. That's when I started to work for Harrison as I helped settle the finances between him and his partner."

Intuko nodded and moved down the wall, pointing to another picture of Harrison and Steven standing in shorts by a tent, clutching onto their Bibles. "You did some sort of tent ministry?"

"After that, Harrison decided to run evangelical tent gatherings. Of all the cities in Canada, Vancouver has the weather. He started with small gatherings and they just kept growing and growing until we were literally bursting at the seams."

"Is that when he started Divine Intervention?"

"Not right away. He landed the job with BCTV first. The television people picked up on his charisma. The show originally took place in the television studio. They taped all the shows in less than a month. They did sixty-five shows, sometimes five shows a day, giving Harrison time to preach on Sunday and carry on his business. The show became so popular that we put up more tents, held more services and within time made enough money to build Divine Intervention."

"What happened to his land? Did he sell out?"

"It's just an investment right now. Eventually, we want to build a private home, a rehab centre for those trying to get off drugs and alcohol." Steven glanced at his watch. "Have a seat. I've only got a few more minutes."

For five minutes Intuko asked questions about the financial situation of his church, what he could do to make things easier. Steven answered the questions like a bonafide accountant. Chris listened, nodding his head from time to time, taking notes.

"I hope I've been of some help." Steven stood.

Chris handed the notebook to Intuko.

"Absolutely. Thank you for your time." Intuko didn't stand.

"I have one last question," said Chris. "Do you have church cars?"

"We have vans. We use them for picking up Sunday school children and for youth trips, things like that."

"Vans? I thought I saw a...black Mercedes the other day with your church logo on it. I thought maybe you were sponsored by Mercedes." Chris grinned.

Steven laughed at Chris's joke. "Harrison owns a black Mercedes but it doesn't have the church logo on it. It's his personal car."

"I thought it was him," said Chris, "although I was surprised he was in that end of town. And even more surprised that he picked up a street girl. I guess you guys must do Street Ministry too."

"I think you must have seen someone else's car." Steven walked toward the door. "We're involved with helping the homeless but we operate from the church. Dinners, gym space, that sort of thing."

"Why would Harrison pick up a girl then?" Chris kept steady eye contact with Steven.

"I'm not sure what you're getting at." Steven furrowed his brows as if puzzled.

"A street girl got in Harrison's car the other night."

"Sometimes...family members like Hope and–and others drive the car. So do I, sometimes. But...you must be mistaken. Lots of people drive Mercedes' and he has been out of town. Anyway, I hope I've been of assistance with your church."

Intuko stepped forward and shook Steven's hand. "Thanks for your help."

When they were at the door of Campbell's office, being ushered out rather quickly, Intuko turned back to look at the pictures hanging on the wall. Something nagged him.

"Churches often have splits," said Intuko smiling, trying to ease the tension that had been created. "Did the board member Reverend Fleming split with start his own church?"

"No," Campbell said. "Mr. Black got into condo development and politics."

Outside the church, Chris asked, "What do you think?"

"Campbell did seem baffled, really confused on the Mercedes questions, but he didn't deny anything. He even said he and Hope drove the car sometimes." Intuko paused, pressing his lips together. Then Intuko said, "His wife looks an awful lot like Hope Fleming. I may have made a mistake in Bailey's."

"Are you cutting this guy slack?"

Intuko shoved his hands in his coat pockets, glancing back at Divine Intervention Church. "He honestly tried to help our church. I'd hate to think of him or Hope being involved. The people we need to meet with are Harrison Fleming and I think condo-developer, city council man, Brad Black."

Chris jabbed him in the ribs. "I already made us an appointment for day after tomorrow with Fleming. Earliest I could get. I convinced little-miss-redhead in there to pencil us in."

As soon as he was in his car, Intuko phoned Susan to find out that Sarah was quiet but fine. Susan handed the phone to Sarah, who in a low voice that Intuko could hardly hear, asked one more time about her dream catcher. He had to go back to the office anyway, so he promised he would get it for her and be there in an hour or so.

Hazel didn't look up from her computer screen when he walked in.

"Hazel, you're still here."

"Someone has to be here to run this church."

"I'm sorry. Would you like some tea?"

Hazel glanced up from her computer screen and peered over the top of her glasses. "Your face looks a little better, although it's starting to bruise. I still don't know what happened to you."

Intuko touched his nose. "It'll heal soon."

She got up from her special chair. "I'll make the tea." She

plugged the kettle in. "I've been organizing the meeting you want but everyone I ring is asking what it's all about and I've just been telling them, I don't know. I have to tell them that because I really *don't know* what it's all about."

Intuko went to the counter to retrieve two mugs.

"Harry Snell, he said to me, 'Hazel, what's this meeting all about?'"

Intuko dropped a cube of sugar in one mug and put a bit of milk in the other.

"People are busy Intuko. They need to know why they're being called to come here in the middle of the week when the regular board meeting isn't scheduled for another two weeks."

"I'm resigning, Hazel."

"Then when I phoned Agnes...what–what did you say?"

He turned to Hazel. "I said I'm resigning."

"But you can't do any such thing. What will become of the congregation?"

"Don't worry. I've been doing some thinking. This church has been good to me and I'll stay until we get a replacement. A good replacement. I won't leave anyone in the lurch."

"But–but...no one can replace you. You just can't up and leave because... because you have a woman in your life. That is downright shameful."

"A woman?"

"I know where you were today. At that Susan woman's house. All morning. When you should have been here fixing the leaky roof. And your nose probably looks like it does because–because you got caught by her husband or boyfriend."

"This has nothing to do with a woman, Hazel. And I promise you, I will sit down and tell you everything. But not today. I can't. I still have so much work."

"*Hrmuff.* I hope you don't expect me to help you with your letter of resignation. I don't have the time as I have too much to do." Lips pursed, she sat and began clicking the keys

164

on her word processor, the sound punctuating the silent tension that circled the small office.

He sighed and went into his office where he flopped in his desk chair and phoned the police station.

"Detective Anderson."

"Ah. Intuko. I was hoping I wouldn't hear from you."

"I need to see you tomorrow."

"I'm swamped. I've got a lot of interviews so I won't be in the office much." He paused. "Guess I could squeeze you in mid-morning. Meet me at Tim Horton's on Columbia at ten-thirty."

"I'd prefer to meet at your office, behind closed doors."

"What's this all about?"

"I like your coffee better."

"Our coffee tastes like mud."

"I'll bring two Starbuck's over then."

"I thought you were going to butt out of this."

"How do you take your coffee?"

"I wish you'd listen to me. One cream, two sugars. But make it Tim Horton's."

When he hung up the phone, Intuko winced knowing Anderson was going to lecture him good about the gun. He had no choice, it had to be checked, and the only way was through the police. This, he had to hand over to Anderson.

Tapping his pencil on his desk, he racked his brain. None of the clues made sense. Was it Hope and Steven they'd seen that night in Bailey's? If so did it matter? Perhaps it was just a liaison of sorts? Had Harrison killed Lola? Why though? Or was it a different Mercedes? But if it was Harrison's Mercedes it had picked up Charlie so Harrison was somehow involved with a street dealer. Or had Steven picked up Charlie? Or even Hope? And what about this Brad Black?

The bruises on his face were shooting sharp pains through his eyes and into his forehead. With his elbows on the desk he tried to massage his scalp. But the pieces of the puzzle refused to fit together.

Jimmy stood at the bar, beer bottle in hand. He watched a few of the big shots stroll in, dressed in their straight-laced-suits, white starched shirts and ties. They nodded their heads to the back of the room where Mr.-fuckin'-ego sat. He hated that guy and his I'm-the-greatest attitude. He wasn't nothin' but he thought he was somethin'. The asshole must have snuck in the back door 'cause he had a drink already.

Jimmy downed the rest of his beer, thumped the bottle on the counter, and put his finger up to order one more. Once he had a fresh cold beer, he made his way to the back of the bar, to the farthest corner of the room.

"Got in a little fight, eh?" One of the men at the table said while lighting a cigar.

"No big deal," said Jimmy.

"Sorry about your girl. But it was rather convenient for us. A john does her in and we're off the hook. She won't talk now."

"She was my best girl." Jimmy smacked the table with the side of his fist. "You guys are bastards. She brought in good cash."

"Lighten up, Jimmy. We didn't touch her. We're not that stupid. We don't want the cops near us. She's a hooker who got killed by a john. Anyway, we've got a huge shipment coming in this time. Biggest ever. You'll make enough for two girls like her. What about her kid?"

"She's gone. No one will look for her as no one cares. When's it in?"

"Could be three days, a week, or even tomorrow. Keep your phone on and your dealers posted."

The three men got up from the table and walked out of the bar, leaving Jimmy alone. He finished his beer, thinking. That minister fuckin' took the CZ75 auto pistol he'd won in a poker game against Mr.-Ego who thought his shit didn't stink. He'd finally beat the idiot, like really beat him and taken his gun right out from under his nose. Now, that fuckin' little twerp of a minister had it. Light, eighteen rounds. For that he would pay.

SEVENTEEN

Angie threw her hair net off, tousled her hair, and headed for the door.

"What's your hurry?" asked Iris.

"I gotta use the phone."

"Go girl, line-ups at this time of night are long."

Angie ran down the hall, through the rotunda area to find that she was tenth in line.

She waited, tapping her foot, wringing her hands, twisting her hair. Finally, she stepped toward the phone, knowing she only had two minutes to talk. She took out the paper with the number of Princess Street United Church, drumming her fingers on the wall as she listened to the ringing. She heard a woman's voice.

"I need to speak to Intuko. Right away."

"Please hold and I'll put you through."

Angie counted in her head, the seconds winding down. When she reached fifteen, she thought she would scream. Then twenty.

"Intuko, here."

"Intuko, it's Angie," she said in a rush.

"Angie! I was going to come visit you again tonight."

She thought she detected a little lift in his voice. Warm air ran through her body.

"Did you find Sarah?" she whispered, not wanting anyone to know anything about her life.

"We did," he said quietly.

The blood rushed through her body like a mad tidal wave,

making her light-headed and extremely happy. "*Where was she?*"

"We got her from school. She'd been dropped off."

"Dropped off? Is she okay? Is she hurt?"

"She seems fine."

"Where is she now?" Angie talked fast, knowing her two minutes would be up soon.

"With a friend of mine. Bathed and in clean clothes."

"Don't let her go, okay, don't let her go."

"Would you like to see her?"

"What, you mean, you bring her here?"

"Yeah."

She pressed her hand to her brow. Sarah, here, at the prison. What would she think? She had to make a decision fast. "Bring her. I'd like to see her," she blurted out.

"She doesn't know about her mother yet. She thinks she's gone away somewhere."

"Oh shit. Poor kid. Don't tell her. Let me do that. I knew Lola."

The phone clicked. Her time was up.

Dream catcher in hand, feathers soft against the palm of his hand, Intuko jumped two steps at a time to reach Susan's front door. He rang the doorbell.

Susan opened the door. "Come on in." She wore faded jeans and a yellow sweatshirt, and her hair was pulled back in a ponytail. She looked fresh like a spring daffodil.

"I've got Sarah's dream catcher," he said.

"They're watching *Arthur* right now. I'll get her."

"Wait a minute." Intuko touched her arm. "There's something I need to talk to you about."

Facing him, she looked up, gazing into his eyes.

"I talked to Angie today. She wants to see Sarah tonight."

Susan stepped back, pulling away from his touch, averting

her eyes to glance out the window. When she finally looked back at him, she straightened her posture and smiled. "I think that would be good for Sarah," she said. "A familiar face might give her some grounding, especially, someone who cares for her."

"That's what I thought but I wanted to run it by you first. Angie also wants to tell her about her mother. Do you think that's a good idea?"

"Yeah, I do." She nodded. "Her mother's dead and she needs to know. It's better coming from Angie, a friend, seeing as she has no family right now."

"I'm thinking of searching for her family. Her father was Inuvialuit."

"Is that like—Inuit?"

"Yeah. The Inuits in the western Arctic, where I'm from, are actually known as Inuvialuits. In broader terms we're all Inuits."

"Just not Eskimos, right?"

Intuko nodded.

"Hilary came home from school after studying the Inuit and told me Eskimo was *politically incorrect*. I don't even think she knows what that means." She smiled. "Have you eaten dinner yet?"

"You don't have to make anything for me."

"It's just spaghetti. We can talk while we eat. Then you and Sarah can go see Angie. I'll even give you some ice for your face."

Susan peeled potatoes.

"Hilary's glued to the television," whispered Mary, saddling up beside Susan. "She won't hear anything we say even if we yell so...tell me. What's going on?"

"Nothing."

"Nothing, my ass. You don't peel a dozen potatoes when

dinner is already over and just two of you live in this house."

"Did you ever think I may be making Shepherd's Pie to freeze?" Susan put down her potato peeler.

Mary took her by the elbow, leading her to the kitchen table. "I'm making you tea."

Plugging in the kettle, Mary said, "Come on Susan. Talk to me."

Elbows on the table, Susan let her head fall into her hands. "I don't know what I'm doing."

"About what? The minister?" Mary sat two mugs on the table.

"No, well, that too. I'll get into that in a minute. This is far more complicated." Susan lifted her head, pressing her fingers against her temples. "I have a child staying at my house tonight," she whispered. "A child I've never met until today."

"You've got the murdered hooker's child?" Mary's eyes widened to the size of dollar coins.

Susan exhaled loudly, nodding her head.

"Holy Hannah. How'd that happen?"

"Intuko found out she was being dumped at her school and I went with him to get her. Now she's here with me."

Mary thumbed down the hall. "I didn't see her."

"She's gone for a few hours. Intuko took her to see Angie at the prison."

"What are you going to do with her?"

"I don't know." Susan slowly shook her head.

"Does she have family?"

She bit her bottom lip. "I'm not sure. Intuko said something about her father being an Inuit from the western Arctic. But I don't think he's ever been involved in the child's life."

"How long do you plan to keep her?"

"Overnight, anyway. But we can't keep her indefinitely.

171

Can you care for her in the morning, just until Intuko gets here? I've got to work at seven. He's going to take her to school and pick her up."

"Sure, I can pour cereal for two." Mary stood up. "I think we need something stronger than tea." She took both mugs to the sink and dumped them.

"There's an open bottle of wine in the fridge," said Susan.

Mary retrieved the wine, sat back down, popped the cork, and poured two glasses. "Cheers," she said.

Susan clinked Mary's glass. "What am I cheering to?"

"You. You're amazing, taking a child in like this."

She tried to smile but wound up grimacing. "I let him kiss me."

"Oh, my, gawd. Really? The minister?"

"Yeah, the minister," Susan said each word deliberately, slumping in her seat. She rapidly tapped her fingers against her forehead. "How could I have been so stupid?"

"What's stupid about it? He's a sexy guy."

"Yeah, he is. But I kissed him and now…I don't think I'm interested in him."

In front of her small distorted mirror, Angie brushed her hair for the tenth time, maybe twentieth, then snugged it into a ponytail. With her hair pulled off her face, she looked pale. She pulled at the elastic, letting her hair fall around her shoulders.

What would Sarah think, seeing her in prison garb? Angie wished for jeans, a sweater, and shoes instead of slippers.

The officer knocked on her door to escort her to the visiting area. Angie picked up the card she had made for Sarah, wishing she had a present for her. With the screw dogging her heels, she walked the distance to the visitors room with sweat beading then dripping from her forehead.

Before she even reached the door to the visitors lounge,

she saw them through the window, sitting together, his arm around her shoulder, looking uncannily like father and daughter.

Sarah spotted Angie first. For a split second she stood still, as if her little feet were hammered to her spot on the floor with a nail, then suddenly she ran, her little legs spinning like an egg beater, her hair flying back like a horse's mane.

Angie almost fell over at the impact of Sarah's jump into her arms. Little arms immediately circled her neck in a tight almost strangling embrace. And Sarah's heart! Angie could feel it thumping, frantic-like.

"Sarah," she said softly, pressing her face into Sarah's hair and closing her eyes, "I'm so glad to see you."

They held tight for few minutes before Angie pulled back, trying to loosen the child's vice grip around her neck so she could look at her face.

"You look beautiful, Sarah! Look at your hair, it's all combed and washed." She ran her hands through Sarah's hair that fell like velvet to her shoulders. "You look like a queen."

"Do you really think I look like a princess?"

Angie pinched Sarah's cheek. "I didn't say princess. No one wants to be a dumb princess, always trying to find a prince. I said you look like a queen. You want to be the one perched on the throne giving the orders and don't you ever forget that."

Sarah reached up to touch Angie's hair, her little fingers pushing strands, finding a home for them behind Angie's ears. "You look different too. Where are your nice clothes?"

"They took 'em away from me. But when I get out, I'll get them back. You and me, we'll go shopping together just like old times. I see you have some new clothes though." Angie put Sarah down and tickled her tummy. "Take off your coat and let me see what's under there."

"It's a top with a rabbit on it. I wore it for you 'cause I know you like Peter Rabbit."

While Sarah took off her coat, Angie glanced at Intuko who stood off to the side observing the action. He caught her eyes, shoved his hands in his pockets, and walked towards them.

"Hi, Angie," he said. "It's good to see you again. She, uh, sure seems glad to see you."

Angie cocked her head, staring at his face. "What happened to you?"

"Nothing much."

"It doesn't look like *nothing* to me." Reaching up, she gently touched his nose, running the tips of her fingers under his eyes, electricity passing from his skin to hers. Immediately, she withdrew her hand and looked around. The officer didn't notice as she was too busy picking lint off her pants. Angie stuck her hands by her side. "I think maybe you were in a fight. It looks sore."

"It's not that bad."

She glanced back at Sarah who now had her coat thrown in a crumpled heap on the sofa. "She's an amazing kid. Isn't she?"

He nodded. "She sure is."

"Come here, Sarah," she said, sitting down, patting the worn sofa. "Tell me about school."

"I drew a picture today of the trees with no leaves."

"Oh, a getting-close-to-winter picture. What else?" Angie put her arm around Sarah, drawing her close.

"Tomorrow I'm going to show Miss Clark my dream catcher."

"Is it keeping your nightmares away?"

"Yeah, a little." Sarah paused. "Angie?"

"What?"

"Do you know where my mom has gone?

Angie sucked in a sharp breath. Intuko squeezed her shoulder. "Do you want me to stay or go?" he whispered in her ear.

"I'll be okay with her." This was it. She had wanted to be the one to tell Sarah about Lola and now she had to live up to her word.

She watched him walk away before she said, "I've got something to tell you Sarah."

"About my mom?"

Sarah looked up at her and the emptiness, the hollowness in the child's brown eyes made her turn away for a moment, gather her strength.

"Yeah." She kissed the top of Sarah's head. "This is about your mom." She hesitated but only slightly, the truth had to be told. "Look at me Sarah."

Sarah lifted her face, staring into Angie's eyes.

"She won't be coming back. You're going to have a new place to live."

"Did she go to the joint like you?"

"No."

"Where is she then?"

"Sarah, your mom's dead."

"Can I live with you?" The words were said with such little emotion that Angie was taken aback.

"Oh, Sarah, I'm so sorry. Not right now you can't." She pulled Sarah onto her knees, hugging her tight.

Sarah swivelled in Angie's lap and touched her cheek. "Can I later when you get out of here?"

"I hope so." She clasped one of Sarah's hands and kissed it.

"Where am I going to live now? At Hilary's?"

"I'm not sure about that either."

"I don't have to go back and live with Jimmy, do I?"

"No, you won't ever go back there."

"Can I live with Intuko?"

"Intuko? Would you like to live with him?" Angie

glanced at him, over on another sofa, drinking a cup of something he'd purchased from the visitors vending machines, waiting for any kind of signal that he could come over. Sure enough, as soon as he saw her look his way he immediately arose and walked toward them.

"How's it going over here?" he asked softly.

"We're okay," said Angie, rubbing her nose along Sarah's cheek.

He nodded and looked at her, eyebrows lifted, questions in his eyes, and she nodded as if to say, I told her, both of them acting like actors in a silent movie.

He sat down.

"Do you have a mother, Intuko?" Sarah asked quietly, looking to the floor.

Intuko shook his head. "No, my mother died a long time ago."

"My mother is dead too."

Silence.

Sarah turned to Angie. "When can you get out of here?"

"Soon, I hope."

"Hey, Sarah," said Intuko. "I brought some money to buy you something." He pointed to the vending machines. "See over there. There's chips and candy."

Sarah took the change he offered and ran toward the machines.

As soon as Sarah was out of earshot, Angie turned to Intuko. "She wants to know where she's going to live."

"I don't know what to do. Did her mother have any family?"

"Lola's mother was a junkie prostitute who died when Lola was a kid. She told me she did the foster thing for a while but couldn't hack it and ran away. At thirteen, Lola was on the streets. No one *ever* wanted her. My guess is that her mother's family never even knew she had a kid. Sarah was Lola's family." Angie put her hand on Intuko's arm, digging her nails in slightly. "You have to keep her for me. I'm the one who cares."

He put his hand on top of hers. "It's not that simple."

"What's not that simple? Lie. Say you're her father or uncle, you can pass." She saw the officer glancing in her direction so she pulled her hand back.

"I think I should look for her father's family."

"Don't, please. What if someone comes forward and wants her, someone who doesn't deserve her?"

"I've been doing some research and–"

"You have to talk fast, here she comes."

"They often grant indigenous children to their kind to give them back their sense of heritage. If I don't find family, the courts may feel I'm the best person to be her guardian because we're both from the western Arctic. But to prove my case, I have to prove she has no family. I have to play by the law."

"No, you don't!"

"Are you two fighting?" Like a small kitten, walking on padded feet, Sarah had appeared all too quietly.

"I don't want to hear fighting. I hate it! I hate people yelling!"

"Sarah, stop, okay. We weren't yelling." Angie held her by the shoulders and gently shook her."

"No, I won't stop! I don't want to." She put her hands to her ears, crouched on the floor in a tiny ball, knees pulled to her chest and rocked back and forth.

Almost as if he moved in slow motion, Intuko bent over and lifted Sarah, who didn't fight but remained in her tight ball. He sat her on his lap, holding her close, pressing her cheek against his chest, wrapping his arms solidly but tenderly around her body. Then he started to sing, a low chanting song that obviously came from his childhood, the Inuit words beautiful, peaceful, soulful.

Sarah stilled and slackened, uncoiling, allowing her body to mould into his as if she was a soft piece of clay. It was as if they were the same, were one.

Angie stared, mesmerized, the drone of his song keeping time with her heart which pounded steadily through her skin. She moved closer and reached out to stroke Sarah's hair, every fibre feeling like raw silk. How could this little girl endure any more pain? She felt sick to her stomach knowing that while Sarah's life spun out of control she was locked inside, unable to really help. This man singing was her only hope.

When Angie returned to her unit, she flopped down on the worn out sofa to watch some mindless television. The fight started as usual about what to watch but Angie didn't get involved. Tonight she couldn't care less.

Deep in thought, she barely watched the television images flitter across the screen. She didn't want to be a mother like Lola, often forgetting her own child existed, dumping her kid for drugs, letting the child fend for herself. She glanced at the rest of the women, whose eyes were glued to the small box, and she felt the desperation creeping through the walls like sap oozing from a tree, liquefying into one big mess.

If Intuko found Sarah's relatives, Sarah would be lost to her. The child would disappear from her life like a puff of smoke. Angie had to convince Intuko to stop searching, prying into the past, digging up what he shouldn't dig up.

With her hand resting on her stomach, she imagined she felt a little bump. Her baby. A knee, a shoulder, as small and as smooth as an ocean washed pebble, the kind she'd picked up on English Bay Beach when she'd roamed the streets with Lola looking for food.

The beach garbage cans were always full in the summer, everyone buying food, bringing picnics, then tossing it all away after they couldn't eat because of the heat. Lola and Angie used to share food if they found something good, like a fresh loaf of bread or a hamburger with just one bite out of it. Sometimes they would find fruit, like a bag of oranges where only a couple were bad but the rest were perfect. Once they had found a whole birthday cake with writing on it and they sang Happy Birthday to each other while eating the cake with their hands.

Lola had only ever dreamed of having a baby, being a good mother. Having a little girl to dress up, take to birthday parties and walk to school.

Suddenly, the strange woman Angie had encountered earlier appeared, gliding noiselessly down the hall. She wore some type of fur boots with tassels and beading. Over her white tunic dress, the woman donned a royal blue knee-length parka with fur around the hood and bottom and white and red beading stitched on the front. Because the parka had not been zipped up, she spotted the carving hanging around the woman's neck, shining as bright as a glow-in-the-dark toy. Only it wasn't a toy; it was a powerful depiction of mother and child.

"Why are you dressed like that?" Angie whispered.

"I'm preparing to go home. Your actions will take me there."

"Hey, girl, who you talking to?"

Angie heard the voices in the background, laughing, felt the fingers poking her.

"Look at loser Melville, she's off in fuckin' la-la land."

She heard the noise but couldn't stop staring.

"Soon I will dance with my people." The woman smiled and pulled at the bottom of her coat to zip it up, her long hair hanging in front of her face. "Please, tell my Intuko to follow his instincts. Tell him to remember what his grandmother, my mother, taught him. He should follow his fox. And tell him his grandmother said, 'Do not fear the journey.'"

Angie felt a hand on her shoulder. "Hey, Melville, your

eyes are bugging out of your head. Give it a shake."

Angie did shake her head, bringing her back to the room where women in grey sweats watched television.

"Where were ya?"

She shrugged. "Nowhere. Just thinking." There was no way she would tell Intuko to follow his instincts, she didn't want him searching for Sarah's relatives.

EIGHTEEN

Sarah remained quiet on the ride home. The early darkness of a late November night fell like a heavy quilt, covering Intuko and Sarah.

Intuko stared ahead through the beams of his headlights at the white lines on the road and the red taillights, clenching the steering wheel. He glanced at Sarah, looking small and alone, her head barely high enough to see out of the window. Her grip on the door handle was so tight, her knuckles shone in the dark like little pearls.

He flipped on the heater, even though it barely worked. The air blowing through the vents hit the silence like a high-speed fan. "It'll warm up in a few minutes. Sometimes it takes time," he said.

"I'm not cold." She stared straight ahead.

"Are you hungry?"

"No."

More silence.

"Were you happy to see Angie?"

"She looks different. Am I sleeping at Hilary's tonight?"

"Yeah. Are you okay with that?"

"I don't care." For the first time since they'd gotten into the car, she turned to look at Intuko, their eyes catching in the dark of the car, his probing for how she was really doing, hers big circles of white and dull brown.

"She seemed happy to see you," he said. "You two are special friends."

She turned her head to stare out the window becoming

silent once again. Not another word was spoken until he drove the car up beside the curb at the front of Susan's house. He parked behind Chris's car, and remembered his date with Mary. Coffee must have led to something else.

Walking up Susan's sidewalk, Intuko reached for Sarah's hand and she, without hesitation, wrapped her little fingers into his. With his free hand, he knocked on the door.

Susan opened the door wide. "Hello there. We've been waiting for you."

There was no spark in Sarah's facial expression, only blankness as if she were a piece of paper without lines or writing. "I'm tired and I want to go to bed," she said.

Susan glanced at Intuko and he knew she had questions.

"Do you want a snack first?" asked Susan.

"No," said Sarah. "I just want to go to bed."

She looked down the hall then at Susan then back at Intuko. "Could you say goodnight to me?"

"Of course I can," said Intuko.

Susan glanced at him. "I'll get her dressed first." She turned and followed Sarah into the bedroom. Hilary, who wasn't as eager as Sarah for bed, crawled into Susan's bed with her latest chapter book. After Susan had said good night to both girls, she came out into the hall and motioned for Intuko to go into Hilary's bedroom.

He quietly padded down the hall and entering the room, lit with just a night-light, he found Sarah curled up in a small ball, her knees touching her chest and her head facing the wall. He slowly walked over to the bed and sat down on its edge.

"I've come to say good night, Sarah," he said.

No answer.

He rubbed her back. Such a heavy load for anyone to bear, let alone a child. "You sleep well tonight and I'll be here to take you to school tomorrow."

"Sing to me again," she whispered. "Like you did at the

182

jail. I liked that song. Sometimes my white fox sings a song to me, sort of like the one you sing, maybe it's kind of different, I don't really know, but I hear it when I go to sleep."

"You have a white fox?" Intuko stroked her hair.

"Sing to me. Please."

The quiet desperation of her small voice made Intuko sing in a low chanting cadence the song his grandmother had taught him so long ago. Singing the words he had known so well, he wondered about Sarah's white fox, her background, and he reached out to stroke her hair and rub her back. She sighed under his touch and a warmth crept into him, into his blood, making it run like a river when the ice was melting because the sun was high in the sky for twenty-four hours.

Her eyes closed, her breath slowed, and he knew she was asleep. He leaned over and kissed her cheek. "Sleep tight." Then he bowed his head in prayer, for Sarah and her soul, sending his message of love and protection to her white fox and her God.

When he opened his eyes, a vision of her, dressed in a parka with beaver fur around the hood, framing her round face, shone like a lit candle in his mind's eye. Then he saw Angie's face, smiling, also dressed in a parka. She held her hands out to him and he…

He shut the door quietly and found Susan in the kitchen cleaning up.

"Is she asleep?"

"Yeah, finally."

"Have you time for a tea?"

"I think so."

They didn't utter another word until Susan had the tea ready and they were seated at the table. She poured the steaming liquid, first into his mug then into her own. He picked up his mug and wrapped his hands around its warmth. Only the kitchen light above the table was on, casting a circle of light around the table. The rest of the house lay in darkness. Intuko had never witnessed the silence of sleeping children before, the magical ambiance created from the hush.

"Angie told her about her mother today," he finally said.

"I gathered that. What was her initial reaction?"

"Unemotional."

"She needs help, you know. We can't do this on our own. Sarah needs professional counselling."

"I know that."

"Foster parents have taken courses in dealing with children like her. There are a lot of good ones out there who really care about the children."

"I know that too."

"We need to call someone. The sooner the better. I'll do it if you'd like."

"No. I'm going to try to find her family. I've decided I'm going to go North sometime soon. If I don't find family or if they're not suitable, I want to petition for legal guardianship."

"Do you know what you're getting into? Raising a child is hard work." She took a sip of tea and when she placed her mug down on the table the ceramic hitting the wood sounded more like metal banged against rock. Then she reached forward and tenderly placed her hand on top of his.

"Intuko," she said softly, "I know you're torn about all of this."

He squeezed her fingers, feeling nothing more than friendship.

"How is Angie handling her situation?" she asked, pulling away, changing directions.

"Okay, I guess." He leaned back, crossing his arms, shrugging his shoulders.

"If she gets sentenced, she may have to give her baby up," said Susan, elbows on the table, hands clasped in a prayer-like pose.

Intuko sat up straight and stared at Susan in disbelief at what she had just said.

She dropped her hands and leaned forward. "You don't know she's pregnant?"

He spun his cup around, staring at the inside, the tea sloshing around. Angie, pregnant? He looked up. "What...what happens in a situation like that... when a woman is pregnant and she's in prison?"

"Depends on her sentence. She may have to give the baby up for adoption."

That's why Angie had been so adamant about not letting Sarah go to a foster home. This woman could possibly lose two children now. His heart shrivelled as he absorbed her pain.

"She's gotten inside of you–I can see it in your face," Susan spoke softly.

Intuko thought he saw a fleeting bit of pain in Susan's eyes but then it was gone as quick as it came and she picked up the teapot, pouring tepid liquid into his mug.

Silence enveloped the room like a halo of fog. He heard her breathing, felt her presence.

"I may need to borrow some of your parenting books," he said with a small smile.

"If you want to go North alone, I'll keep her until you get back. But that's it. After that we have to do something. I don't want to keep her indefinitely. I've already got my own child. Mary said she'd help for a few days."

Intuko nodded.

More silence.

"I heard," Susan spun her mug, "from Chris that you're thinking of resigning from the church. Are you sure you made the right decision?"

"Yes," he whispered, "I've made the right decision." He dropped his head into his hands.

When he looked up, he caught her concerned gaze in the

lone light that shone above the table. "When you're not doing your best work and you're being bogged down by the little things, it's a sign you're not looking at the big picture."

"I only went to that church because of you," she said. "You're a wonderful minister."

"Thank you. But..." he sighed deep from the bottom of his chest, exhaling his breath as if it was pumped out of him, "I'm being told to make changes."

More silence.

"You're a wonderful person," he said. "Do you know that?"

"Would you like some *hot* tea?" Susan got up from the table and walked over to the kitchen counter.

"I'd better get going. I have an early date in the morning to take a beautiful little girl to school."

"It's been a long day. I'm as bushed as you." She picked up his coat, handed it to him then flipped on the outside light.

Leaning on the doorjamb, he looked at her standing in the rim of light, her fresh skin glowing, her hair pulled back to enhance her face. He reached out and she came into his arms, without hesitation, like she was a sparrow landing freely on a branch. A surge of comfort flowed between them but he had no desire to kiss her or press her body closer to his. When the hug split apart, she opened the door and they said good-bye.

He walked away from the door, toward his car, his still damp coat hanging over his shoulder, the night air chilling his skin, bringing him back to his reality. He had to go to a lonely, sparsely decorated apartment that was not really a home. He looked upward to a sky void of stars and a glowing moon, to have the pattering of mist softly hit his face.

He didn't want to go to his apartment. Not tonight. Susan's apartment still had a light on in the kitchen and for a brief moment he wanted to rush back into the warmth of her cozy home and into the warmth of her arms.

But that would be wrong.

He drove cautiously down the street, wondering where he should go, when he thought about the quiet sanctuary of the church. It provided a surrogate for him; a tentative foster home.

The church slept in darkness, bedded for the night, except for the front light that spread a dull shine on the wet steps. He unlocked the door and stepped inside, where he stood for a moment, allowing his eyes to adjust to the dark. Once he was sure he could find his way without stumbling, he removed his shoes and socks and walked barefooted into the sanctuary, the place for holy worship. As he slowly walked down the aisle, he gently touched the newel post on the end of every pew, their ornate designs chiselled smooth to create beauty. He saw the tattered hymn books, some scattered on the seats, some placed in their stands.

Suddenly, he saw his white fox, darting through the hymn books! It bounded from one book to another.

He blinked in shock. His fox was gone! Twice it had visited him now.

Shaking his head, he wondered about Sarah and her fox. Was all the talk about foxes making him delusional?

At the front, he found the matches and lit a candle, its incandescence radiating a fiery circle of light, creating shadows on the walls. He watched the shadows, mesmerized how they danced to their own beat, oblivious to time and space.

Finally he knelt in prayer. "Oh, my dear God, my Creator," he whispered, his hands clasped over his face, his head lowered, "I'm so sorry for my actions today. Please forgive me. I need your guidance more than ever now."

He opened his eyes and stared into the flickering flame. He saw the North: dancing, drumming; the northern lights; a vast whiteness in winter, a forever light in summer; animals roaming, birds flying, tundra blooming, night descending. The images shimmered and moved in his mind just like the candle flame.

He got up from his kneeling position and went to the front of the church to stand behind his pulpit. He stared out to the dark empty seats. Then he turned to look upward and sideways and behind him, taking in everything. The stained glass cherubs, the beautiful architecture of the vaulted ceiling, the windows, the pews, the floor and the ceiling again. He was resigning, leaving this home soon.

He laid down on the floor in the fetal position, curled his knees to his chest, and closed his eyes.

He needed to sleep.

Susan sat at the kitchen table drinking re-heated tea. What she needed was sleep, in her bed. The oak sled bed with the white cotton bedspread she had bought after her split with Eric. It had been the one thing she had wanted and the one thing she had splurged on for herself. The only thing.

She'd never had a man in her new bed and tonight, had the circumstances permitted, she may have invited Intuko to stay. But she had Hilary. And now Sarah. And her separation from Eric was still too new. She couldn't help wondering though, what would it have been like for her to take Intuko's hand, guide him to a darkened room where he could have undressed her piece by piece? The thought of curling up beside a warm body gave her erotic shivers.

Crawling under the covers, she reached for Hilary who had fallen asleep, and pulled her against her body. A loneliness crept through her, the aching secreting from the depths of her being. His kiss had felt good but not right. She was still vulnerable. And it wasn't really him she wanted, but someone to fill the void. After an emotional day like today, she'd wanted someone strong to hold her, touch her, waltz and tango in her big double bed.

She snuggled closer to Hilary. Someday, with someone, the time would come again.

The lights went off in Angie's cell, all except her night-light. She didn't want to be alone in the dark, anyway, with her thoughts racing like mad demons through her mind. She couldn't get that man off her mind–his touch, his skin, his smile. How he sang to Sarah, holding her as if she were his own, calming her.

A good man like that wouldn't want her.

He was a minister, she was a stripper. The word gave her goose bumps–she never wanted to do that job again, ever. She rolled over, pulled the covers up to her chin, and curled into the tiniest of balls...her only escape from the real world.

Childhood memories surfaced when the lights were low. Usually, Angie thought about all the bad things, but today, she remembered the time her mother had sat on the end of her bed and read a story to her. Peter Rabbit. Her favourite childhood story. She had loved the part where he'd tried to hide in the watering can, only to get soaking wet. That was the only time she could ever remember her mother being nice to her. The day she gave her the book.

Angie cupped her stomach, desperate to feel the life inside her.

NINETEEN

"Do you know where Sarah came from?" Hilary whispered to Mary as soon as Susan had walked out the door for work.

"What did your mom tell you so far?" Mary placed a bowl of oatmeal in front of Hilary and sat beside her at the kitchen table.

"That she comes from a poor family and there's no one to take care of her properly."

Mary watched Hilary dig her spoon into the bowl, skimming the melted brown sugar from the top of the oatmeal.

"That's kind of the story, Hil."

"Is that Intuko man going to be my mom's boyfriend?" Hilary took a mouthful of oatmeal and before Mary could think of an answer said, "Can I have some juice, please?"

"Apple or orange?"

"Apple."

Mary walked over to the fridge, thankful for the time it took to pour a glass of juice. When she plopped back down, she looked at Hilary. "I can't say for sure about your mom and Intuko. Would it bother you if your mom did have a boyfriend?"

"Kind of."

"Do you miss your dad?"

"Yeah. I wish they'd get back together. Oh, I think I hear Sarah." Hilary looked at Mary and said, "I bet she missed her mom and dad last night, too, even though they're poor."

* * *

Intuko took a breath and knocked on Susan's front door, nervous as to how Sarah would act towards him now that it was a new day. He shrugged his shoulders trying to get the kinks out of his body. Waking up in the wee hours of the morning on the cold, hard, church floor had stiffened his muscles. When Mary opened the door, her eyes sparkled like copper pennies and he couldn't help but smile back.

"Your face looks a little better this morning," she said.

He put his hand to his nose. "How's Sarah?"

"Better. She's quiet but that's to be expected. Hilary is able to deal with her the best out of all of us. But, she does seem excited to go to school. Would you like some coffee?"

He shook his head, "No, thanks. I stopped and picked one up on the way over here."

Mary nodded and glanced at the clock. "Time's a-wasting. I'll get Sarah for you."

While waiting for Sarah to appear, he tapped his foot and jingled the change in his pocket. He could hear some coaxing going on, but within a few moments she appeared, dressed in a nice little blue outfit. Her combed dark hair hung to her shoulders. He walked toward her and squatted to eye-level with her. "Morning, Sarah."

Big, brown eyes stared back at him.

"I've come to take you to school. Do you have your dream catcher?"

A glimmer, like a sudden surge of power passing through a dying light bulb, flashed across her face then, it was gone. She nodded. He gently took her hand in his. "Let's go."

She nodded again.

"Here's her backpack," Mary said. "I packed her a snack. I wasn't sure what your plans were for the day. I've got some writing to do but will take care of her this aft if you need me."

"Thanks."

With Sarah safely buckled in the front seat, Intuko raced

around to the driver's side of the car, the damp wind nipping through his jacket. "It sure is cold out," he said getting in the car.

Sarah didn't respond but looked straight ahead and fiddled with the red ties on the backpack.

"Did you sleep good last night?"

She nodded.

All the way to the school, he tried to get some sort of conversation going with her, to get her to open up a little, but every question was met with either a one-word answer or no answer at all. Finally, they were at the school and he carefully helped her out of the car and took her hand. "Come on."

"You don't have to walk me," she said.

"I don't have to, but I want to."

"My mom only ever walked me once."

They ambled across the field hand-in-hand, dodging the puddles, Sarah clutching his fingers. Memories of his first days at residential school surfaced and he felt sick to his stomach. No child should have to feel this way.

"We have to wait for the bell," she said. "This is the kindergarten area. Next year I'll go through those doors." She pointed to the doors on the other side of the school.

"You'll be a big girl then. Grade one. Are you looking forward to first grade?"

The bell rang and Miss Clark opened the door. Intuko squatted down and kissed Sarah on the cheek. "I'll be back at eleven-fifteen to pick you up."

She tilted her head to the side. "You're going to pick me up, too?"

"You betcha. Now, go show Miss Clark your dream catcher."

Intuko arrived at the church to messages but only one he listened to twice. From Chris. He had done some snooping around concerning Harrison Fleming and his old partner, Brad Black. There didn't seem to be a major legal fight before the split. Chris's final sentence had been, "I smell a conspiracy of some sort."

So did Intuko.

Angie had mentioned Black and now here he was linked to Fleming. Were Fleming and Black involved in the drug ring? Partners maybe? And Lola. Did Lola know too much? Had Fleming shot her? Or Black? Were they both involved in her death?

Intuko's day timer sat open on his desk. He glanced at his schedule. Detective Anderson at ten-thirty, Sarah at eleven-fifteen, art class at four-thirty, board meeting at seven-thirty. Such a busy day. Would he have time to visit with Black? If he worked hard, as it was just past nine, he could draft his resignation letter this morning.

One try after another, paper piled in the recycling bin, he wrote and rewrote. Deep in thought, he heard Hazel arrive but she didn't peek her head in his door to even say hello.

Pounding away at his computer keyboard, he jumped when his phone rang; Hazel had obviously opted out of taking messages for him. Without taking his gaze off the computer screen, he picked up the phone, crooked it in his ear, and kept typing.

"Hello," he said quickly, still typing.

"Intuko, Chris here. You got my message about Brad Black?"

He stopped his mad typing and pushed his chair back and away from the computer screen. "Yeah. I did. Something's weird here. How did Lola fit in is the big question for me."

"I wouldn't be surprised if Campbell's involved too. If Lola did get in Harrison's car that night, I think the question is– was he the one who killed her? Or was someone else driving his car? Campbell said he drove it sometimes and so did Hope.

Maybe Hope's involved too."

"Maybe Lola found something out and the cops were after her to tell and Harrison and Black felt they had to kill her," said Intuko. "She said she walked in on Jimmy with his rich friend once. She was scared. Jimmy's in on all of this somehow, but he didn't kill Lola–of that I'm convinced."

"Something else," said Chris. "I found out that land of theirs, from their old ministry, is in White Rock. Remember the pictures in Campbell's office. I wonder what they use it for now, especially if they're in cahoots together. Why the big split, the big production if they're still working together?"

"Maybe they started that long ago and it was all a front."

"That's what I was thinking."

"There's something else I can't figure out," said Intuko scratching behind his ear. "I can't see men like this getting their suits dirty killing Lola in an *alley*. She might have been killed somewhere else. Or they hired someone. Maybe a low street seller who would do anything for some cash or drugs. Listen, do you have a street address for that land? It might be worth a drive out. And I think we should visit Black."

"Yeah. I agree."

Intuko tapped his pencil on his daytimer. "I've got some time early afternoon."

"I'm pretty swamped," said Chris. "I can't get to that land but I've got time to pop in to see Black as I'm going to be in the False Creek area and that's where his office is."

"Okay. You go see Black. I'll take a drive. Have you already made an appointment?"

"Who needs an appointment?" said Chris.

"Okay, okay. Do it your way. Let's connect later tonight. I've got my art class and a meeting at the church. But after that."

"Sounds good."

Hanging up his phone, Intuko wondered how he was

going to fit one more thing into his day. His watch beeped. Nine-thirty. Thirty more minutes to do this letter.

At exactly ten-thirty, Intuko walked into the police station with two coffees and two apple fritter donuts.

"Okay, Intuko," said Detective Anderson, ripping the tab off the take-out lid, "besides the fact that you were in a fight, which I'm not going to ask about because I really don't want to know, why are you here?"

Intuko sipped his coffee first, before reaching into his coat, pulling out the towel. He laid it on Anderson's desk, opening it to reveal the gun.

Anderson jumped, hitting his coffee, sending it flying on the floor. "What the..." He quickly picked up his coffee, slamming it on his desk, spilling it everywhere.

"I found this at Jimmy's," Intuko spoke slowly. "Lola's pimp. I think it might be the murder weapon."

"Damnit, Intuko. You don't just take a gun from someone's place. What were you thinking? You could have been killed!"

"That it might be the murder weapon."

"You've been watching too much television!" Anderson picked the gun up by the towel. "CZ75 auto. Nice gun. Might be imported from Eastern Europe." He put it down and eyed Intuko. "How did you pick it up?"

Intuko grimaced. "My hands."

"Bare?"

"Yes."

"Great. Your prints will be all over it."

"Can't you dust it for other prints? Can't you find if it matches the gun that shot Lola?"

Anderson stood, shaking his head at Intuko, looking like a pot of boiling water ready to bubble over. "We didn't have a search warrant to take this," he hissed through gritted teeth.

"Which means," his voice picked up volume, "this evidence could *never be used in court*."

Intuko hung his head. "I never thought about that."

"You didn't think about a lot of things!" After flicking his hands at Intuko, Anderson sat down, leaning back in his swivel chair. He vibrated his lips, sounding like a horse going out to pasture. Then he leaned forward, took a bite of his donut, wiping the sugar from his mouth. "I'll use up a few favours to get it checked out, even though my supervisor will hang me in a noose if he finds out."

"Maybe if we work together on this, we could figure out who killed Lola. What do you think?" Intuko picked up his donut and handed it to Anderson. "I'm not hungry."

"I think you should butt out." Anderson took another bite of his donut. A huge bite. "But that's obviously not going to happen. What do you know?"

"Lola got in a black Mercedes the night she was killed."

"Okay. And you also have Charlie getting in a black Mercedes."

"Yes. The Mercedes belongs to Harrison Fleming. What is he doing with Lola, a hooker, and Charlie, a street dealer? How is Harrison connected? Street-like ministry is ruled out–Divine Intervention only operates from the church. Did he kill Lola that night? Or maybe he hired a killer. Steven Campbell maybe? Or a street seller? And did you know Brad Black and Harrison Fleming were partners way back when?"

Anderson rocked back on his chair, balancing it on two legs. "What does Brad Black have to do with any of this?" he asked, rubbing his chin with one hand, setting his balancing act off ever so slightly.

"I heard his name circulating."

"Circulating? He's on city council, Intuko," said Anderson, still rocking on his chair, annoying Intuko. "I wouldn't throw his name around without proof."

Intuko didn't say anything.

"His name can't be just thrown around in space."

"Okay. Point taken. Can you search Harrison's car? For blood, fingerprints, hair fibre."

Anderson thumped his chair down so it was sitting on all four legs again. Then he ate the rest of the donut, narrowing his eyes, chewing, thinking. He swallowed. "Do you watch every cop show there is? We can't search the car yet. All the evidence is hearsay. Did you see her get in the car? Did you get a license number? No, you didn't. You only got the license when Charlie got in the car. We don't know if that was the first or last car Lola got into or if she even got into Harrison Fleming's car. If we go ahead with something like searching his car, we could jeopardise everything we've done so far. Anyway, all we have is your word that Charlie got into a Mercedes. Lola could have gotten into a black car owned by someone else."

"Yes, but don't you think it could somehow be connected." Intuko talked with his hands to make his point. "Shouldn't you be searching any car you may think she got into?"

"We work with evidence, not big huge whopping maybes. I'll sleep on this one. From now on, don't you dare do anything without consulting me first."

Intuko stood outside Sarah's class, with all the other parents, mostly moms, feeling…special. He puffed out his chest, like a proud peacock with a plume of feathers. When the door opened, the children came streaking out.

"Walk, don't run, please," said Miss Clark.

He watched Sarah look around, almost desperate, but when she saw him, she beamed from ear to ear. He waved and walked over to her.

"You *did* come," she said, squinting up at him.

"Of course, I did."

"She worked hard today," said Miss Clark, smiling down at her. "Sarah, why don't you show Intuko your classroom?"

"Would you like to see it?" she asked, looking up, her brown eyes filled with hope.

"I'd love to." He took her hand and she led him to a class filled with numbers, letters, and posters of animals. He walked around holding her hand, listening to her soft little voice tell him about her fall picture, the math she could do, all the letters of the alphabet and the few words she could read.

After leaving the school, Intuko treated Sarah to a hamburger meal at a fast food joint, the plastic toy enthralled her, absorbing her attention, and after they finished eating, he took her over to Susan's. He asked Sarah if she wanted to go for a drive but she said no, she wanted to watch *The Lion King*. Susan wasn't home but Mary came up from downstairs and put on the video for her. He made a mental note to get a video machine soon, stock up on some kid's movies.

The drive out to White Rock took just under an hour. After leaving the city the scenery became rolling, lush green farmland that made the city seem so compact, so dense. Barren tall trees swayed in the distance, leaves covering the ground below them.

He followed his map, driving down a well-traveled dirt road. Leaning forward on the steering wheel, he relaxed as no one was riding his bumper, wanting him to speed up. Only a truck, which hauled hay, and a big old blue Chrysler car with the exaggerated fins, batman type mobile, passed him on the other side of the road, coming from the direction he was going.

He bumped through the potholes for a few minutes before he slowed the car down to nearly a halt in front of a big peach stucco house. Did he have the right address? This looked residential. Nice green lawn. Garden. One car and a big truck with some writing on it were marooned out front. Intuko squinted to read the side.

"Spiritual Retreat Centre," he said to himself. "How interesting." He parked the car on the side of the road and stepped out. Time to pay a little visit.

He knocked on the door. At first there was no answer then a woman appeared at the door. Her ash-blond hair hung to shoulder length, her skin glowed with a pink fresh-scrubbed tinge, and she wore dark jeans and a bright lime-coloured sweat top. She smiled at Intuko, and he tried to guess her age. Mid-forties perhaps.

"Can I help you?" she asked.

"Yeah, um, I was wondering about your Retreat Centre." Here I go again, he thought, stumbling over little white lies.

"We're closed right now. Until May. We always close from Thanksgiving through to May long weekend."

"Oh, I'm sorry," he said. "It's just that I'd heard such great things about your Centre. Do you think you could maybe show me around anyway? I'm a minister myself and I might be able to refer some people to you."

"Sure. Let me get my coat."

Yet another white lie. While he waited, standing on the front porch, he observed the front yard. Everything seemed neat and tidy: flower beds in order; plants trimmed; fences painted.

When the woman stepped outside she said, "My name's Joanne, by the way." She stretched out her hand. "Joanne Venus."

"Intuko," he said, shaking it, feeling like a fool for not introducing himself first.

"What church are you from?"

"Princess Street United."

She nodded although he detected the confusion in her shoulder shrug, as if she knew no one at Princess Street United had the money to come to a Retreat Centre.

"Come on round the back," she said. "I'll show you where we hold our classes and house our guests.

Intuko followed Joanne around the side of the house and was surprised when he saw a wonderful little duck pond, five rustic buildings that looked like back woods cottages and one bigger building, also charmingly rustic. It must be the centre where everyone congregated. The ducks quacked when they heard them coming, scattering and splashing water in all directions. A golden dog came running out from the woods, wagging its tail when it saw company.

"Don't mind her, she's rambunctious and overly-friendly. Best people dogs, though. Her mother was a gem."

Scratching the dog's ears, Intuko asked. "What do you do at your Retreat Centre?"

"Rebirthing. We also do yoga, meditation, and writing workshops. We study crystals, learn about Tarot cards, make spiritual alters, ritual baths. We hold new moon and full moon gatherings. And we take walks in the woods. People are free to take part in what they like."

"Do they come here for extended periods of time?" he asked, watching the ducks settle, floating like royalty on top of the water.

"We have package deals. A week is the longest. Some come for the weekend."

"How many acres do you have?" He stared at the buildings and the property.

"Fifteen."

"Lot of work for you. You must have a partner."

"My son, Eric, lives with me, helps me maintain the land, and keeps the property groomed. I guess one day he'll get sole ownership. I think that's what he's hoping for."

"Well, he does a good job for you. The place is immaculate. Is he here now?"

"He just left. You probably passed him on the road. He

had to pick up a few things in town."

Intuko nodded and walked over to a cedar fence that appeared to be the dividing line between properties. Standing under a magnificent willow tree, he leaned against the railing, and looked into the distance. Set back in the trees he could see an old building, which looked to be boarded up. "Anyone live there?" he asked, pointing to the building.

Joanne laughed. "Does it look like I have neighbours?"

Intuko turned, and smiled. "No."

"That land just sits there," she said.

"Who owns it?"

Joanne looked Intuko square in the eye. "You ever heard of Harrison Fleming?"

"I have," said Intuko. "I've seen his show."

"He doesn't do much with his land, except visit now and again. I think he wants to build some sort of rehabilitation centre, but most neighbours around here aren't happy about his plans."

"Are you?"

"No. I've done a petition. We don't want our area sullied with the likes of what *he'll* bring here. Hookers, drug addicts, and drunks. At least that's the way he's talking. Sure won't be good for my business."

Back in the car, Intuko waved to Joanne who stood on her front porch. Everything seemed above board. But perhaps "seemed" was the operative word. Once again, he checked the address Chris had written down and it compared to the lot number on the fence post. He scratched his head. Had Black sold his land to this Joanne Venus? Was this another wild goose chase like the night in Bailey's?

He started his car, watched Joanne wave one last time before going inside her pretty peach house. The narrow dirt road, with ditches on either side, didn't give him much space to

201

turn around so he drove ahead, deciding to turn around in the overgrown gravel driveway of the vacant lot beside the Retreat Centre.

He braked and was about to shove his gearshift into reverse when he happened to glance at the flat-topped, boarded-up building that stood in the distance like an eerie haunted house without the spirals and gables or black fence.

He put the car in park and peered next door; Joanne wouldn't be able to see him through the trees. It would be safe to take a quick peek. Quickly walking up the gravel road, he tried to stay light on his feet, remembering his days running beside the dog sleds, hunting for caribou with his grandfather. When he approached the building he slowed to observe his surroundings. Weathered but still readable, he spotted a sign that said, "Seed of Life." Harrison held his tent worship here. Had this been an office of sorts?

Intuko tiptoed up the porch and tried the front door. Locked. He circled the building looking for some way to see inside, a crack, a broken board, anything at all. On his second time around the house, he found a slightly loosened board and tried to pry it off. Within seconds he had a small opening. He wiped the grime from the window with the cuff of his sleeve, until he had a circle the size of an orange. Inside he saw nothing but a few chairs, an old table and stacks and stacks of hymn books.

Had they left this abandoned? Simply shut the ministry down, leaving the building with remnants of hymn books?

Suddenly he heard quacking sounds. Someone must be in the back yard next door. Without even glancing over, he ducked his head in his coat, shoved his hands in his pockets, and hurried to his car without drawing attention to himself.

TWENTY

By three-thirty in the afternoon, after looking in on a content Sarah, and after promising to tuck her in again at night, Intuko was back at the church to prepare for his first carving class. From his closet, he pulled out the box of supplies he was going to take to the prison, wondering if Angie would show up. He needed to talk to her again about Sarah. He had to go North. For Sarah's sake. The sooner the better for everyone involved, especially Sarah as she couldn't settle too much if she had to be moved again.

Kneeling down, he ran his fingers along the carvings he was taking for demonstrations, every piece unique, every piece someone's creativity.

Today, he would go inside the prison–past the visiting room–to see where his mother spent her last days. He fingered the soft, moose-leather strap of the necklace he wore. The whalebone carving of a woman and child she had carved now hung between his breast-bone instead of being shoved in the back of a drawer.

He rubbed the carving of the tiny baby with the wide-cheeked smile between his fingers, wondering if his mother had ever carted him around on her back, papoose style. His recollections of snuggling with a mother under fur blankets were vague. This necklace had been carved and created by an innocent version of his mother.

The afternoon light was the colour of a shark's skin and the barbed wire and thick metal fence surrounding the prison grounds looked as menacing as a shark's teeth.

Getting out of the car, Intuko opened the trunk to retrieve the heavy cardboard box filled with his teaching tools: files, mallets, dust masks, sand paper of different grades, and geologist pics. Susan had ordered the soapstone, the softest and easiest stone for beginners to manipulate, from a specialty store in Edmonton.

He wiped the sweat from his brow, rested the box on his knee and pressed a buzzer to be let in. Grace, the Program Supervisor, met him and after he and his box were thoroughly checked, and he had explained the reason for every tool, he made his way through the metal scanner.

"Stop a moment, please," he said quietly to Grace as he walked by the waiting room. He put his box down. Although he had been here twice already to see Angie, he had purposely shut the old visions of his mother out. But today, with her necklace hanging around his neck, he remembered their last visit.

"I'm sorry, is the box heavy?"

"I just need to…look." He stared at the far corner of the room, the one where he had sat, waiting, twisting his fingers, for his mother to be escorted to him.

As if he was reliving that day, she walked through the door. Trance-like, he watched her body move to exactly the place he had last seen her. The sight of her mesmerized him, for she looked real.

On that day, he had desperately wanted her to ravish him with hugs and kisses, say sorry, and hold him like a little boy— even though he had been a teen. He had wanted her blurry eyes clear, her calloused brown skin soft and her skinny body covered in thick, warm flesh. From her distant, opaque eyes and her drooping yellow skin that covered her hard bones like a wet paper bag, she wasn't long for this world. Hugging her had been like hugging a spindly tree in the cold of winter.

He refused to see the blatant signs that day; her rancid smell, hollow sound and steel touch. He had left the prison numb and returned to his small place. At that time in his life, at the age of fifteen, he was fending for himself. There had only been one phone in the run-down crowded house he lived in. Most of the people he lived with were unemployed and smoked marijuana most of the day. One of his relatives had found the room for him, when he'd wanted to move South to get away from residential school. He was to finish his high school on his own.

Intuko would lock himself up in his room to study as he wanted to make something of his life. When the phone rang later that night, and someone screamed at him to answer the *damn thing*, he knew…bad news–no one ever called him. After walking the length of the hall, he had picked up the dangling phone and heard the words, "Your mother is dead."

Intuko shook his head, for he now saw his mother standing, not sitting, and she was dressed in a royal blue parka and crow boots and her arms were reaching out to him.

"*Quviatchangniaqtuami*; I will be happy," she said.

He stepped toward her.

Sweet coercion had caused her to end up in prison. The white men came to the North and built rigs out in the sea where his people caught food. They brought in material possessions the Inuvialuits had never seen before. The men she started to hang around, the ones with smooth words and money must have convinced her to leave. That must have been the reason she left her children. He wiped his eyes.

His vision changed. She sat slouched again, dressed in her drab prison clothes, staring into space.

For all of Intuko's life he had always respected his culture's ways even when the black robes drilled it into his mind that he was a pagan and a heathen. But in a desperate, futile search for what she could never find, his mother had ended up here. In this prison. *Trying to escape being the real person you are born to be leads to disaster.*

Always.

She was gone, disappearing like a blown out candle flame. Again.

Intuko picked up his box and looked at Grace, a handsome woman with a big smile and wide hips. "Which way now?" he asked.

"Are you all right?" Her eyebrows bunched together. "You look as if you've seen a ghost."

"I'm okay." Intuko assured her. He *had* seen a ghost.

Intuko followed Grace through more doors, flinching each time he heard the distinct sound of the lock catching. After walking down a few more corridors and through a few more doors, he found himself entering a large open area, round in shape with high ceilings. The second floor had a railed hallway and, on the other side of the hall, doors with little glass windows. Those doors must lead to the cells where the women were locked at night.

What did his mother's last home on this earth look like? Did she hang pictures, set up house? The thought of his mother sitting on a bed, crying with a photo of him in her hands gave Intuko a strange sort of comfort.

Benches and large pots of greenery perched precariously in the middle of the rotunda. Women, all dressed in the grey sweats Angie wore, loitered, many of them smoking. He looked for Angie but couldn't see her anywhere. Would she keep her promise and come to class?

When Grace unlocked a door, he quickly assessed the room, noticing there was sufficient counter space for the women to work and lots of shelves for storage. In the corner the soapstone, piled in a big lump, looked like nothing more than a mound of rocks. That would soon change. He hoped.

"There should be enough ventilation in here," Grace said.

206

He immediately walked to the windows with bars on them, noticing they had already been opened. Filing stone created an enormous amount of dust and the only way he'd said he could run the program was if they had an adequately ventilated room.

"This should do," he said.

"I'll make sure the windows are open before every class. And we've made some rules. No one will be allowed in here unless they ask first and then a blue will have to unlock the door. And every time someone leaves the room they must be frisked." Grace pointed to a little black box hanging from the ceiling. "We've also had cameras installed so we can keep an eye in here at all times."

Out of the corner of his eyes, he saw his first student. He smiled broadly, making Grace turn around.

"Angie," he said, his spirits lifting, his body jittery. He didn't even have his coat off yet and she was here. "I'm so glad you came."

"I'm not much of an artist," she muttered.

"Everyone's an artist. And carving is storytelling in stone. Everyone has a story."

Grace gave a little wave. "I'm off."

Intuko and Angie stood a few feet apart. She twisted her fingers, he shuffled his feet.

"How's Sarah?" she asked.

"I got to go into her classroom today. Now there's an artist. She puts me to shame."

"Have you thought any more about what you'll do?"

"Angie," he stepped toward her. "I have decided to go North. When, I don't know, but I have to. I couldn't live with myself if I didn't. It would be like taking something that wasn't mine."

"But you're not doing that. She's mine." She tapped her fingers on her chest.

"I'm not saying she's isn't. I just have to clear the channels so you won't be hurt in the future."

She bit her bottom lip and looked away. Intuko put his finger under her chin, turning her face to his, gazing into her eyes.

"If I just take her, they can come and take her back," he said. "If I do my homework then they can't. This will save us all pain."

"And it may cause pain." She stepped away from him.

"Angie," said an older grey haired woman who had just walked into the room. "I didn't know you were coming to this class."

Angie rotated on her heels. "Iris, hi." She forced a smile. "What the heck."

"Yeah, might as well do art as smoke in the rotunda or watch television. I figure I can miss the *Young and Restless* one night a week."

Every woman took a piece of stone, looking at it carefully to see if they could visualize it as anything other than a big lump of unformed rock.

Intuko had brought along animal magazines and real carvings to help them with their decision. When they did decide the shape, he showed them how to chisel their stone to give it basic form. Within time they would file for more definition, shape with all different grits of sandpaper and, the final touch, much later, would be to shine their carving with floor wax.

He walked around the room, showing each individual woman how to work the raw material, his mind focused, his body energized, his soul vibrating with enthusiasm for life. He'd left his art for too long.

He picked up a piece, touching its hard contours, knowing that only by manipulation and time could it be carved to be the texture of smooth silk, shaped in the form of something magnificent. How easy it was to change stone, how hard it was to change humans. So many resisted the filing, shaving and sanding, the defining, preferring to keep the exterior unformed, unfinished and hard.

When he stopped by Angie, he moved as close to her as he could without anyone noticing. His thigh touched her thigh. She continued to work on her piece, the beginnings of mother and child. Instinctively, he touched his mother's necklace. She put her file down, picked up her carving, holding it away from her face so she could really look at it.

"That's a good start," said Intuko.

"Thanks." She turned and obviously caught sight of the necklace that was around his neck. *"Where did you get that?"*

"My mother made it. A long time ago."

"It looks…familiar." She looked back at her carving. "I'm giving this to Sarah when I'm finished. I just hope I have it done by the time I get out of here."

Six men and two women sat around a table, and their voices reduced to a hush when Intuko entered the room. He stood before them, firmly holding the copies of his letter. He cleared his throat. Some of these people had been on his board for years; it was their social life, their way of giving to the world, their service to humanity. And they believed in him.

He took a deep breath, sat down at the head of the table and slid each person a copy of his letter. The only sounds in the room were the shuffling of bodies trying to get into comfortable positions, the odd snuff or cough and the flipping of paper. Silence would have been easier to take than the cacophony of sounds.

After he gave them ample time to read through his letter, he cleared his throat. Eight pair of eyes looked at him.

"I understand," he paused, "that this may come as a bit of

a shock to some of you."

"It's more than a bit of a shock," said Bill Temple who sat on his right-hand side. "I don't think any of us saw this coming. Does this have anything to do with your face? I mean, if someone beat you up or you did get into a fight that is no reason to resign. Forgive and forget, you know, it's what this church is all about."

"This here church needs you."

"We don't have an assistant to take over."

Intuko raised his hand to quell the mumbling. "Please," he said softly. "Although I have explained everything in the letter, I want to tell you my reasons in person."

The noise-level dropped to silence. Intuko could hear every board member breathing. He took a deep breath, exhaling a sigh. "Please believe me when I tell you I have done a lot of thinking about this."

He turned to Bill Temple on his right-hand side. "These bruises on my face, Bill, are just the catalyst, the open door."

His gaze moved slowly around the room, meeting the eyes of every person in turn.

"I will not leave you without a proper replacement, I promise you that. But over the past few days I've learned some things about myself and I need to deal with some parts of my past that I have neglected and hidden."

Bill coughed.

Intuko cleared his own throat again so he could continue.

Then for twenty minutes he talked–words he never had planned to say. His life became an open book, his past revealed, his wounds left gaping. Everyone sat still, grasping onto every word. At the end of his speech he slowly looked around the table, holding each member's gaze in his for a few moments before he moved on to the next. Then he placed his elbows on the table and clasped his hands together. No one spoke and two men at the end of the table turned their heads to wipe their eyes.

This church, these people, his congregation had been his home, his life, his identity, all had been wrapped up in his job. And now he had officially resigned.

After a few minutes, everyone arose and came over to him to shake his hand. Then they all poured themselves another cup of coffee to better discuss the future of the church.

When the last person left, he headed back to his office to get his own coat. He found Hazel there, waiting with tea and homemade cookies.

"You look tired," she said.

"It was a lot harder than I thought it would be."

She passed the plate of chocolate chip cookies in his direction. "I'm sorry for how I've been acting. It's just that I'll miss you. We'll all miss you."

"Change is hard," said Intuko, taking a cookie. "I love your cookies."

"That's why I made them. What will you do?"

Intuko bit into the cookie, chewing thoughtfully. "I promised the board I'd stay on for six more months," he said after swallowing. "Then I don't know. I have enough money saved to be comfortable for a bit. But that's it."

"Intuko?"

"Yes." He looked at her.

"I know some of this has to do with your face being the way it is but...does any of this have to do with you being back at the prison and your mother?"

He shrugged. "I think so. I don't know."

"Chris...he told me about the girl." Hazel's facial features softened, her eyes showing obvious concern. She touched his arm in a motherly gesture. "What are you going to do with her?"

"Lola asked me to care for Sarah, Hazel, when she came in that day. I know in my heart I need to look for her relatives.

Her dad, Lola told me, is supposedly from Inuvik."

"Will you go there?"

"I have to."

"Promise me something."

"What?"

"That when you go North, you don't just go for her, you go for yourself as well. You need to go home, Intuko, to figure out *your* life."

He smiled at Hazel. "You know me so well. And you always know the right things to say."

Intuko met up with Chris at Hank's after lulling Sarah into dreamland, kissing her cheek and tucking the covers under her chin. Susan was being a good sport but she told him she was tiring of the situation. This couldn't go on much longer. It wasn't fair.

"We could have met at the church," said Chris, sipping a beer. He glanced at the woman on stage.

"I thought we might see Charlie." Intuko propped his elbow on the bar. "We need to talk to him. How does he know Harrison Fleming? I wonder if he was contracted to kill Lola. The other thing is—he put something in the drugs he sold Angie. She bought from him. Was he trying to kill her? And you know, Jimmy may not have killed Lola, but he's involved in this entire drug scene, I'm sure of it. When I last saw Lola, she talked about Jimmy and his friends." Intuko paused. "Now what did you find out about Black?"

"Swanky office, man. Tenth floor, huge glass windows, and I mean all windows, overlooking False Creek. Leather seats, the works. Even a bar in his office. Of course I declined."

"Did he offer?"

"Nah, but I still declined." Chris winked at Intuko.

"So you sweet-talked his secretary and got in to see him?"

"Wasn't easy. I got the standard movie line, 'Mr. Black is a very busy man.'" Chris mimicked. "She was protective, and, this is the clincher–it was so obvious that she's got something going with Black."

"Come on Chris, let's get serious here. How can you see that in a five minute meeting?"

"Intuko, I sat outside his office, chatting with this blond babe for half an hour. I listened and watched. Body language. Facial expressions. I went at her with questions about Black, his family, children, and although I admit she was good, had all the right answers, she wasn't that good. I tell you, I could smell something going on between them. She had the odour of a girl in over her head with her boss. Underneath that silk blouse of hers, the smell of sex was dripping. And I just bet it's kinky stuff too. I could sense and sniff it."

Intuko shook his head. "What was he like when you were in his office with just him?"

"All business. Curt. Busy. I only got about three feet in the door."

"What did you talk about?"

"At first I did my over-eager student spiel about wanting to be just like him. I said I was working construction to find out how everything ran at the bottom level. Then I told him he was my hero, you know, all that crap. He didn't buy it and told me to leave, I was wasting his time. So I asked him point blank if he still stayed in touch with Harrison Fleming."

"What did he say?" Intuko took a sip of his Coke.

"He didn't answer. I think I stumped him. Then he got mad and really told me to leave.

"Again."

"Yeah, again. So I asked him if he owned a black Mercedes. That got him confused 'cause I changed directions so quickly. He answered that one though with a booming 'no.'"

"I hope you left after that."

"I moved about a foot." Chris nodded. "But at the door, I turned and asked if he'd heard about Lola."

Intuko thudded his elbow on the table, dropping his head in his hands and closed his eyes. Black, by now, could have Chris's number. Chris could have put himself at huge risk with this visit and it was all Intuko's fault.

"Hey." Chris shook Intuko's wrist. "Don't you want to know what he said?"

Intuko looked up. "You never should have gone there. You've said to me over and over these men are dangerous, leave it to the police. Why don't you listen to your own advice?"

Chris took a swig of beer then gave a crooked smile, raising his eyebrows. "You and your *investigation* have kind of got the old adrenalin flowing."

Intuko shook his head at Chris.

Chris leaned in and whispered, "For a split second, Black didn't say anything when I asked about Lola. Intuko, he knows her. I saw it in his eyes. He covered real quick and phoned security. I took the back stairs."

"Do you think he killed her?"

Chris shrugged his shoulders. "It's possible. He seemed surprised I mentioned her name. What does he need Lola for when he's got his blond secretary? Unless, they're into the real raunchy stuff. Or unless Jimmy works for him and he gets a deal with her. Maybe he happened to leak something to her then decided to knock her off." Chris scanned the bar, stopping when he hit the far side of the room. "Charlie's over there, by himself," he said quickly. "I think we should wait until he goes, catch him outside."

Intuko glanced quickly in Charlie's direction, then turned back to Chris and nodded. "Okay. Keep talking though, till we see him leave."

"So what'd you learn out in White Rock?" Chris asked,

keeping his eye on Intuko and the back of the bar.

"Black seems to have sold his portion of the land. Harrison still has his. I wished I'd known that before you went to see Black, you could have asked about his land. When he sold it, why, how–all of those question. I did find out the *who* question–he sold it to a woman named Joanne Venus."

"Her last name is *Venus?*"

"She runs a Spiritual Retreat Centre. A new age deal. Her son Eric helps her out."

"What's his last name, Aquarius?"

"The weirdest thing, Chris, is that on Harrison's land there is an old abandoned building. All boarded up, but locked. Why would someone lock an abandoned building?"

"So no one could live in there." Chris arched his eyebrows and patted Intuko on the back.

"Okay, okay. But it doesn't make sense. There's not a lot of street people way out there. Why lock the place?

Chris downed his beer.

Intuko tore his little bar napkin into small pieces.

"He's leaving," said Chris.

Intuko picked up his fleece-lined jean jacket and headed to the door. Stepping outside, he breathed fresh air. Enough smoky bars for him. Charlie stood about twenty feet away from them, glancing up and down the street.

"I'll handle this at first," whispered Intuko. "But I'll need a bouncer."

He walked over to Charlie. "I think you may have dropped this." Intuko held out a twenty dollar bill.

"Thanks man," said Charlie, stuffing the twenty in his jacket pocket.

"You look familiar." Intuko snapped his fingers a few times. "I know," he said shaking his finger. "You told me about the girl in the alley."

Charlie squinted, stared at Intuko's neck, probably

searching for the collar he had on that day. "What are you talking about?"

"Angie Melville. I called the ambulance for her."

"Don't know no one by that name." Charlie scanned the streets, up and down, his eyes little slits of fear.

"Why did you put lethal amounts of ecstasy in the cocaine you sold her?" Intuko spoke low and with as much menace as he could muster.

"What the fuck you talkin' about?" Charlie stepped back, looked around, obviously wanting to take off but Chris grabbed his coat at the neck.

"Hey, let go," hissed Charlie.

"Not until you tell us."

"I don't know nothin'."

Chris lifted Charlie off the ground, his feet dangling, swinging back and forth like boats in the wind. "We know you know something."

"Who are you guys?"

"We're not undercovers." Chris put him down, gripping the neck of his jacket even tighter and shaking him a bit. "We're friends of Angie's."

Charlie glanced up and down the street, biting his lips, moving his eyes back and forth in their sockets. "Angie asked too many questions," he finally whispered. "About Lola. And Lola's kid. They took the kid so Lola would shut up. She walked in on Jimmy. Scared the shit out of her. Then suddenly…she's dead. Angie was gonna get herself killed asking so many questions about Lola."

"Did someone tell you to knock Lola off?"

"Me? No way. It wasn't fuckin' me. I liked Lola." He rapidly shook his head.

"What about Angie? Did someone tell you to kill her?"

"No, man! I had to protect her. Get her off the streets. I didn't know she was scamming. I didn't want to make her go to

the joint. She's better off in there, though. They might have done something to her."

"Who were you protecting her from?"

"I can't. They'll kill me."

"Did you see Lola the night she died?

"No. No."

Chris tightened his squeeze on Charlie's jacket. "You did so see her. She got into Fleming's car, just like you did."

"He goes by Gibby." Charlie's yellow-stained, rotten teeth chattered like stones in a tin can and the whites of his red-streaked eyes burnished in the dull night.

"Who goes by Gibby?"

"Fleming does. Now let me go. I've told you pricks enough."

Chris eased up on the jacket, gave Charlie a gentle push, telling him to get lost.

Intuko watched Charlie walk away at a fast clip, almost as if he would break into a run at any moment. "I'm glad you let him go."

"If I didn't, Intuko, we might have been responsible for a murder."

TWENTY-ONE

The next morning Intuko picked Sarah up for school then once she was settled in her classroom, he phoned Chris.

"What time you want to meet?"

"I just got a call. Fleming cancelled. Or Gibby to the underworld. He's gone out of town. Business. I rescheduled for Monday."

"Monday! That's four days from now."

"That's all I could get. The guy's busy."

"Where's he off to?"

"South America. His assistant said it was missionary related. I have my doubts."

Intuko flipped the page of his day-timer. "This sort of puts a hold on things." He paused. "I may…go…up North," he said slowly, methodically, tapping his schedule. "All I need is a couple of days."

"Go today. It's Thursday. Get Joe from Street People Ministry to come in for Sunday. He's due for his yearly talk."

"Yeah," said Intuko, thinking. "That might work. I'd have to fly to Edmonton then Yellowknife then Inuvik. I bet I could get a flight this morning or mid-afternoon and get a connecting later this afternoon." The thought of being in the North by dinner seemed surreal. He hadn't been home in years and now… he was planning it all in a day. The irony of jet travel.

"I'll do some digging," said Chris.

"Find out all you can about Harrison Fleming, a.k.a Gibby."

"Anything else?"

"Brad Black. His connection to Harrison now. Why he sold his land to that Joanne. Who is this Joanne? Is Venus her real last name? Sounds highly unlikely. And Steven Campbell. What's his story? How is he involved in all of this? One of these guys killed Lola. And it seems they're all a part of the larger picture. This could be huge." Intuko paused. "But Chris, don't go see any of them, just check up on records, newspaper articles, stuff like that. Talk to other people but stay away from them. I think they're dangerous men. I mean, look what happened to Lola. I'm getting bad feelings from all of this."

"Will do boss." Chris paused then said quietly, "Hey, good luck, eh. I'll be praying for you."

And I'll be praying for you, thought Intuko.

Immediately after hanging up from talking to Chris, Intuko booked his flight.

Then he called Susan and Mary to make arrangements for Sarah. Susan was less than enthusiastic but glad he was moving on the situation. He wished he could visit Angie but his flight was leaving at eleven, and visiting hours didn't start until evening. He tried calling her, getting the desk receptionist who informed him that leaving a message was the best he could do.

He left a list of phone numbers for every place he would be staying in the Arctic with Susan, Mary, Hazel, and Chris.

He went to his apartment and packed a small bag.

On his way out to the airport he decided he had time for a visit with Detective Anderson.

Anderson met him at the front desk. "Intuko, no coffee today?"

"I have to go North for a few days. I wanted to let you know in case you tried to get in touch with me."

"Nice of you to check in." He rolled his eyes and crossed his arms.

"Any news…on the gun," whispered Intuko.

"Two sets. Yours and Jimmy's. But it has been confirmed by ballistics as the murder weapon. Unfortunately, it's tampered evidence."

"I don't think Jimmy killed Lola."

"Why do you say that?" Anderson, holding his fingers under his pits, tapped them against his body.

"She was his best girl, she brought him money. Why would he want her dead?"

Anderson nodded, ruefully. "Sometimes you make sense."

"Is it Jimmy's gun?"

"Not registered. It's an overseas import. We'll keep working on that."

"Do you think someone could have hired Charlie to kill Lola? That's why he got into Fleming's car?"

"You ask far too many questions, Intuko."

"What about the car?"

"Can't do right yet. I have nothing to go on except she got in a black Mercedes. Lots of people drive that kind of car. It's worth a tail though and it definitely is a piece of evidence I'll hang on to."

"You're doing a good job," Intuko said seriously.

Anderson raised one eyebrow in a comical gesture. "Thanks. I needed to hear that from *you*. You know, Intuko," Anderson said patting Intuko on the back, "You're okay. Have a good trip. And thanks for dropping by, keeping me informed. You're holding up your end of the bargain."

Next Intuko drove to Sarah's school. Miss Clark allowed Sarah to leave class for a few minutes so he could talk to her. He told her he had to leave for a few days but he would bring her back something special.

When she looked at him she said, "Next time, I want to go with you."

He kissed her forehead. "I promise you that will happen."

Handing his boarding pass to the gate receptionist, Intuko wondered if he would ever be able to fulfill his promise to Sarah. There was a strong possibility that by the time he got home, Susan would have looked into the child services route and Sarah could be heading for a foster home. Earlier this morning, he had phoned to find out how he could adopt Sarah but that's all he had time for. One lousy phone call with someone who explained about the masses of paper work. If he did find Sarah's relatives they would have the first right to the child.

The plane took off with its usual noise and lifting feeling. Intuko peered out the window at the Fraser River with all its boats, filled with logs, moving up and down its length. The day was cold and dreary and the window so small it was impossible to see the mountains. He leaned back in his seat, closed his eyes. Vivid images flashed in his mind, drumming and dancing, drinking and poverty. Good and bad, they were all there, clicking like a slide show.

He flew to Edmonton, waited for an hour then caught the next plane to Yellowknife.

Flying into Yellowknife for his last stop-over, Intuko sat up straight and stared out the window at the lights from the town sparkling like raw uncut diamonds in the darkened polar sky. They stretched quite a distance and looked much like the bright lights of the big city. Yellowknife was no longer a small town, it had grown. But the North hadn't changed, winter remained dark.

He remembered the long winter days, bundled in a parka and fur boots, trudging from the residences to the school in the dark and coming home to his little room later that day, also in the dark. His parka had been royal blue and his grandma had sewn caribou around the hood...or was it beaver fur?

He only had a short time to wait in the Yellowknife Airport before he caught his connecting flight to Inuvik. People walked by him, and he wondered if he would see someone he knew, but he didn't, so he pulled out his note pad and started doodling, writing names. Lola in the middle. Surrounding her was Jimmy, her pimp. Intuko crossed his name off. Joanne Venus. Harrison Gibby Fleming. He circled his name and tapped his pen on each and every letter. Intuko hadn't met the man yet so he couldn't draw any conclusions. Campbell. Black. Charlie. He crumpled the paper and threw it in the garbage. He was going in circles, with not enough information for any conclusions.

Walking across the pavement towards the lobby of the Inuvik airport, Intuko was chilled by the cold winter winds and he turned his collar up to cover his ears and shield part of his face. As soon as he entered the warmth of the small, one-room airport he rubbed his ears and looked around. Immediately, he spotted his cousin's smiling face. Intuko had phoned him to meet him at the airport, even though they hadn't seen each other in years.

As young boys, they had fished and harpooned seal, hour upon hour during the summer months. And in the winter at school, this cousin had protected him, sticking up for him on the playground, fighting the other boys who picked on him. This cousin took the beatings from the priests after they had been caught fighting.

"Tom," said Intuko, holding out his hand. "It's been too long." As adults, the grip between them was firm and faithful regardless of the time apart.

Tom grinned at Intuko. "You've been in the South too long. You've forgotten how to dress."

Intuko slapped his cousin's back. "How long has it been?"

"You want me to do the math? You were the one who got the good grades in numbers. I was the fighter."

222

"Yeah, you were the fighter all right."

Outside, Intuko threw his bag in the back of Tom's truck and rubbed his hands. "I forgot how cold it gets here."

Tom shook his head at Intuko. "You're dressed like a *tanik*. Let's get you home to clothes and caribou soup."

Driving down the main street of Inuvik, population thirty-three hundred, they had to pass the now boarded-up residential school. Right beside that old school stood a newer elementary school. Outside, under bright streetlights as the day was dark, children ran around dressed in their parkas, crunching snow, playing tag and being children. Just like children should be allowed to do without the black robes watching over them like hawks over mice.

"That residential school ain't worth nothin' now," said Tom.

"It wasn't worth anything then either." Intuko liked watching the children play.

"That's for sure. What they did to us was wrong ya know."

"I know. One culture has no right to say another is wrong."

"Ain't that the truth."

At his cousin's house, the caribou meat in the soup bobbed amid rice and hunks of potato. Intuko managed to scoop a big bone, fully covered with meat, from the bottom of the pot. Slicing the meat into slivers he let it melt in his mouth like it was some decadent foreign food.

Before heading outside again, Intuko dressed in Tom's fur-trimmed parka. He also wore a pair of mitts made of wolf fur and tall lace up, caribou-hide boots. Maybe he would have Auntie apply her traditional sewing methods to make a masterpiece for Sarah. Tomorrow he was going to Tuk to visit Auntie.

* * *

When Angie received Intuko's message, just before lunch lock-down, she crumpled it up and threw it in the garbage. What a jerk! She'd seen him last night and he said he might go–why didn't he have the guts to tell her he was leaving the next morning? He'd saddled up beside her yesterday, complimenting her on her art, saying nice things when all along he was conniving to leave in the morning without telling her. All men were the same. They did whatever they wanted not giving a hoot about anyone else's feelings.

She hated him right now.

She threw herself down on the thin mattress of her bed, crossed her arms above her head, digging her face into her flat pillow that smelt of bloody bleach. No luxuries in this joint.

She picked up the pillow and threw it across the room. If she were on the outside, she could have taken Sarah, moved, enrolled her in a decent school, bought her some new clothes, kissed her goodnight every night. Now she wasn't even going to get to see her for a few days because *he* had full control over that situation as well.

Angie punched her mattress. Tomorrow she had to go to court. Her hearing had been bumped.

Her lock clicked.

"Time to go back to work," said the officer, opening her door.

Just after noon, Chris, on a break from work, walked into Hank's and peered through the smoke. He'd been here more times in the past few weeks than he'd been in the two years since he'd met Intuko. The place was less than half-full. He remembered Hank's burger platter being almost as good as White Spot's.

Dressed in a Santa's elf costume, Candice was on, bending over to reveal nothing underneath the short, red skirt but garters and lace panties. As far as Chris was concerned it was a little early for Christmas as it wasn't yet December.

He stared around the bar. No one he knew. Not even Charlie. He'd hoped to catch him again. He ordered a beer and watched Candice until she finished her set, gathered her clothes and strutted off the stage.

A cheeseburger later (loaded with layers of raw onions) Chris slugged back the last sip of his Coke. Still no one he knew. Until Candice, fully dressed with a big bag slung over her shoulder, walked toward him.

"Hi there," she said.

"You look as if you're done for the day."

"I'm just doing one set." She scanned the bar, her eyes shifty slits, and her mouth tight. "My little guy and I are going to a Christmas party later," she said without looking at him.

"Christmas party already. It's only November."

"It's one of those things put on by the city council for single moms. They always have it the end of November." She gave him a little smile, letting her bag drop to the floor.

"Can I buy you a drink?" he asked.

She paused to scan the bar, again. He wondered what was wrong, why she kept looking around. Finally she turned and said, "Yeah, I'll have a double rum and Coke."

"Double?"

"Yeah, what the heck." She shrugged.

With no waitress in sight, Chris walked to the bar to order the double rum and Coke for Candice and a Coke for himself.

When he returned she asked, "So, who are you seeing these days?" She lit a cigarette, her hand shaking.

"An older woman. How about you?" He played with a plastic stir stick.

She took a long, hard sip, almost downing the entire drink before answering. "No one," she said quickly. "Well, I had someone but it's over."

He looked at her, wondering why she was telling him this stuff. "What...happened?" Did she just want to talk?

A glaze covered her eyes. She took another sip of her drink. "Darn good drink. Tastes like a triple."

"Maybe Hank snuck a little extra in for you," said Chris.

"The guy was no good." She took a good drag of her cigarette and blew the smoke out in a huge hurry. "No good at all."

"What do you mean?"

She forced a smile. "You're cute, you know. Real cute."

"As cute as the guy you dumped? You did dump him, right?" Chris arched his eyebrows.

She turned her head.

"Hey." He put his arm around her. "I'm sorry. Tell me who the guy is and I'll beat the crap out of him for you."

When Candice picked up her glass her hand shook so much she spilled rum and Coke down her chin.

"Candice, talk to me. What's going on?"

She bit her bottom lip and scratched at the back of her neck. It was then he saw the bruises surrounding her neck. He had to grit his teeth as he abhorred men who beat women.

She stubbed her cigarette out. "I'm scared," she whispered.

"Scared of what? What did this guy do to you?" His voice was low.

She closed her eyes and shook her head. When she opened them, she looked him straight in the eyes. "I didn't know nothin' when I first saw him. I swear I didn't. He got all pissed last night and he spilled. Drunk talk. He was so out of it, I'm sure he don't remember." She scratched at her neck. "But if he does."

Chris leaned over and lowered his head toward Candice. "What did he say?"

She downed her drink. "I gotta go."

He touched her arm. "Tell me."

She looked up, her eyes welling. "On Wednesday there's more coming in. Crack and heroin from somewhere south." She glanced around the bar then leaned in. "This guy likes a girl on those nights 'cause he's all worked up ya know." Candice stopped, closed her eyes, pressing a trembling hand to her sweaty forehead. "He goes too far. Does real weird stuff." She was shaking. "I've said enough. Anyone sees me talking like this to you and tells him we're both in trouble. I gotta go."

Chris tried to catch her by the forearm, get her to tell him more but she pulled away, picked up her bag and took off out the door. After watching her leave, he threw his own coat over his shoulder and when he turned to wave to Hank, who had a bunch of books spread out on the bar, he saw a man way at the end of the bar staring at him.

"Thanks Hank," Chris said knowing the guy still eyed him. "The burger was great."

"Glad to hear it." Hank waved then went back to his papers.

Chris got the heck out of Hank's. That guy gave him the creeps.

TWENTY-TWO

That night from Inuvik, Intuko phoned Chris but got no answer on either his cell or his home phone. He left a message on his home phone as Chris had no message service on his cell. Worried, he also called the church. No answer there either, but why would there be? It was not a youth night.

Making sure his own cell phone was charged, Intuko decided to head out to the Inuvik Hotel to ask questions about Sarah's relatives. He'd questioned his cousin about Kevin Kudlak, trying to be discreet, and his cousin had scratched his head, thinking he may have known him years ago.

The outside of the Hotel hadn't changed much since he'd been a child visiting Inuvik from Tuk in the summers when he was off school. In his early teens, they would sometimes sneak away from residential school to go to the Hotel, but if they were caught they got beat bad for the evils of drink.

Opening the door, he peered through the smoke, smelling the stale beer. Red terry-cloth table cloths covered small round tables, some with broken legs. The wooden floor, dirty from wet snow, creaked as he walked over to the bar. He thought he recognized some of the people but he didn't stop to say hello. He had a mission to accomplish, the extent of his visit to the hotel.

He walked up and ordered a Seven-up. The bartender raised a sarcastic eyebrow but slid the drink in his direction anyway.

Then Intuko waited, sipping his drink for five minutes before he said, "You wouldn't know where I could find Kevin

Kudlak?"

"Who?"

"Kevin Kudlak."

"Never heard of him." The bartender yelled down the bar, "Hey, Sam, you ever hear of a Kevin Kudlak?"

Sam, an old weathered white-guy, probably a rig worker who never left, with few teeth in his head lisped, "Kudlak. Lots of 'dem in Inuvik." He swallowed a sip of draft beer. "Dat guy gone." He waved his hand. "All drunked up, hit a ditch."

Intuko walked down to the end of the bar, not wanting to yell like the bartender did so the entire bar could hear everything he had to say.

"Would you know anything about his family?"

"Nope." Sam gummed his lips together. "Some 'uder Kudlak's died in a fire."

Fire, accident. This guy was a dead end. Intuko left a tip on the bar. From the RCMP detachment office or from the government offices on Mackenzie Road he could probably dig up some information on the Kudlak's. He probably could have checked this information in Vancouver but...then he wouldn't have come North.

He slapped Sam gently on the back. "Thanks, man."

When he turned to leave, he saw her, propped up in the corner, drunk as drunk, fat, unkempt, slobber dripping down her chin. Ruby. His sister.

He almost choked on his own breath. Hesitantly, he walked over to her.

"Ruby," he said.

"Who's dat?" She lifted her head, weaving, eyes covered in a blue film that resembled skim milk.

"Ruby, it's Intuko."

"Intuko. Long time no see. Wadch' you doin' here?"

"I came to see Auntie. I'm going to Tuk tomorrow for a

visit."

"You ain't been round dese parts for years."

"No." Intuko shook his head. "I haven't Rub."

"Buy me a drink, would ya."

"I can't Ruby."

"What good are ya, den." She flopped her head back, rolling her eyes into the back of her head.

Intuko stared at her for a split second, feeling sick to his stomach, then abruptly turned and headed to the door. He had to get outside.

The air outside was frigid, colder than Intuko could remember. With no light pollution the constellations showed clearly, almost as if shown through a magnifying glass. He breathed in, the cold sinking deep, jabbing at his lungs. His sister was still a drunk. Life in the North was still harsh. Breathing out, his breath sat in front of his face, a cloud of white frosty air and silver crystals.

He pulled the hood from his parka over his head, feeling the fur tickle his skin. It smelt raw, natural, pure, bringing back memories of the land extending for miles, hunting caribou. He thought of Sarah. She had Inuvialuit blood in her; it flowed through her even though she'd never been North.

Blood was blood.

She had awakened something in him; old songs, indigenous words, visions of a land that he had forgotten. Her eagerness to hear him sing had reminded him of his upbringing. His true soul. Lola had been right to ask him to care for her, and he had to return Sarah's heritage to her as she had returned it to him.

Angie lay on her bed listening to her cell door lock. She clamped her jaw tightly together, top teeth grinding against bottom teeth, and closed her eyes. Every time she closed her eyes she thought of Lola, saw a picture of the two of them sharing a bottle and telling stories. Lola drunkenly talked about having a baby, wanting a little girl she could dress in fancy little dresses and take to birthday parties at nice homes where people owned furniture and ate dinner together at night. Angie told her she talked crazy and that kind of dream life didn't exist. Now, Lola was dead. Never would she have her fairy tale life or any life for that matter. Angie hated thinking about Lola but hated thinking about her own childhood even more, and her own unborn baby.

Night set in and with it came a darkness that was unlike any other darkness Angie had ever felt. It was almost worse than her first few nights on the streets. The black stalked her like a sniffing, long tailed rat, crawling over her head and along her body making her want to scream. Its dark beady eyes shone, looking inside to steal her guard, her only defence in life.

She awoke screaming, howling like a wild animal in pain caught in a trap. Trembling, gasping for breath, she sat up. She quickly looked around, half expecting to see the woman in the long dark hair. But only shadows danced precariously, provocatively.

Someone rapped on her window. "Are you all right in there?"

Angie got up, her legs feeling like the vanilla pudding they'd tried to give for dinner, and walked toward the door. The voice sounded like her mother. She used to beg Angie to come to her bedside and unzip her dress or comb out her hair. Usually, she smelled of booze, stale cigarettes and vanilla-musk perfume. As a four-year-old, Angie would ease her mother into bed and tuck the covers under her chin. Then she would pad back to her own room where she tucked herself in. Those innocent years had passed in a blur and as she got older she ignored her mother calling to her, plugging her ears instead to muffle the begging, cajoling voice. By the age of eight, she hated everything about her mother, even her vanilla-musk perfume.

The voice at the door wasn't her mother and Angie wasn't four years old any more, aching for her mother to read her a bed time story.

"Are you okay in there?" an officer said quietly as she opened Angie's cell door. Angie knew her name was Susan Peterson and that she was temporarily looking after Sarah.

"Yeah."

The officer nodded and was about to shut the door when Angie said, "Wait, Guard. How's Sarah?"

"She's fine."

"Any news?"

"News?"

"From Intuko. Up North?"

"Not yet. He just left today. I'll let you know when he calls though. He did try to reach you. Wanted you to know he left."

"I bet," said Angie.

"It's true," said Ms. Peterson. "For what it's worth, I think he cares about you and your outcome."

"Why? Why would anyone care about me?"

"You care about Sarah. Maybe what goes around really does come around. Don't blow it with him, he's a good man."

After her door locked again, Angie crawled under her covers. The light outside her cell went out and once again she fell into the black hole of night. When she lay between the sheet and scratchy blanket, the strength coming from her big talk seemed to fly away like a crow with a mouthful of garbage. Her bed felt like a pool of liquid. She couldn't help think about what that officer had said about Intuko.

He cared for her.

Then Angie thought about her parents. Were they still together? Was her mother still a beautiful woman having fancy parties? Or did the abuse of the vodka she snuck in her orange juice every morning, show on her face? She'd probably had plastic surgery to take away any unsightly lines. She hadn't seen or talked to her parents in almost ten years. What would they say if they found out she was having a baby?

Tomorrow she went to court. Angie squeezed her eyes shut. Wanting to sleep. But she couldn't.

Opening them, she flinched.

For sitting on the end of her bed was the woman again, in her blue parka and fur boots. Around her neck, hanging from a strap and resting on the wool of her coat, was the carving of the mother with the baby on her back. Same as Intuko's.

"Who are you?" Angie whispered.

"Who am I—that's a good question. For my entire human life I didn't know who I was because I tried to be someone else."

"Everyone thinks I'm crazy because of you."

"Since I died, this is where I've had to live. I'm a prisoner to this room, to the earth, and…I want to be free, to walk where I belong. I want to go back to my home to rest among the foxes, caribou, tundra, and snow. My freedom will only come when I have helped someone else, and so far every woman who has occupied this room has not been able to loosen themselves from the chains that bind them. I believe you are different."

"No," whispered Angie.

The woman took off her necklace and laid it on the bed. "This is for you."

Angie stared at the carving then she reached out and touched it, letting her fingertips glide over its smoothness. "You're making me crazy."

The woman lowered her head, almost in a prayer-like pose. "I don't want to do that. I know that feeling. I want to help you love, find fulfilment as a human being and in turn share that others. Like the man, the one who carves."

"How do you know about him?"

When the woman looked up, Angie caught her eyes. Such sadness. Tears slowly ran down the woman's cheeks. Angie shivered and moved back, toward the wall, to get away from the pain.

"I didn't give him the love he deserved. I regret it terribly. Please, tell him I love him." The woman disappeared.

Angie flopped back on the bed to stare at the ceiling, clutching the necklace in her hand. Dry tears pooled in the desert behind her eyes.

In the morning, first thing, Intuko tried Chris again, hoping to wake him. No answer. He left another message on his answering machine. And another and another.

Then he dressed in his parka and mitts and trudged downtown. Intuko spent the morning searching records, finding everything he needed within a few hours. Last night, old Sam in the hotel had told the truth; Sarah's paternal family was dead. There had been a fire.

He phoned Susan, told her the news and told her to tell Angie as he could only leave messages, never get through to actually talk to her. He asked her if she'd seen Chris. Not recently, she said. But she'd ask Mary.

Then he talked to Sarah. She seemed withdrawn and she wanted him to come back so she could go see Angie again; she'd made her a present at school. Could he pick her up from school on Monday? He said, yes, of course, he would be back by then and he'd bring her something.

Even though he had everything he needed to help his case with Sarah, Intuko felt ill knowing this child had no family left. He understood the life of an orphan.

He almost felt as if he should cut his trip short to see if Chris was all right, but yet he wanted to visit his home, say hello to his Auntie.

Stand on his childhood land. Tuktoyaktuk land.

After all these years, he couldn't fly all this way and not go to Tuk.

Angie looked at the judge dressed in black, gripping his mallet with a vice-grip and smacking it on his wooden desk. He shovelled the people in and out of the courtroom as if they were meat in a packing plant. He reminded her of her father.

Angie's childhood memories brewed inside her like a batch of the bad wine some of the women at the prison tried to make by hoarding fruit and letting it rot. She watched a guy with hair down to his shoulders and rings in his nose get sentenced to eighteen months for theft.

She knew full well when she stood before the judge she would have to act subdued and sorry if she wanted a lighter sentence. But she was sorry. Sorry for not being there for Sarah, sorry for Lola, sorry for…she touched her stomach. She sat tall in her seat.

She closed her eyes. A baby, at this precise moment, was growing inside of her and if things went badly today she might never…she couldn't go there.

"Angela Sarah Melville." The name boomed from somewhere making Angie jerk in her seat. The lawyer on her left stood and nodded for her to follow.

She stood. This was it.

TWENTY-THREE

By mid-afternoon, the sun, now a tiny arc on the horizon, looked much like the embers of coals, hours after the burning flames of the fire had disappeared. Intuko's cousin, Tom, veered the truck from the main snow-covered road to the ice road. Earlier, Intuko had repeatedly tried Chris but had gotten no answer, even Hazel hadn't seen him. And Susan hadn't been able to reach Mary. Mary wasn't scheduled to babysit Hilary and wasn't home to answer Susan's call.

Feeling the need to remain silent, Intuko stared out the truck windows at the land spread out like a desert of whiteness, flat and untouched, the snow in the distance pure, absolute. He marvelled at the blue-grey ice they traveled on, at the hardness of the river water, and its ability to hold their truck and the bigger semi-truck that passed them on the other side.

They bounced over and through the ruts in the road, the ice having been chipped from the pressure of vehicles. By the end of the winter months some of the ruts would be huge craters, large enough to damage the bottom of a car or truck.

The long slick road stretched out in front of them, distending like a huge tentacle. Initially, the road traveled along the Mackenzie River, evergreen trees with their branches laden with snow stood stoically on either side. As they continued their drive, the trees thinned until they drove past the tree line and the vegetation turned into low rambling, unruly brush. It sprawled out, resembling large brown and white cotton balls or snow-covered over-sized prairie tumbleweeds.

Within an hour or so, the river bed widened and they

headed toward the mouth of the Arctic Ocean. Finally, Intuko said, "Could we stop for a few moments? I need to stand outside."

"Sure thing," said Tom.

He drove the truck over to the side of the road and Intuko stepped out. When his feet hit the ice he looked down and saw layer upon layer of a crystalline formation. With his head down, he walked, staring at the ice below him. After thirty feet or so, he stopped and looking up, the wind hit him like a hammer, smacking his skin, the temperature being at least forty below, if not colder with the wind chill factor. He pulled his hood up so the caribou fur surrounding the hood pressed against his reddened cheeks.

He walked even further away from the truck venturing onto the virgin snow, and toward the beginning of nowhere.

The sun in the west appeared as a smidgen on the horizon line, its yellow hue smeared with orange and a tinge of violet. He sucked in a deep breath of cold air, remembering the hunts with his grandfather, running beside the dogs, never winded, free as a lone bird flying high in the sky. He had only been around Sarah's age then. Only his grandfather, so set in his ways, had used the dogs. Even then, ski-doos were used for hunting, making life easier. No more dog lines to untangle, no more dogs to shoot because they couldn't keep up. Life had to progress, Intuko understood that but...did the freedom have to vanish?

He looked into the distance, into the infinity of snow and timelessness, and immediately knew his answer. Man was chained by his own self and freedom today was as tangible as it was yesterday. This land was still undaunted.

He thought about Harrison and Hope Fleming and how they might be involved in crime. And for what? Money? And Hope possibly involved with Steven Campbell. Infidelity. And Brad Black, city council man. Condo developer. Why did he need money from drugs? Or did the drug money buy all his condos? And he thought about Lola. Sweet Lola. What made her sell her body for money? Why had she been left with so few choices in her life?

The sun reflecting off the snow created patterns, lines and circles were scattered haphazardly, everywhere and anywhere, creating crazy blueprints in the snow. Every one different. Just like people. Intuko stared at the deviations in the snow remembering a time when he would weave a story from the different patterns on his way home from school. Now he couldn't remember one single story he'd created in his own imagination. Where had all his dreams gone?

Suddenly the snow crystals warped, turning to pictures. Jimmy, Steven Campbell, Hope and Harrison Fleming, Brad Black, and Joanne Venus all huddled in a circle. Charlie stood with Lola and Luc and Elizabeth. Lola smiled, her teeth straight. Then they all joined together to stand in a circle, linking arms, rocking back and forth.

The picture faded and changed to Hope and Harrison standing, clinging to each other. Intuko's white fox surrounded them, circled them, holding them together like glue. His fox stared at them, without snarling or raising a lip and started to run around them. Faster and faster. Hope waved to Steven. The fox jumped over the hymn books at Princess Street United Church. Drums sounded in Intuko's mind. He felt himself sinking, lower. Was he going to the Lowerworld? Was he going on a shaman journey?

He heard a horn beep, jolting him back to the present. He waved to Tom and walked back to the truck. What were the spirits trying to tell him?

Inside the cab the heat blasted through the vents and he sat back to contemplate his visions and the rest of the journey.

"Tuk's not far," said Tom quietly.

"Yeah," said Intuko. "So much is coming back to me. I

haven't been on this road in a long time."

They passed old landmarks along the banks, fishing huts, rock formations, small cabins deserted for the winter. Intuko remembered traveling this exact same route by boat during the summer months to go to Auntie's cabin. It had been one room with an outhouse out back but they had fished and harpooned seal all day. The thought of her smiling face, her leathery skin weathered from time and life, made him smile. "We're almost there." He pointed out the window.

"Yup, one more bend and we'll see the smoke from the houses," replied Tom. "You're awful deep in thought, Intuko."

Intuko nodded. Then he proceeded to tell him about Lola and Sarah. And all his clues regarding the murder.

"Think of it like a hunt, Intuko. You know where the herd is but you gotta focus on the right animal, the one you know you can shoot. If you focus on the wrong animal, it gets away and you're left with nothin'. Sounds like you got the herd, but you're too focused on the herd and not the kill."

Intuko nodded his head, thinking.

Tom drove straight off the ice road and onto the main road of the tiny hamlet of Tuktoyakatuk. Population 950; just a micro speck on the big map of the human race.

Their first stop was Auntie's place. She lived in a house that looked the same as every other house for they were shipped up in pieces from the South. Do-it-yourself houses. All the houses stood on stilts because of the perma-frost. Three ski-doos were parked out front of her house and a deer lay on the front lawn stiffened from the cold, dried blood frozen on brown fur.

"Come on, Intuko," said Tom, patting him on the shoulder. "Auntie is going to be so happy to see you. She asks about you all the time."

Intuko walked up the rickety stairs and into the one-level, two bedroom house. A black wood-burning stove stood at the entrance like a large statue and provided enough heat for the entire house.

"Intuko!" A little woman shuffled down the hall. "It 'as been long."

"Auntie!" Intuko bent over and hugged his aunt. Her back curved more than he remembered, her teeth were now completely gone, her lines etched deeper in her brown skin, but she smiled, lighting up the room with her welcome for her nephew...as if he'd never left. The years dissolved into a tiny moment in time. And Intuko was home.

That night in Tuktoyaktuk, Intuko attended the drum dancing competition at the community center. As soon as the ceremonies began he became mesmerized by the dancing of the young children. They danced for their hamlets, in full gusto, hoping to win some coveted points. The solid primary colors of their costumes, the music, the way they silently moved, their bodies shifting, flying in perfect harmony to the sound of the beating caribou drum overwhelmed him.

Religion had tried to destroy this part of the Inuit culture, but now, years later, it was fortunately being brought back. By the children. All their parkies were ornately embroidered and adorned with fur, which they helped sew with their mothers and grandmothers.

Traditional values gave a person a sense of pride. Intuko straightened his shoulders.

After the children danced, they posed with pride for pictures, their beaded headdresses poised like tiaras on their foreheads.

Sitting along the side on an old wooden bench beside an elder, Intuko couldn't help but overhear the older man talking to a young girl of probably eight or nine. "We haven't done this sort of thing for over forty years," his voice feebled, "and you, my child, are bringing back a lot of wonderful memories to an old man. Thank you. Thank you for dancing."

The next morning, Iris was already in the kitchen, humming away to herself, when Angie arrived, still in a state of shock. She grabbed her hair net off the peg.

"How are you today?" Iris asked.

"Lousy."

"You'll be okay."

"How do you know if I'll be okay or not? You live in this body?"

"I've got some news," Iris said rather perkily, like a fresh brewed cup of coffee.

Angie was about to retort when she saw the smile that covered every inch of the woman's face. "What's up?"

"I had me a visitor last night."

"Yeah, so." Angie put on her apron and went over to the board to see what her job was for the day.

"My daughter came to see me," Iris said softly.

"Your daughter?" Angie turned to look at Iris. "I thought you didn't know where your kids were." She took a head of romaine lettuce from the refrigerator.

"She went through some agency to find me," Iris said. "I can't believe it. She says she's going to stay in touch and come visit me every month. She's done real well for herself. The family she went to were good to her. But she still wants to have some kind of relationship with me."

Instead of shredding lettuce, Angie stared at Iris who had a mound of chicken in front of her and was tearing the skin off the raw meat, her arms moving like a mixer on high speed.

"You should see her," said Iris, her words a steady stream of thought. "She's pretty, nothing like me. And smart too. She goes to college, you know. She might have my eyes though. I know we're going to have to take it one step at a time. She still calls the people who took her in Mom and Dad. That hurt but,

241

hell, at least I've seen her and I'm going to see her again."

Angie leaned forward, her belly touching the counter and for a second just stared at her lettuce as if it might at any moment jump and skip out of her sight. Then she glanced up and said, "I'm happy for you, Iris."

Iris stopped de-boning the chicken to study her face. "You really mean it, don't you?"

"I wouldn't say it if I didn't."

"Things have a way of working out, you'll see."

If only Angie could believe that.

First thing Intuko did when he awoke was phone Chris's phones. Still no answer. Where was he? He phoned him at his place of work but found out there hadn't been any construction work for a few days because of the weather. Intuko checked with Hazel once again and she hadn't seen Chris either. At the Correctional Institute he left an urgent message for Susan.

Intuko had to get home to Vancouver. He'd done what he had to do in Inuvik and he'd visited Tuk. He tried the airport in Inuvik, in the hopes of getting a flight out later in the evening. There was one flight out but his cousin had some work to do in Tuk and by the time they drove the ice road back, Intuko wouldn't have time to get on that flight. He thought of hiring a little plane to fly him back to Inuvik but his resources were so limited. He called anyway to the one pilot he knew only to find out they couldn't get him back to Inuvik in time either.

His stomach in knots, he dressed warmly in his cousin's parka and went out for a walk. He pulled his hood up to shelter his face, the snow crunching under his feet as he headed down the main road.

He curved off the main drag to walk along the frozen shoreline of the Arctic Ocean. Like a lone hunter, he stopped to view the landscape, imprint it in his mind for when he returned to Vancouver. Just staring ahead at the vast whiteness stilled his mind, allowing him to conjure up other images and sounds like...laughter which rang in his ears like church bells. It was the sound of his mother's voice, calling him in for some *muktuk,* whale blubber.

A whale had been harpooned and the families had cut it up to share and distribute. *Muktuk* had always been like candy to Intuko and he eagerly sucked on his treat, letting the fat from the blubber run down his chin. His mother had been young then, maybe twenty. In the North it wasn't at all unusual for a girl to have a baby at thirteen.

The laughter in his mind stopped. He shook his head and turned, looking away from the icy ocean to the small hamlet and its sparse buildings. Up on a hill and directly to his right hand side, there was a small cemetery. Tiny white crosses, all close together, (as the perma-frost made it impossible to actually bury the dead) were lined up in rows. The church had set up the cemetery. His people preferred to offer the bodies of the dead to the spirits out on the land. He trudged away from the icy shore, walking up a small bank to reach the cemetery. Searching its grounds, he couldn't find a cross with his mother's name on it, anywhere.

He found a small open spot with no cross and knelt on the ground, the hard snow digging into his bony knees. He wanted to bury her, to let her be free from the confines she died in, give her life again. He wanted her to live in spirit in this magnificent land where she had been born. He bowed his head.

When he finally raised his head, he noticed he was not alone in the cemetery. On the far side stood an elder of the community dressed in traditional parkie adorned with beading and tassels. On his hands he wore white fox-fur gloves.

Intuko moved toward the man and his feet crunched the ground beneath him, crackling the air with sound. At first when he approached the stranger, neither of them said anything, at least not out loud. Finally, Intuko said softly, "Do you come here often?"

The elder slowly nodded. "It is where I journey."

"Are you communing with the spirits?" Intuko spoke quietly knowing the subject of spirits was still considered by many to be taboo.

The elder's eyes narrowed and he pressed his lips together.

Intuko continued, "I believe the spirits are communing with us right now. They are watching over our talk, rejoicing in our meeting."

", yes. So much has been taken from us. I have seen so much hurt to our people. But always, spirit lives." The elder raised his arms and looked outwards to the white desert of timelessness.

Intuko nodded, inhaling to absorb the powerful energy surrounding this man. When he exhaled he said, "My grandmother taught me about the spirits. But she died before I went on a journey. I think, lately, I've been close to leaving, traveling to the Lowerworld."

Again the man eyed him, although this time not as warily.

"Are you a shaman too?" Intuko asked so quietly he was sure he hadn't been heard.

The elder looked at him and slowly raised his fingers to his lips. "*Shh.* Yes, my man, I am one of the last. When I go, there will be no one. My heart feels sad, we are losing this part of our people."

A sudden wave of energy flowed through Intuko like a zapping of electrical wires. "No," he said. Then he took a deep breath to slow down his breathing. "That…is where you're wrong." This was why he was back here. "I will be returning to visit here from time to time, maybe even stay. Will you teach me the ways?"

"Ahh." The elder nodded, evenly and said surely, "I was called here today by the spirits. They knew. You go, my boy, and listen. Not with your head, with your heart. The spirits will help you find love with the right lady, the one you truly love, and they will tell you who killed your friend, so you can honour her spirit too. Then you come see me and I will take you on your journey."

Then he turned and walked away, leaving Intuko speechless.

TWENTY-FOUR

Sunday morning. Jimmy arose. He put on a pair of black pants and a clean shirt, gelled his hair back with a black comb and grabbed his leather jacket. A fat, dark-haired woman still slept in his bed and he kicked her side. "Be gone by the time I get back," he hissed.

The cold air outside felt like a hurricane against his throbbing headache. Too early to be up.

When was the last time he'd been to church? Had he ever been to church? There was always a first for everything. He had to find out if that little prick of a minister worked at Princess Street United Church. That's the only info he'd found out about the guy. Geez, he wanted to knock out his knees to get back his CZ75. The sharpest, sweetest gun he'd ever had.

He spun his tires, squealing away from the curb.

Sunday morning. Before he boarded his plane at the Inuvik airport Intuko phoned Chris, praying as he punched in every number on the phone. Chris answered after the second ring, his voice booming with energy.

"Where have been?" Intuko barked without even saying hello.

"Intuko, good to talk to you too."

"I've been worried sick about you," said Intuko. "Where were you?"

"I took off for a few days. Went up the coast to Squamish. Had to get away."

"Alone?"

"No. Not alone."

"Who with then?"

"What is this, the third degree? Mary came with me. We were having such a good time we stayed at a B&B."

Intuko sighed. "I'm sorry, Chris. I don't mean to delve into your private life, but man oh man you had me scared. Did you get my messages? Why didn't you have your cell on?"

"It died on the way up and I didn't have my charger. And yeah, I got all nine messages you left here. We drove back this morning for church. I literally just walked through the door ten minutes ago and I was going to call you on my way to church."

Intuko looked out the window of the airport and saw people boarding the small aircraft he was to fly on. "I'll be back in Vancouver tonight," he said. "I'm glad you're okay."

There was silence on the other end for a second before Chris said, "I had to get away, Intuko. I had some bad vibes. I'm sorry I worried you. Thanks for caring."

Monday morning. Intuko and Chris met outside Divine Intervention Church. The rain slopped in the dull grey clouds like water in a balloon.

"It's good to have you back." Chris slapped Intuko on the back. "I've got news for you." Chris whistled through his teeth.

"What's up?"

"Jimmy, Lola's pimp, was at church yesterday."

"What? At Princess–"

"Yeah. Weird eh? He only stayed for around ten minutes though. As soon as Joe got up to speak, he left. I think he was looking for you."

"I took his gun."

"*You what?*"

"I took a pistol when we had that–"

"Geez, Intuko. Why would you do something like that?

247

Where is it now?"

"With the police. It matches the gun that killed Lola. But I don't think he killed Lola. Tell me what you found out before we go in this church."

"You make me nervous."

"Me! What about you? Taking off like you did."

"Okay, okay, are we even now?"

"I was stupid taking the gun, I know," said Intuko. "I just saw it and grabbed it. Did you find anything out before you went away up the coast?"

"I had a weird chat with Candice. She told me she found out from this jerk she was dating that there's a big shipment of drugs coming in Wednesday. I guess he was so drunk she doesn't think he remembers telling her."

"Wednesday? Anderson needs to know this."

"She also said this scumbag likes his women on the nights the drugs come in. Said he goes too far."

"Too far?"

"I think Candice was implying he killed a girl."

"Was it Lola? *Who's the guy?"*

"I tried to get her to tell me. I even went to her place later on, but she freaked on me. Totally lost it. I'm thinking he's someone we all know. But I gotta leave her alone. She's got a little guy."

"Can you get her to talk to the police?"

Chris shook his head. "She's freaked and I mean freaked."

"Don't talk to her any more. I don't feel very good about this." Intuko's stomach felt sick. "Is that why you took off? Did you think the guy was on to you?"

"Yeah," Chris said softly.

"You got to be careful. Anything else?"

"I found a newspaper article, in the White Rock Times, on Harrison Fleming and the Seed of Life Church. It mentioned his first wife Joanne. I made a few phone calls and found out

Joanne Venus used to be Joanne Fleming."

"Are you kidding? She was married to Harrison? The guy's had two wives."

"Yup. Apparently, they must have been married during the Seed of Life time and split the same time the church split. I figured that out when I read another article on him, in the Vancouver Sun Saturday religious section. It was all about his Divine Intervention and he was listed as engaged. Hope apparently is the daughter of a preacher from somewhere in the States. It's interesting that Joanne lives on Black's portion of the land and not Harrison Fleming's. I think there may have been some hanky-panky going on between her and Black. Maybe that was the cause of the split. But that's just an assumption."

"She has a son," said Intuko. "He works for her."

"Yeah, his name is Eric G. Venus. I looked up the Spiritual Retreat Website and he was listed as a partner."

"Was Black listed as a partner?"

"Nope."

"I wonder who this Eric's father is. He doesn't go by Fleming or Black." Intuko pursed his lips for a moment. Then he asked, "Do you think the split could have been calculated? A fake move to give them all the perfect set-up to operate a drug ring?"

Chris shrugged, surveying the massive Divine Intervention Church. "I don't know." He shoved his hands in his pockets. He winked at Intuko. "Come on old man, let's go see what we can find out. But promise me, you won't take a thing."

Intuko and Chris followed a woman down the same hall they went with Steven Campbell but made a right turn instead of a left. For this morning's visit, Intuko had returned his collar to his neck, and he moved his neck, tugging at it, trying to make it comfortable.

When they entered the big library-type room, Intuko saw Harrison Fleming sitting in an over-sized, moss-green and rust plaid chair with Hope Fleming standing behind him, hands on his shoulders. Harrison arose and stuck out his hand.

"Praise the Lord. How wonderful to meet another man of faith. It is truly remarkable that our Lord can bring us together like this."

"Amen," said Hope.

Harrison's handshake was firm enough to almost crush the bones in Intuko's hand. "I feel privileged to meet you, both of you."

Intuko took Hope's hand in his, her handshake limp. She gave him brief eye contact before she bowed her head.

When Chris shook hands with Harrison, he did so with such gusto that Intuko thought they both might get some sort of whiplash.

"Have a seat and we'll bow our heads in a wonderful word of prayer to Our Lord and Saviour Jesus Christ." Harrison ushered them to a plush, moss-green, leather sofa.

Hope sat in an uncomfortable-looking, wing-backed chair and Harrison returned to his over-sized chair. Hope looked younger than on television, and exotically darker with her hair flowing to her shoulders, curving into her face, her dark eyes rimmed with perfect make-up and her lips crimson like beets. She sat with her hands clenched in her lap, her back completely straight. Before he closed his eyes, Intuko tried to find the connection between her and the woman in Bailey's.

"Dear Lord and Saviour Jesus Christ, we gather here today to sing our praises to the heavens, to you our God," Harrison's loud voice boomed.

Intuko opened his eyes, (he couldn't help himself), and watched Harrison raise his shaking hands to the sky and Hope whisper, *Amen, Amen,* over and over. Intuko caught Chris's gaze, he also had his eyes open. Chris raised both eyebrows and faked a slice at his throat with his hand.

Intuko nodded his head then scanned the room. On the wall, he saw a framed-in-gold version of the picture outside the church, Harrison and Hope and children. There were also other family pictures; Hope and the children; Hope and, (he presumed), her parents; a wedding picture of Hope and Harrison; Harrison and possibly his parents; and an older picture of Harrison standing in a field holding a little boy of around five on top of his shoulders. Harrison looked younger in the picture, no grey hair yet, and he appeared happy, his hands wrapped around the child's ankles for support.

Harrison's prayer reached a fevered pitch and Intuko squeezed his eyes shut to ignore the cosmetic words, saying his own silent prayer, thanking God.

"Amen."

"Amen."

"Amen." Intuko raised his head. Hope and Harrison, as if rehearsed, lifted their heads at precisely the same time and smiled, pearly-white teeth shining in the fluorescent lights.

"Now, what can I do for you gentlemen?" Harrison folded his hands in his lap.

Intuko went into his poor church spiel, building Divine Intervention to the hilt, hoping for some sort of advice from such a successful church on the music program and board structure. Chris listened, nodded his head and added a few words now and again.

For the most part, Harrison's suggestions were valid and helpful and Intuko made notes, wanting to make a few changes before leaving, make the transition for whoever took over easier.

After fifteen minutes, Harrison stood, leaned over and grabbed Intuko's hand in both of his, shaking it firmly. "I hope I've been of some help. Thank you for coming. The Lord be with you."

"Amen," said Hope.

Intuko smiled. "I think I should be the one thanking you. You've helped me a lot. I'd love to buy you coffee one day, hear your stories about your tent ministry. I've been out that way, driven by your land."

Harrison smiled, as if reliving pleasant memories. "That was a wonderful time. We saved so many people under those tent awnings."

"You went from Seed of Life to your tent ministry. Did you keep the name for your tent services?"

Harrison shook his head, wistfully almost, his gaze resting on the wall. "It had to be changed."

Both Chris and Intuko followed Fleming's gaze to the photos framed on the wall. Intuko walked over to the pictures, pointing to the photo of Harrison holding the boy on his shoulders. The child looked like the child in the photo in Campbell's office.

"Is this the land? Where you held your tent ministry?" Intuko couldn't help study the boy in the picture, how he held Harrison's hair in his tiny fists to keep from falling, how he smiled for the camera, how happy he seemed to be with Harrison. Intuko thought of Sarah, how much he wanted to see her, pick her up from school and take her for lunch and to the mall. Today they were going shopping for a bed, a dresser, movies, toys and food. Kid food.

Intuko stepped back from the photo to see Harrison move toward Hope, link his arm through hers, pat her hand. Chris moved closer to Intuko, to look at the photo.

Fleming nodded. "We'd like to build a rehabilitation centre on that land now," said Harrison. "The architectural plans are drawn already. We want it to be more than a detoxification centre, though. We want it to be a place where those inflicted can heal and find the Lord."

"We know of a woman who was murdered recently." Chris tapped the photo. "She would have done well to be at your rehab centre." He turned to Harrison, looking him square in the eyes. "Her name was Lola."

Intuko studied Harrison, expecting to see darting eyes or a flinch, any indication that he recognized the name. Nothing. The guy was a great actor.

"We should stay in touch," said Harrison. "Working in the East side of town, you would know of those needing help."

"You ever frequent our area? Drive your black Mercedes around the block, visit the shelters?" Chris, nonchalant in his approach, amazed Intuko with his fox-like quickness.

"Not enough, I'm afraid," said Harrison, shaking his head. He surveyed his room, his desk, the files piled neatly. "There is so much to do here." He pressed his lips together and knitted his brows, thinking.

Chris and Intuko exchanged glances while waiting.

"I don't think I'd want to drive, anyway," Harrison said, finally. "I'd want to walk, reach out a hand to help. Sometimes I feel so bogged down by paperwork and I know I'm not doing what the Lord intended me to do. I reached so many more people when I was with the tent ministry."

"I know what you mean," said Intuko, thoughtfully.

Chris returned his gaze to the picture. "How do the neighbours feel about your plans?"

"We're praying they'll see them through." Harrison looked at his watch. "I'm sorry gentleman, I have another meeting soon. I've enjoyed your visit. You've made me think."

"Who's the boy?" asked Intuko.

The room hushed, a still silence taking over, as if the molecular components of the air had stopped moving for a moment. Finally, Intuko heard Harrison breath, pushing the air back into motion.

"That's my son, Eric," whispered Harrison. "He's one

lamb I pray for every day."

"Amen," said Hope quietly.

Angie smoked a cigarette in the rotunda. She'd quit for a few days but after the judge ruled her case, she'd started again. She drew the smoke deep into her lungs, slouched in her seat. What difference did it make now?

Loud-mouthed Sherry sat a few seats down. Angie cringed listening to her grating voice. There wasn't a soul she liked in this crummy place. She took another drag.

"I heard there's crack coming in tomorrow," said Sherry.

Angie slit one eye to see who Sherry was talking to; a mousy-looking, skinny woman whose hands shook as she tried to smoke. "Can you get me a fix?" the woman begged, desperate.

"I made a call. My friend will visit and hoop it for me."

"I need some. Bad. I need some." The woman trembled, sucking so hard on her cigarette Angie thought she might swallow it whole.

Sherry leaned back, thinking she was the big-shot.

The woman ran a finger through her greasy hair. "Please. I'll do your laundry for a week."

"Two weeks and you got a deal."

Angie saw Intuko and Sarah in the visiting room before they saw her for another open visit. For a moment she stood at the window and watched them; their heads bowed together, a book open in Sarah's lap, Intuko running his fingers under the words while reading aloud.

Sarah didn't need Angie.

Angie was about to leave, head back to her cell when Sarah suddenly looked up, pointing in her direction. Angie gave a feeble wave and forced a smile.

Sarah came running.

Angie squatted down, hugging her, closing her eyes when she smelt the fresh, fruity aroma of her hair and felt the shammy-soft little hands circle her neck. She nuzzled her nose into Sarah's hair.

Sarah was the one to pull back first this time, pushing away to look into Angie's face.

"Are you sad?" Sarah asked tilting her head, touching under Angie's eyes.

"Why would I be sad when I'm seeing you?"

"I brought you a present." Out of her pocket, Sarah brought an animal figurine she'd made out of clay. It had big pointy ears, a long tail, out-of-proportion legs and a circle for a body.

"It's beautiful, Sarah. Thank you." She held the precious present in her hand, gazing at it for a moment. Then she smiled, wrapping her arms around Sarah again, letting her hands mould into the curve of her back.

"It's a fox," Sarah whispered in Angie's ear. She pulled back, touching Angie's face. "It'll protect you, tell you things. Intuko bought me a new bed. Do you think it will fit in your place?"

"I dunno," said Angie standing.

Intuko, who stood watching the scene, smiled crookedly at Angie and moved forward.

"Hi," he said. "It's great to see you."

She stepped back, not wanting him too close. "Sarah says you bought her a new bed."

"And he bought me a Gameboy." Sarah pulled out her lime green electronic game, showed it to Angie then sat on the sofa, her face buried in the small screen.

Turning her back on Sarah, Angie spoke low to Intuko, "I suppose you heard my rap."

He nodded, remaining silent.

"She gonna stay with you?" she asked.

"I'm working on it. I have a strong case."

"Why didn't you tell me you were going up there?"

"It was a quick decision. A meeting got cancelled so I was able to leave."

Angie nodded, biting the side of her mouth, while looking away. Answers. Everyone always had answers.

"She won't be out of your life," Intuko said, reaching for her hands. "I won't let that happen."

"Yeah, right," Angie said flatly, crossing her arms.

"Sarah needs you. Wants you. Time will pass. You'll be out quicker than you know."

"That's easy for you to say. You're not here day in and day out. You're not the one who's going to lose..." Angie closed her eyes, touching her finger to her forehead, bowing her head.

Intuko moved beside her. "I'll be there for you."

She looked up, into his eyes. "Why?"

"I want to."

She shook her head. "I've done nothing but mess-up my whole life. And now when I have a chance to make good, I've messed up again. Please, don't get involved with me."

"I don't care about any of that. I want you in my life and so does Sarah." He shifted his weight. "That was quite a present she made for you."

Angie attempted a smile, opening up her hand to display the clay fox. "I'm going to put it on my desk."

He nodded then suddenly shook his finger, thinking of something he had to say. "I forgot to tell you, I talked to Charlie the other day."

"Charlie? I think that bugger laced my–"

"He wanted to protect you, thought you were in danger."

"Yeah, well. That wasn't his decision to make now, was it?" Angie flopped down on the sofa beside Sarah, their legs touching. Sarah slid under her arm, smiled up at her then went back to her game.

"He did the wrong thing," said Intuko also sitting down, looking a little more at ease. "But he did it for the right reasons."

"Yeah, but that's still wrong. Believe me, I know that now. I did what I did for good reasons but I'm paying big time."

"Do you ever hear anything in here? About what's happening on the streets?" Intuko spoke evenly, in a low voice.

"What do you mean?" She cocked her head, interested in his change of tone, his probing question.

"I'm still trying to find out about Lola." He mouthed the words, so Sarah wouldn't hear.

Angie pulled Sarah closer to her, kissing the top of her head. Thinking. Sherry and that woman. She'd heard something...but...ratting was not cool. Not cool at all. Anyway, it probably had nothing to do with Lola. She'd already ratted on Charlie. She stroked Sarah's hair, gazing into space.

"Angie, Lola is dead. And I think it has to do with the drugs. She knew something or just got in the wrong car. But she's dead."

She shrugged her shoulders when she looked at him. "I can't help."

"If you can, please tell me."

"Hey Angie, you want to play this game with me?"

"I'd love to." Angie pulled Sarah on her knee, completely turning her back to him.

Angie waited in line for the phone. With the money she'd made working she'd bought a phone card. She hoped he was in his office. Ever since he'd left, she'd had a splitting headache.

After three rings she heard his voice.

"Intuko, it's Angie," she whispered.

"Angie? What is it?"

She glanced up and down the hall. No one but no one could hear her, or else she'd be beaten to a pulp.

"Angie, tell me."

"Shipment tomorrow night." She hung up the phone without saying good-bye, heaved a sigh of relief, looked around, coast was clear, then, feeling ten pounds lighter, she walked toward her unit to see what everyone was watching on television. Hopefully, she'd get there in time to see a rerun of Friends.

TWENTY FIVE

The next day, Intuko and Chris sat in Intuko's office behind closed doors comparing notes.

"Angie said tonight. Tuesday."

"Candice said Wednesday. Tomorrow."

"I think we should go to Anderson with this. Immediately."

Chris nodded his head. "Most definitely. I'm glad to see you're finally getting smart about this. Handing it over to the right people."

"Me? You're worse than I am now." Intuko paused, drumming his fingers on his desk.

"What are you thinking?" Chris broke his thoughts.

"My cousin said to stop looking at the herd as a whole. Find the right one and zero in. I'm not hunting very well these days." Intuko stood and grabbed his coat off the hook. "Let's go."

"No, you go alone. I'm meeting Mary for coffee. Phone me with the outcome."

Detective Anderson sat at a very messy desk drinking coffee and eating some sort of breakfast egg fast food deal. Ketchup ran down his chin. A hockey bag overflowed in the corner, hockey sticks leaned against the wall.

"Intuko, what's up," he said, his mouth full of yellow egg.

"I've some information you might be interested in." Intuko cleared the chair of files, placing them on the floor, and sat. He leaned forward, propping his elbows on Anderson's desk. "I've heard... there's a big shipment of drugs hitting the streets today or tomorrow."

Anderson swallowed before asking, "Who'd you hear that from? And the word drugs is a broad term. Define."

Intuko thought of Angie, how breathless she'd been on the phone, and he knew that call had been tough for her to make. "Rumour inside the Women's Corrections was today. Rumour on the streets, tomorrow." He clipped his words. "And I'm guessing heroin and crack cocaine."

Anderson raised a questioning eyebrow, studying Intuko. "Okay. Junkies locked up get desperate. Street talk has more validity. I can't work with guesses. Anything else?"

How to say what he had to say? Intuko hesitated.

"I don't have all day," said Anderson, slurping his coffee.

"I think Harrison Fleming and Brad Black are involved in this drug ring. And I think if you can catch them, then we'll find out who killed Lola."

Anderson crumpled his wrapper and threw it in the garbage. "Who was your source on the street?"

Intuko gulped.

"I've been in this business a long time," said Anderson slowly, "and we hear a lot of things. Most of which is not true."

"Candice," said Intuko quietly. "She's a stripper at Hank's."

"I'm not sure I know her that well. How'd she hear?"

Intuko took a deep breath. "She was with a guy, he got drunk and talked. She says he was so drunk, he'd never remember talking. Or so she hopes."

"Who was the guy?"

"She wouldn't give us the name. She's scared. I think it's because he's a public figure."

Anderson played with his lower lip for a moment, putting it into major contortions before he placed both palms on the table and said, "I'll go to narcotics with this. Suggest they get extra tails. That's all I can do."

"You're sure."

Anderson stood. "Look, Intuko, this is serious stuff, narcotics has a game plan and has been working on this operation for a long time now. But what we do behind these walls is confidential otherwise we jeopardize our hard work. One slip and we've lost. So, go home. Take a shower. Your job is done, leave the rest to us."

The day, once again, sported a dreary grey. Intuko walked up the little hill to the corner of Main and Hastings, past the phone booths where a young man with chains on his jeans and a black toque on his head talked on the phone. On the dirty concrete a woman sat with a cardboard sign and tin can in front of her saying she needed money for her baby.

Intuko stopped at the lights and glanced across the street to see Elizabeth prancing around in her crown. He shook his head, wishing there was somewhere Elizabeth could go for help besides a prison. There wasn't enough money to help mental disorders, and until they committed a crime, they were on the streets. The light turned to green and a walk signal flashed. He stepped off the curb.

Suddenly, he saw his fox darting through Elizabeth's coat. He thought of the North, his visions in the snow, seeing Elizabeth, and he picked up his pace turning to the right instead of the left.

"Elizabeth, how are you today?"

"I'm a queen you know."

"And you're a beautiful queen. You see any more princesses lately?"

She stopped. "Princesses?" Her eyes widened. She looked like Lucille Ball.

"Yeah, princesses. Like Lola."

Elizabeth tilted her head upwards. "Some of the princesses go away in a blue carriage with bi-i-g wings." Elizabeth started to dance again. "Maybe they fly to the ball."

Intuko walked away thinking blue car, blue car. Elizabeth said they went away in a blue car.

Intuko stood outside Sarah's school, leaning against the wall, talking to Chris on his cell, waiting for the school bell to ring.

"Anderson's right," said Chris. "I would think Candice is more reputable than the women in the prison. Why don't we take a drive out to White Rock tonight? I'm curious to see what's out there. Maybe we can meet up with Harrison's ex-wife and son as well. I'd like to meet him. We could do a bit of prying."

"I have Sarah to think about."

"I'll ask Mary to baby-sit. What time is your appointment today?"

Intuko looked at his watch. "Not until one o'clock."

Intuko glanced at the clock in his kitchen. Ten to one. He downed a glass of water, placed the glass on the counter then picked it back up. That wouldn't do. He couldn't have a thing out of place. He stuck it in the cupboard even though it was dirty, telling himself to remember to wash it later.

He sat down, but his knee shook so he had to stand.

"Intuko, what's wrong?"

"Sarah!" He almost jumped out of his skin.

"When is the lady going to be here?" she asked.

"Soon. Eight more minutes."

"Is she nice?"

"I'm sure she's very nice." He squatted down. "I don't want you to worry. She just wants to see if this is a good place for you to live. Why don't we read for a few minutes on the sofa? You get your favourite book."

"What if she doesn't think so? Who will I live with? Please, not Jimmy. I saw him today at the school."

He glanced at Sarah who had one thumb shoved in her mouth while the other hand was busy twisting her hair round and round her finger.

"Jimmy? I bet that was someone else you saw," he said.

Sarah shook her head back and forth, her hair swinging in her eyes. "No, it was him. I saw him. I know I saw him. And he followed us home too." The child was close to tears.

He placed his hands on her shoulders to calm her, and to calm himself. Was Jimmy following him? Why didn't Sarah say something in the car? This was not the time to ask the child about Jimmy; she couldn't get upset.

"Come on, let's read that book. Everything's going to be okay, Sarah. Everything's going to be okay."

The doorbell rang.

Night fell early in late November. Intuko had Sarah in pyjamas when Mary arrived to baby-sit. He kissed her goodnight before he left for White Rock with Chris. He promised to bring her back a treat for snack at school the next day.

The drive took a little more than an hour because of the night traffic. Finally, Intuko inched his car down the dirt road toward the Spiritual Retreat Centre.

"Man, is it dark out here," said Chris.

"I brought a couple of flashlights," replied Intuko. He pointed to the peach stucco house. "That's where Joanne lives." He slowed down. "I don't see the truck."

"What truck?"

"She has a truck with her logo on it. It was in the driveway last time I was here."

Intuko drove a little farther to the vacant lot, Harrison's

land. "There's the boarded up Seed of Life." He pointed down the driveway.

"Some lights are on at Joanne's place," said Chris. "Aren't we going to see her?"

"This is the place I want to check out first." Intuko leaned over to look out Chris's passenger-side window. "The boarded up building."

"Why?" Chris rolled down his window.

"I want to get in that building and look around. I'll park the car out of sight. I'll hide it in those trees." He pointed further down the road. "Then we'll go and see if we can get in. I brought some tools."

"Why don't we go see Joanne first?" Chris looked back at the peach house.

"I did that last time and I think she watched me come over here. I don't want to arouse her suspicion. She'll never know we were here if we check the building first. We'll take a quick check then we'll go visit her."

Intuko parked his car, at least a hundred yards down and out of sight. They shut their doors quietly.

"I robbed a few stores when I was young," said Chris. "This crap-your-pants adrenalin I feel now is how I felt then."

"That's a way to put it."

"I think we should go through the fields instead of walk along the road," whispered Chris.

Tall, overgrown hedges lined the one side of the property and they tip-toed close to the branches, trying to stay out of sight of the road, in case someone came driving down.

A car did go by and they both fell to the ground, laying flat in the long grass, hidden from sight.

"Geez, my heart's thumping like crazy," said Chris.

Slowly, they arose and tip-toed toward the building.

They were about to move away from the hedges and walk right up to the house when a truck without its headlights swerved into the driveway.

Intuko and Chris dropped to the ground again. They watched the truck drive up to the front steps. "Come on," whispered Intuko. "Let's move closer, see what's going on."

On hands and knees they crawled toward the old abandoned building and when they were close enough to see the action they lay on their bellies and watched.

A few lights went on and Intuko saw a man dressed in black open the door of the old building and go inside. When he came out he flashed a light on the truck and said, "All's clear."

Intuko squinted to see what was written on the truck. Spiritual Retreat Centre. "That's Joanne's truck. What are they unloading?"

"I'm not sure," whispered Chris. "They're bringing in boxes of...hymn books. I think that's what it says on the boxes. They look like ants unloading food they're moving so fast."

"Can you see Harrison anywhere?"

"No, I can't. But he wouldn't get his hands dirty. He's sitting in an office somewhere, talking on a phone, collecting money. Maybe he's with Black and they're running this out of Divine Intervention. It's the perfect set-up."

They heard another vehicle coming up the driveway, also with its lights off. When the person stepped out, the interior light went on and Intuko noticed it was a dark vehicle, old Chrysler maybe, with...fins on the side.

"Elizabeth said something about–"

"."

Chris and Intuko watched, mesmerized by the speed at which the men moved. They all wore black gloves and unloaded boxes with the utmost efficiency.

"Call Detective Anderson," Chris whispered. "My gut says these are not hymn books."

Intuko suddenly remembered something. One night in the

church, his white fox had run through the hymn books. It had been trying to tell him something but he didn't listen, he had been so absorbed in his own pain that night. And then later on that night, he'd almost gone on a shaman journey but he had made himself stop. Why? He shook his head–he couldn't remember. Now here he was, in the woods, on his belly, like a serpent, trying to right wrong. Why hadn't he listened?

He reached in his pocket, fished out his cell phone and punched in Anderson's number, whispering for the police to get out here right away. Send reinforcement. He shut off his phone, hoping Anderson would believe his message.

They watched for another fifteen minutes or so before another car drove in the driveway, again with its headlights off.

"It's the Mercedes," Intuko said.

"It's not Harrison though," whispered Chris. "It's a woman. And it's not Hope."

"It's that Joanne Venus."

"Why is she driving his car, they've been divorced for years?"

"Might be working together. I think we should go back to the road," said Intuko. "Meet the police."

Intuko pressed his hands on the ground to push up when he felt something cold against his head.

"You're not fuckin' going anywhere, preacher-boy," a voice threatened in his ear. "I knew I'd catch up with you sooner or later. I want my gun back."

Jimmy.

"I've been following you for days. And the kid," he hissed quietly. "Couldn't believe my luck when I tailed you coming out here. Especially when you decided to take to the dark woods."

"Yeah, get up," another voice quipped in, sounding equally raunchy.

Two against two.

Only two had guns and two didn't.

How could Intuko not have heard them behind him? He was a boy who used to sneak up on caribou. He'd lost his touch.

Jimmy and his sidekick pressed the guns into Intuko and Chris, jabbing them to move away from the house and the road and into the woods. They moved through the long grass. In the dark.

"Where are you taking us?" asked Intuko.

"I'm going to write a note," Jimmy spit in Intuko's ear. "And sign your name. Say you took off 'cause you couldn't manage the kid."

"You'll never get away with that," said Intuko.

"Or maybe I'll just beat the shit out of you like you did to me and if you say a word to anyone, I'll get the kid. During school. She's supposed to be dead, anyway, the little fucker."

Intuko stumbled. Chris beside him kept walking, his hands balled into fists.

They approached an old run-down barn-like building and Jimmy shone a flashlight on the door. He pushed Intuko against the building face first then he pushed on the door. It swung open.

Jimmy pushed Intuko inside. Chris got pushed in as well by the big, burly guy.

Noises, odd noises sounded from the darkened building. Animals?

"Turn on the lantern," ordered Jimmy.

Once the big guy did as he was told, a rim of light circled the inside of the building. Stacks of piled hymn books leaned against the wall. And in the middle were new-looking tables. And drug scales and other drug paraphernalia. Intuko heard Chris beside him gasp, choke, cough then, spit on the floor.

When he turned to look at Chris, he saw Candice. Completely nude, tied up and gagged, lying on the floor staring wide-eyed at them. The fear in her eyes sank through Intuko's skin and muscles. Bile rushed up his throat. Her eyes, red and swollen from crying, begged for help.

"Shit!" said Jimmy. "So this is how that asshole parties."

"We're in trouble," mumbled the big guy. "Man, they said stay fuckin' low with the pigs. This is the kind of shit they hunt for."

"We have to kill them all," spouted Jimmy.

"We...we can't do that," stuttered the big guy. "Everything will bust wide open and I don't want no damn murder rap."

"But she's seen us, you idiot. So have these two losers. They mention one word and we're screwed. And if we fuck up the big boys' operation we're as good as dead meat. If we do this without gettin' nailed we're cool. They'll link it to hallelujah-man."

While Jimmy and his bruiser friend nattered at each other, Intuko glanced at Chris, his hands clenched in fists to his side. He glanced sidelong at Jimmy and the guy behind him. Intuko knew Chris was thinking of something.

"Move it." Jimmy slammed the gun into Intuko's side, shoving him toward the back of the barn.

They moved forward. Toward Candice.

Slowly, a millimetre at a time.

Intuko looked at Chris. Chris looked at Intuko.

"I knew I'd get you, you fucking prick," Jimmy hissed in Intuko's ear. "I don't care what he says I'm going to kill you for stealing my gun. And I'll finally kill the kid too."

Surging with adrenalin, Intuko eyed Chris. Chris, his body rigid, eyed Intuko.

Then suddenly, Chris snapped around. His feet flying in the air. A high kick. To Jimmy's hand. The sound cracked through the air.

Intuko lunged at the big guy, spilling him down to the

ground. The guy's gun landed in a mound of dust somewhere. His head banged against the floor.

Intuko turned to see Jimmy wavering, still holding his gun.

Chris charged, knocking Jimmy to the ground.

They rolled, Chris grabbing Jimmy's hand trying to get at the gun. Jimmy kept it out of reach. Chris kept clawing at him to get the gun.

Intuko dove to the ground and crawled on his hands and knees toward them. Maybe Chris could get the gun to him. If Intuko could get it out of Jimmy's hand. They were still two against two but only one gun now.

Then Intuko felt a foot on his hand, a boot, crunching his bones.

And he heard the gun shot.

Intuko looked at Jimmy and Chris who were now separated, each lying still. Was one of them shot? He watched as Jimmy sat up, the gun still in his hand. Chris lay perfectly still. Intuko crawled on his hands and knees.

He saw the blood on Chris's shirt. He remembered the smell of blood after a hunt. So distinct. But this was human blood.

Intuko inched forward, toward the lifeless body, toward the best friend he'd ever had.

"Chris."

Intuko had never thought about dying before, not until this moment in his life when Chris lay bleeding on the ground. He wondered what happened in the after-life. How much of what was written in the Bible was true? He wondered if he'd get to see his mother, his grandmother. He wondered about God, Jesus, doubting Thomas. Lola. Would he see Lola? This had all started with her. She'd died at gunpoint. Just a hooker. When she really had been a human being, a physical body, a beautiful soul with emotions and feelings. And what would happen to little Sarah?

When he reached Chris, he cradled his head in his lap and started to sing, softly. He pressed his fingers to Chris's wound, the sticky blood, to stop the life from gushing out of a healthy body. And he talked. To God. His white fox. And his Grandmother. He asked her to help, use her medicine to save a dying man. He told his mother he loved her no matter what she had done. He told Lola he was sorry he didn't avenge her murderer. He prayed for someone to take Sarah, guide her, and give her a home.

He could feel the gun, again, digging in his skull and a deranged man swearing in his ear, telling him to get up.

Then sirens screamed. Cars screeched to a halt.

Intuko kept singing.

"The pigs are here!" The big guy grabbed Jimmy by the arm. "This guy's singing is freakin' me out. Let's get the fuck out of here!"

The big guy swung the barn door open. "Come on, Jimmy, I've got some bros over the border. We can make it there before this blows. He waved his gun at Intuko and Chris. "Even if these guys talk, we ain't done nothin'. Come on man, let's blow this place." He took off in a run.

Jimmy glanced quickly at Intuko then followed. They would probably run through the fields, hide, then get in their cars, drive back to the city, pack and take off, thinking, hoping, no one could ever find them.

Intuko laid Chris's head gently on the ground, and crawled over to Candice and untied her. He took off his coat and wrapped it around her shaking, sobbing body.

He crawled back to Chris. Slowly, tenderly, he lifted his head. Onto his lap. Singing…singing…

TWENTY SIX

When Intuko went to visit Chris at the hospital the next day, after driving Sarah to school, Chris was sitting up reading the newspaper, wincing every time he had to move.

"Detective Anderson came by earlier." Chris gave the paper to Intuko.

"Was that good or bad?" Intuko sat down on the edge of the bed and picked up the newspaper although he'd already read every word, twice over, this morning.

"Both. He gave me a good lecture but he said good work. They wouldn't have wrapped it up without us. One more day and the drugs would have been on the streets. They needed to catch them in the act." Chris grimaced. "I'm sure you got it last night too. He's made me think though. I might go through to be a cop."

"You, a cop?" Intuko paused. "You'd be a great cop."

Chris smiled then grimaced again. His torso was tightly bandaged, limiting his movement. But still he fidgeted. "I'm sure you've already read the paper."

Intuko nodded, picked up the paper anyway and stared at the front page. There was a big picture of Joanne Gibson Fleming Venus and her son Eric Gibson Venus in the back of the police cruiser, coats over their heads. The G. in his name stood for Gibson and he was known as Gibby. He was Fleming's son but had never gone by the name Fleming. Gibson was Joanne's maiden name. Venus was a name she and Eric had chosen when they opened the Spiritual Retreat Centre. It meant Goddess of Beauty. Eric chose the name. Sex was part of the Spiritual Retreat Centre.

The city was up in arms as the entire drug operation was linked to millionaire Brad Black and a silent partner of his in the condo development. Paul Redman. There was a photo of Black with Redman, both with their lawyers, both ready to fight in court, denying anything to do with Candice or Lola. There was a smaller insert photo showing the open hymn books filled with drugs. There was no mention of Jimmy. He must have made it over the border. Charlie wasn't mentioned even though Intuko had found out they'd pulled him in for questioning late yesterday afternoon grilling him for eight gruelling hours. They'd taken him after Intuko had talked to Anderson in the afternoon. He'd been cut a deal to talk.

The police had been tailing Fleming for a few days and had come up with nothing. They'd also been collecting evidence on Black for months. Anderson said narcotics had enough to nail Black.

"I hope this Eric and his mother Joanne remain in prison for life." Chris shook his head in disgust.

"They made home videos, the police found them tucked up in the rafters." Intuko sighed and put the paper down. "What they did to Lola was despicable. They thought they were smart getting shots of dumping her in the black Mercedes. They wanted to pin everything on Harrison." He stared into space, his throat tightening in emotion as he thought of Lola's last minutes. Did she think of Sarah?

Chris groaned, closed his eyes and leaned back against the pillow. "Jimmy, that bugger, took off. They still haven't found him although there's a warrant for his arrest. Attempted murder. And there's not one link to Harrison Fleming. His son and ex-wife used him. They used his land and he didn't even know it. How sad."

"I guess the deal was if Eric took the job as the overseas mule for the drug operation then Black let Joanne and him live on his land for free. They used Harrison's land as a cover-up because the building was conveniently vacant and Harrison was too busy to ever go out there. That's why as neighbours they were fighting his project. They didn't want their operation to end." He shook his head. "Joanne and Eric thought they were okay using that back building for their sick parties. And the fact is–for a long time they got away with it. I don't even want to think for how long."

"Evidently, they must have had keys to his car too. I have a feeling Steven Campbell knew they took it when Harrison was out of town and didn't do anything about it and he didn't want Harrison to find out. They must have had something on Campbell for him to turn a blind eye to the use of the car." Intuko paused. Then he looked up, shaking his head in disbelief. "How would you handle knowing your own flesh and blood had done something so awful? It must just about kill Harrison to know his son is so despicable."

Chris shivered. "I don't even want to think about it any more. Poor Candice. I think they were planning another sick murder."

"I heard she's flying with her little guy to Toronto today. Hank gave her the money." Intuko walked over to the window. He pressed his hands against the cold glass. "You know, through his fire and brimstone, Harrison's a good man. My cousin told me not to go after the herd, to focus on the right animal. I had them all together in one big herd."

"Do you think Hope's having a thing with Steven Campbell?" asked Chris.

Turning, Intuko smiled sadly at Chris. "I hope we were wrong with that clue, but it may be what they had over Campbell. Why he allowed them to use the car and why he wouldn't talk."

"We are amateurs, Intuko," said Chris, shifting in the bed, trying to get comfortable. "We could have got something wrong."

"Anderson let me know that." Intuko raised his eyebrows, making Chris laugh.

"We're a bunch of bozos trying to do police work like that. I deserve to be in this bed."

"No, Chris." Intuko walked toward him, sitting on the bed beside him. "I should be there. I got you started."

Chris's facial expression changed and he became serious. "If you hadn't of started, you wouldn't have Sarah now. You saved her Intuko."

"Yeah." Intuko sighed, picking at the lint on the bed. "I was so nervous yesterday when that lady from child services came over. I was soaked in sweat. I have a lot more paper work to do though."

"What's up with you and Susan?"

"Nothing. She's a good friend."

"Angie?"

Intuko gave Chris a crooked smile. "I think she's still mad at me for not telling her I was going North."

"Ah, she'll get over that. Women like to get mad at things like that."

Intuko arched his eyebrows. "I'm definitely out of touch." He paused. "I am worried about her, though. What she'll have to go through when she has her baby. I don't know how she's going to handle her situation."

Months later.

The deep sharp pains began in the middle of the night, and Angie curled into the fetal position on her bed unsure of what was happening to her. It was only May 15th and she wasn't due until June 15th. The mild cramping had started in the afternoon and had slowly built to this harsh, debilitating pain.

She clutched her stomach and closed her eyes, not wanting to call out for help in the middle of the night, not wanting her baby to be born at all. The longer her baby remained in her body, the longer that baby was hers and hers alone. She gritted her teeth and willed the pain away. But it increased in intensity and by morning, when her door was unlocked, she was rasping for breath.

The ambulance high-tailed it down the highway.

The sweat dripped off her brow. The pain ripping through her body every few minutes felt like a sledge hammer hacking away at her insides. Sometimes her body burned like a fire, and in other moments it felt like a block of ice, frozen in time.

When she slept, she saw her mother and Paul leering at her. They told her they were going to get married and take the baby. They were the adopted parents. Then she dreamed of escaping, running away through the tall grass with her smiling baby on her back. Then that dream turned into a statue and she became the woman in the carved necklace. A block of bone.

Where was Intuko? Desperately, she wanted him by her side to help her through this wretched pain. She called out for him.

Then she heard someone yell. "The baby's coming now. It's crowning. She's going to deliver vaginally."

Swimming eyes stared at her and yelled her name. "Angie, come on girl, give a push. Your baby wants out. You have to push. Come on, Angie. BP rising! Push. One more!"

Then she finally heard, "You've done it. Good girl, Angie, good girl."

She collapsed against the pillow, her arms and legs feeling like mush. But somehow in her crippling pain, she remembered the last words. She'd only ever been called a good girl by her Dad, years ago, when she was just little.

She closed her eyes to the world until…she heard crying. Almost involuntarily her eyes fluttered open and she turned her head to see a nurse, standing beside her bed holding a small, red, wrinkly, but beautiful baby.

The nurse leaned over. "Would you like to hold her?"

Shaking, she opened her arms to hold the infant. Her baby. She nestled her daughter against her swollen chest and rubbed her cheek against her soft fuzzy scalp. Angie softly kissed the baby's forehead.

They took the baby from her not soon after. Then they wheeled her to a private room where they shackled her with leg irons to the bed.

Intuko visited her with a bouquet of flowers and a handwritten card from Sarah. It said, "I love you, Angie." And on it was a stick drawing of a tall person holding a little stick person's hand and beside them was a baby carriage. Angie sunk back into her pillow and stared out the window, the card falling from her hand to the floor.

"I wish I had escaped a long time ago." Her voice was low and monotone.

"No, you don't." He touched her face.

"Yeah, I do. She's not mine."

"You're wrong. She'll always be yours."

"No. I won't get to raise her. They have to give her away to someone else." Angie licked her dry lips. "She deserves a good home. I can't give her that right now. I've messed up again."

He reached over and brushed his lips against her forehead in a kiss as soft as butterfly wings.

"I need you to do me a favour," she said. "There's a necklace in that drawer. I want you to get it out. I had Susan bring it to me."

Intuko opened the drawer, pulling out a necklace that looked exactly like the one his mother carved. He gasped. "Who gave you this necklace, Angie?"

She licked her lips and took a look at the necklace. "This ghost or spirit."

"What did...she, uh, look like?"

Angie paused then said, "Like you."

"My mother committed suicide in that prison years ago." Intuko fingered the necklace. "She made necklaces like these when I was a little boy, before she left us."

"She told me I was the one who could free her from the prison. She wanted to go home–she said she wanted to go to where she could dance to the beat of the caribou drum."

"What was it you had to do to free her?"

Angie bit her bottom lip, trying to stop the tears from sliding down her face. It did no good. She couldn't stop them. "The woman told me...I had learn how to love."

"Do you think she has now been freed?"

"Yes," Angie whispered.

Intuko reached for a tissue and gently dabbed at Angie's face.

"She said some other things, Intuko. Things I never told you. She wanted me to tell you that your grandmother said to follow your instincts and to not be afraid to go on a journey. I'm not sure what she meant by that. I...didn't tell you any of this because I didn't want you to go North and find Sarah's relatives." She paused before she said, "And...she also told me to tell you...she loved you."

EPILOGUE

Intuko stood in the lobby of the prison holding Sarah's hand tightly in his. When he looked down, he only saw the top of her head because she was so intently focused on the door in front of her. Finally, they saw Angie's blond hair through the little window. Sarah started to jump up and down as if she had to go the bathroom on the spot.

The door pushed open and Angie appeared. She stood like an obelisk, her hair hanging loose like raw golden silk to her shoulders, her eyes wide, full of apprehension, her lips pulled together in a straight line, her chin pointed forward. Dressed in jeans, a purple T-shirt and running shoes, and adorning little make-up, she could have passed for someone much younger, a teenager, but she didn't possess teenage energy. Instead, she was serene.

Her first steps were slow and methodical like an animal moving to new pasture then she quickened her pace when she saw Sarah running toward her.

Intuko watched the greeting from a distance knowing, although he wanted this to have a happy ending much like in the fairy tales, that it would take work. She would need time to adjust to life outside the prison walls.

"I hope I can do this," she said, avoiding eye-contact, looking into the distance.

"Do you want to do it?"

She turned to look at him. "I'm…afraid. I don't think I've ever been afraid in my life, but today, walking outside to the real world, the big blue sky of life, I don't know if I can forget my old ways."

"You don't have to forget to change."

"I hope you're right."

On the way to Angie's new home, a halfway house to help her integrate back into society, they stopped for ice cream cones. Sitting in the park by the swings and bars and slides, Angie watched the freely moving children. She longed to be one of the mothers, pushing the swings.

On the other side of the park, she saw a woman with a baby. Angie stiffened and dropped her cherry ice cream cone into the sand. The baby had the same hair color as her little Lola and the woman, from all the descriptions and pictures they had given Angie of her, looked exactly like little Lola's adoptive mother. When the woman holding the baby turned towards her, Angie realized the baby was too young to be her Lola. Lola was already over a year old. She wouldn't still be in an infant carrier. She might be walking by now.

Angie turned to Intuko with a burning so intense behind her eyes she covered them. "Will there ever come a day when I don't look for her?" she whispered. "I want her in my arms. I want to see her take her first step. I want her to say Mama to me, not someone else. I gave her a letter. It took me days to write. I want her to read it when she's older. I want her to know why I gave her up and that I love her. And always will. Maybe…maybe one day there will be hope for us. Iris got a second chance, maybe I will."

"Life has a way of working things out. You're going to be okay, you know."

"I don't know about that. I hope this hurt goes away one day. I never thought I could ever feel like this. I never allowed myself to feel this way." Angie rested her head on Intuko's shoulder and he gently put his arm around her, pulling her close to him.

From the distance they heard a little voice. "Angie,

Intuko, look at me. Look what I can do."

Cast against a brilliant sapphire sky, shining in a beam of light from the sun like a paragon of beauty, Sarah smiled, swinging upside down from the high bar, her skirt flowing with the breeze. In innocent splendour.

The drum beat rises.

Her head, like the steady pulse of the beating drum, turns to view her surroundings. There are men and women, young and old, dressed in parkies, dancing to the fingers beating against the caribou hide of the drum. In her royal blue parka, she joins the group, dancing like a bird skirting the earth, her feet barely touching the dirt. Up and down, she lifts her body, forward and back she moves her feet. The sun burnishes the sky with its potent spring power. There is bright yellow against blue for hours on end.

Summers are always this way in the North. The world transforms from a silent reverie to an abundant fresh flurry of activity and music. Mating birds sing in harmony with the crackling ice along the shore. On the tundra tufted pearlwort, Arctic lupine, cotton grass and yellow Arctic poppies bloom in an abundance of color.

The woman is heartened after being lifted from the darkened depths that once blackened her soul. She opens her arms to the sun's whiteness that spreads out like liquid from the circle of yellow, reaching for it, embracing it, she feels the heat.

Uqittuq; It is light, she says.

Then she dances.

To the beat of the drum. Her drum.

See Fox Run

Coming Soon from

Exposed Secrets

Lorna Schultz Nicholson

Book Two of the Intuko and Angie Melville series

PROLOGUE

Sunday, July 1ST 11:00 a.m.

The cold metal of the gun dug into his skin. The eyes that stared at him were black with hate.

He closed his eyes. Secrets flashed in front of him: stealing a chocolate bar when he was five, lying to his mother when he was eight, stealing a case of wine when he was thirteen, joy-riding when he was eighteen.

All little mistakes, hardly accountable.

He opened his eyes again, and reached for the gun pointed at his chest.

"Don't! I'll shoot."

He knew the gun was cocked so he moved his hand away. No problem, he'd play a game–pretend to be scared. This person, the biggest secret of his life, would shit before shooting.

"You can't hurt me again. Ever!"

Closing his eyes, he smiled.

"You're nothing but...but..."

He knew the person in front of him was shaking. He laughed.

"You're a bastard. A dirty rotten bastard!"

He heard tears. He continued laughing.

"Stop laughing!"

This was funny. To think this person thought they could

get the better of him. No one ever–

The shot rang clear.

He saw blood, drop after drop; the dark spot getting bigger until it spread to the brown dirt where it disappeared, sucked into the earth. He gasped for breath. Blood gurgled from his mouth, spattering on his clean pressed shirt, his jeans. He looked up and saw eyes in front of him, swaying. He drifted above his body and looked down, watching his body spit blood.

The other person wiped the hunting rifle with a cloth and laid it on the ground, wide eyes revealing shock. Then that person walked away, breaking into a run without glancing back at the man dying on the ground.

Now *that* person had a secret.

One

Summer arrived in Inuvik, North West Territories, in an abundance of colour, bringing with it a sun that shone for twenty-four hours.

Intuko loved the spring sounds; ice crackling along the shore, snow dripping from rooftops, birds garbling from their beds of tundra, all noises that, when put together, sounded like a well-tuned orchestra playing symphony music. But with the melodious music had come the dust balls, mud puddles and dirt that accompanied spring.

Now that it was summer, however, the colours vibrated, shimmering in the heat of the sun. The dry Arctic tundra had turned from mousy brown to lemon yellow, flaming red, tangerine orange and little shoots of deep green emerged from beneath the ground that had been covered in a blanket of white snow since October.

Summer meant creativity, freshness, new birth from plants and animals. Intuko wondered how many polar bear cubs were being born and if they were playing with their mothers far from the shore. The whales would come closer to shore, blowing their air, making gushing, purling sounds. Baby foxes would run and play, sticking their noses where they didn't belong.

And most of the students at Aurora College where Intuko had worked since September had gone on to other things. The spring/summer session was currently running, but it was so much more relaxed as only a handful of students attended classes.

He stepped outside the small campus building painted with murals of ravens and wolves. The vivid colours of Arctic blue, blood red, and jet black blended together to create an artistic Inuvialuit statement.

The building only housed two classrooms; a computer/library room doubling as a make-shift office for the mayor of the town and a broom closet that had been made into an office for Intuko, the supervisor of programs.

Intuko inhaled, staring into the sun that stayed high in the sky all day and all night, letting it broil his skin. Land of the midnight sun.

"Have a good weekend, Intuko."

Intuko opened his eyes, having to squint to see. The mayor of Inuvik, Perry Pearn, stood before him, holding a stack of files under his arms, but wearing a smile on his face. As mayor of the town, he also doubled as a college instructor in business management.

"Thanks," said Intuko. "I will."

"What are you up to tonight?" Perry shifted the files onto his hip.

"My friend is coming in later."

"Oh, right. That friend from Vancouver. Is she on the evening flight?"

Intuko looked at his watch. "Four hours to go."

"Are you bringing her to Canada Day?"

"I think so."

"Why don't you sit with us at the square dance and barbeque?"

Intuko nodded his head. "Sounds good to me, but I'll see

how Angie feels before I make any evening plans. I'm sure I'll see you at the celebrations. Sarah signed up for the bike race."

Perry raised his eyebrows. "I've seen her around town on her bike. She's a going concern."

Intuko grinned, thinking of Sarah, riding up and down the road on her new bike, her hair flying like a horse's mane, pedaling as if she had been born with her legs moving around in a circle. All last winter she had begged him to buy her a bike and had even done chores without asking to make some of the money. Day after day, she'd poured through the Sears catalogue until the newsprint was dog-eared and unreadable. Catalogue shopping was a way of life in the North as department stores didn't exist. Finally, the bike had arrived in a box.

"She can't wait to show Angie how good she is and...she wants to win the medal for her wall."

Perry laughed. "I had those medals shipped. I bet they're not worth more than a nickel a piece."

"They have big meaning to a little girl."

Perry glanced at his watch. "I'd better get home. My little one is no longer interested in a medal for his wall. Or a bike. He wants my car. He's going to some party out of town later with his girlfriend Debbie. Cabin Creek, I think. Bryon seems to be taken by this one."

"Young love makes summer seem real. I'll call to let you know if we're going to the barbeque."

"Don't call, just look for us."

Intuko walked toward home with a spring in his step. Young love wasn't just for the young ones. Old guys like him could enjoy the feelings: the sweaty palms, the flushed cheeks, the flying deer in the stomach.

He couldn't wait to see Angie.

Angie Melville grabbed her stomach when the small aircraft she was in hit turbulence. Why had she agreed to come all this way–to some Arctic town in the middle of absolutely nowhere? She looked out her window, at the land stretching into the horizon and felt as if she were flying to the end of the world.

Angie uncrossed her feet, the thin heel of her beige leather sandal digging into her ankle. The seats were so small she could hardly get comfortable. The plane took another nose dive. She leaned back in her seat and closed her eyes only to have Sarah pop into her view. Angie was making this trip to see Sarah; she hadn't seen her since September and she missed her like crazy.

Opening her eyes, Angie looked out her window again. And...then there was Intuko. Angie hated herself for even thinking that she might have missed him. She wasn't supposed to feel anything for him but friendship.

For three years now Angie had been straight. For the eighteen months in prison and eighteen months on parole she'd toed the line. Intuko had helped her stay straight when he had been around, but when he'd left last fall to live up North for the year, taking Sarah with him, Angie had found living like a good little church-girl difficult.

She'd taken a computer course, but it had only been one night a week and any homework she had easily finished the same night, leaving her itching to do more. She'd even gone ahead and finished extra assignments but her teacher hadn't been interested in looking at them. Overworked and underpaid, she'd told Angie.

On the odd night when Angie was bored out of her mind, she had wanted to go back to her old ways. But then she'd think of prison and her old job as a stripper.

Prison life and stripping sucked. Both reminded her of her life on the streets–the one she wanted to escape–and of Lola, Sarah's mom.

When she remembered the ravished face of her old friend Lola, all twisted into knots from the drugs, Angie would almost cry. For Sarah–who dealt with a junkie mother for the first five years of her life–Angie would stay straight.

The uncertainty of Angie's future, however, did consume her thoughts, making her edgy and sometimes even snappy with people she didn't want to be snappy with.

Angie bit her nails. They used to be long, until she'd developed a biting habit in prison. She stuck her hands in her lap.

Restless, she sighed and traced her finger along the small airplane window. Why couldn't she just relax, enjoy Sarah and Intuko's company, and let her life unfold? With her parole finished, Angie was free to go anywhere, live anywhere, do whatever she wanted. Usually freedom gave her a rush, but this unsettling feeling seemed to halt the rush, rot the thrill.

The pilot came over the loudspeaker telling them they were heading in for a landing. Angie gripped the side of the chair, closed her eyes, and tried to breath. She needed a cigarette when she got off this plane.

Available

November 2004

Where There's A Will

By Debbie Cavanaugh

Gayle Ferguson, reluctant bounty hunter and part time sleuth, is hot on the high heels of a bad-check writing, East Texas redneck. Splitting her time between a paralegal job for a kooky attorney, kids, and her sexy obsessive-compulsive ex, things get really tricky after a clandestine meeting under the school bleachers leading to a scandal, and her investigation into the death of a little old lady.

Threatened by a macho bartender, hurled from a run-away 4-wheeler, hog-tied, hit on by the local mortician, and shot at, Gayle can't help but wonder why her. If that weren't enough, her mother, a PI wannabe, decides to "investigate" as well.

Experience the thrill of
Echelon Press

Meet the author:

 Lorna Schultz Nicholson has been a television co-host and reporter, radio host and reporter, fitness co-coordinator and a rowing coach. Now she is a full-time mother and fiction author who, along with her suspense novels, also writes children's sports novels. Lorna is based in Calgary, where she lives with her husband and three children. She is busy working on her next novel.

Visit Lorna's site at

www.lornaschultznicholson.com

Printed in the United States
21551LVS00001B/88-99

9 781590 803011